Slick!

NON-FICTION BY DAVID PERLSTEIN

Solo Success: 100 Tips for Becoming a $100,000-a-Year Freelancer

God's Others: Non-Israelites' Encounters With God in the Hebrew Bible

Slick!

A Novel

David Perlstein

iUniverse, Inc.
Bloomington

SLICK!

iUniverse books may be ordered through booksellers or by contacting:

iUniverse
1663 Liberty Drive
Bloomington, IN 47403
www.iuniverse.com
1-800-Authors (1-800-288-4677)

ISBN: 978-1-4620-4545-7 (sc)

Library of Congress Control Number: 2011914648

Printed in the United States of America

iUniverse rev. date: 08/26/2011

For Yury

Virtue itself turns vice being misapplied,
And vice sometime's by action dignified.

Friar Laurence, *Romeo and Juliet* (Act 2, Scene 1)
William Shakespeare

*   *   *

Costello: What's the guy's name on first base?
Abbott: No. What is on second.
Costello: I'm not asking you who's on second.
Abbott: Who's on first.
Costello: I don't know.
Abbott: He's on third, we're not talking about him.

"Who's On First?"—Bud Abbott & Lou Costello,
Written by Michael J. Musto

Sana Saeeda

| Happy New Year |

One

More in resignation than anger, Brigadier General Qasim bin Jabaar fondled the electrode intended for intimate contact with the blindfolded shopkeeper. His guest—bin Jabaar preferred the term to prisoner—hung from thick metal chains attached to an iron hook embedded in the ceiling of the windowless, concrete-walled interrogation cell. The cell occupied a corner of the basement directly below the cafeteria in the Sultanate of Moq'tar's Ministry of Security.

Bobby Gatling, the American security contractor hired to advise the Ministry, stepped out of the shadows ringing the cell. Bobby had no authority to prevent bin Jabaar from acting as he wished. He could, however, offer counsel based on hard-won experience ferreting truth from suspected terrorists during a thirty-year Army career.

Bin Jabaar held a hand up like a school crossing guard. "Yes," he said. "I know what you are going to say."

Bobby paused then stepped back.

Bin Jabaar turned to his guest. Colonel Gatling was not the only one put out by the shopkeeper's reticence. He had hoped that nothing more than the impressive presence of the Minister of Security would induce the shopkeeper to cooperate. Bin Jabaar was an imposing man, if not as tall as his American advisor who neared two meters at six-feet-five-inches. He took pride as well in an erect, athletic posture that cut quite the trim figure even in middle age. Bin Jabaar's silver hair, matching mustache and toasted-almond complexion prompted frequent comparisons with the Egyptian film star turned European sophisticate Omar Sharif. His wardrobe affirmed such observations. Even in this dank, chilly cell he wore a

3

well-cut dark blue suit complemented by a custom white shirt and elegant navy-and-crimson silk tie. His ensemble identified a man who gave considerable thought to everything he did. Indeed, he'd chosen his wardrobe to reinforce a well-earned reputation among fellow revelers during what remained of the festive New Year's Eve he still hoped to celebrate.

The shopkeeper whimpered then mumbled the name of one of his children. Of what use was that? Bin Jabaar already knew the names of the man's children, the schools they attended and even their favorite sweets. What he required was useful information. Actionable information. Information that would reinforce his value and that of the Ministry.

Bin Jabaar's disappointment produced a frown. He would have taken umbrage had anyone—the shopkeeper included—suggested he had scowled. He was at heart a warm and gentle soul, a loving husband and a doting father. Family, friends and associates knew him as a man who revered tradition yet easily adapted to the new global order while rejecting its excesses.

That his fierce love of country periodically compelled techniques of interrogation some might construe as distasteful or, in naïve circles, cruel he found regrettable. Even Colonel Gatling, who took a skeptical view of his approach, acknowledged using or approving such measures at one time or another.

But the Persian Gulf presented no end of challenges to a sultanate as small as Moq'tar. What was a patriot to do?

Subordinating his natural sensitivity, he passed the electrode to his assistant.

Stretched out like a lamb prepared for *dhabihah*—ritually prescribed slaughter—the shopkeeper elicited what might have been taken for a bleat as he struggled in vain to plant his feet on the concrete floor.

Bin Jabaar came nearer. "Do you know what the Americans say, Ali?" He modulated his rich, resonant voice as if chatting with a member of the venerable London men's club in which he once had been a guest. "You will not consider it too forward if I continue to address you by your first name, will you?"

"Please," the short, heavyset shopkeeper pleaded in a raspy whisper. The owner of an electronics store in downtown Moq'tar City, he had never before been arrested or, to his knowledge, watched by the Ministry of Security let alone been subjected to questions that left purple welts across his back and thighs. More to the point, he'd done nothing that such treatment should be inflicted on him. Of that he was almost sure.

Bin Jabaar's assistant, unenthused by his summons to duty given that January first had arrived only five minutes earlier, wolfed down the last of a particularly satisfying goat-cheese-and-date pizza delivered by Hungry Herdsman Pizza #4. Facing little prospect of a New Year's Eve celebration, he found solace in the fact that no one chided him for being a vegetarian. Yielding to his professional responsibilities, he tightened the chains.

The shopkeeper uttered a sound midway between *la*—no—and a helpless grunt.

Bobby cleared his throat. He felt like a ghost standing in the corner of a cell lit by a single compact fluorescent bulb in response to the new green initiative to which all government agencies had been committed.

Bin Jabaar smiled, although the shopkeeper could not see him. "An important American," he informed his guest, "once said that extremism in the defense of liberty is no vice." He turned to Bobby. "Is that not so, *habibi?*" he asked, using the Arabic term for "my friend."

"*Na'am,*" Bobby answered in Arabic. Yes. "A candidate for president. Many years ago. He lost."

"Of course," mused bin Jabaar aloud, "what Americans mean by liberty may be quite different from how we define the term here in Moq'tar or elsewhere in the Gulf." He turned back to the shopkeeper. "Philosophical discussions aside, my dear Ali, we can all agree, I believe, that the defense of the nation must be the primary concern of every loyal citizen."

Sweat tumbled from the shopkeeper's forehead like a mountain spring after a hard winter rain. His blindfold sagged under the weight of the moisture it had absorbed. "Please. I know nothing."

"Ah, nothing about *what?*" bin Jabaar inquired. It struck him that Ali might finally have given himself away concerning several recent and seemingly amateurish bombings in Moq'tar City. While doing minimal damage, they suggested a lack of security in the sultanate. This would not do. The matter cried out for resolution. In a region now given to protest and revolution, the potential for disaster lie just below Moq'tar's surface like an improvised explosive device covered by a thin layer of sand.

Bobby again stepped forward.

Again bin Jabaar held up his hand. The squeamishness of Americans puzzled him. Expressions of horror at nothing more than routine procedures at Abu Ghraib and Guantánamo revealed a weakness unbecoming a superpower—if America still was a superpower. Not that he doubted the credibility of this particular American. Although imposed on the Ministry by Sheikh Yusuf, the Sultan's favorite son, the Colonel presented credentials unmatched by anyone in Moq'tar. While warfare highlighted most of Moq'tar's history, the sultanate's relatively new army had yet to fire a shot in anger. The newly reorganized Ministry struggled to gain Sheikh Yusuf's full confidence.

A sound emerged from the shopkeeper's throat suggesting gargling to prevent the flu.

Bin Jabaar folded himself at the waist as if bowing before the throne and lowered his ear to the man's mouth. "What, Ali? Tell me. *Insh'allah*—God willing—this will all end very soon."

"I . . . I . . ."

Bin Jabaar nodded to himself. His guest was weak. Like most Moq'taris now, he was a man of the city rather than of the mountains or desert. Yet although Ali might appear to be at some remove from the still-anonymous terrorists who plagued the sultanate, he offered some hope of a connection, no matter how tenuous.

Most important, the shopkeeper enabled the Ministry of Security to add to its ample statistics relating to the arrest and interrogation of cowardly plotters. Metrics, Sheikh Yusuf insisted, were the hallmark of a modern society.

Bobby held his place but not his thoughts. He had one more card to play. "Perhaps tomorrow, after this man has had a little more time to think, he'll shed some light on the situation. As it is, you still have time to go out with your wife."

Bin Jabaar well knew that the shopkeeper's arrest placed him in a delicate position. It had forced him to renege on his promise to celebrate New Year's Eve at the new Swiss-French restaurant overlooking the Gulf. The owner ran a similar establishment in Davos, where annual ski trips with the children had established a prized family tradition. His wife had looked forward to lovely sautéed veal or perhaps lamb chops Provençal, a fine wine and, this being a special occasion, a stunning dessert. Upon learning of the unwelcome modification to their evening, she had expressed profound displeasure.

Unmoved if somewhat unnerved, bin Jabaar placated his wife's anger by pledging that the urgent business before him would conclude in sufficient time to make a late but deliciously dramatic entrance to an elegant soirée at the home of a well-to-do friend with business connections from Istanbul to Shanghai. The event promised to last until just before morning prayers. Should the shopkeeper force him to betray his oath, there would be hell to pay—for both of them.

"I know you have something to tell me, Ali," bin Jabaar coaxed. His voice hinted at a dangerous impatience without betraying the anger welling up inside him. "You may confide in me. I have only your best interests at heart."

The shopkeeper gasped for air. "I . . . yes. I will tell you."

Bin Jabaar straightened and motioned his assistant to set the electrode down. Having come to his senses, Ali would name names, specify dates and identify materials requested by the bomb makers—or those who served as middle men or connections for middle men in what undoubtedly formed a large and complex web of traitors. If fortune smiled, *insh'allah*, the Ministry of Security would acquire workable leads. If not, he would still compile data sufficient to demonstrate the Ministry's persistence.

The assistant slackened the chains.

The shopkeeper slumped onto a small stool as if his spine was no more rigid than a woman's underthings.

Bobby stepped forward.

This time, bin Jabaar offered no resistance.

"Are you really sure this man knows anything?" Bobby whispered.

Bin Jabaar gently grasped Bobby by the elbow and guided him back into the corner. "Certainty lies only with Allah. The safety of the Sultan, of Sheikh Yusuf, of Moq'tar's sovereignty . . . this is a heavy responsibility."

"It is, indeed. But Qasim," Bobby said softly, "shouldn't you be more focused on getting the Sultan to sign the succession papers?"

Moq'tar's constitution, written at Washington's behest by a Harvard post-doctoral fellow during a summer vacation at Cape Cod "to adapt democracy to regional cultural imperatives," would legalize Yusuf's succession to the throne following the Sultan's ultimate leaving of this world. Death was not a word spoken in His Excellency's presence. The Sultan had sworn to live forever.

"Stability," Bobby continued, "builds security."

"So it does, *habibi*. And so I assure you, Moq'tar will remain stable. The succession document represents merely a formality. Even without it, nothing will change. Moq'taris love Sheikh Yusuf as they do their Sultan. But with security threatened, there can be no stability." Bin Jabaar pointed to the exhausted shopkeeper. "This man will provide information to help secure the throne. And *this* is where my *greatest* responsibility lies."

Bobby leaned closer. "Moq'tar's security is also *my* responsibility, Qasim. Sheikh Yusuf has set Moq'tar on the right course. That's one of the reasons I'm here."

"Most certainly, *habibi*. But the money is good, no?"

Bobby glanced at the shopkeeper. "Times change, Qasim. Moq'tar is transitioning to democracy. Washington expects certain standards to be upheld."

The corners of bin Jabaar's mouth fell. "I appreciate your concern, Bobby. But if Moq'tar stumbles, I and not you will have to live with the consequences." He guided Bobby towards the door, stopped and clasped both of Bobby's arms. "I tell you as Allah is my witness, our guest is not innocent. He will reveal much to us."

"And if you ultimately determine that he has nothing useful to say, that he lies out of fear for his life. What then?"

Bin Jabaar reached up and wrapped his right arm around Bobby's shoulders. "Some things, *habibi*, it is better not to know."

The muscles tightened in Bobby's jaw and neck.

Bin Jabaar patted him on the back as if the two had just shared an amusing story over a glass of champagne. "I must confess," he continued softly, "I do feel somewhat guilty."

Bobby cocked his head.

"I have been keeping you from enjoying this otherwise festive evening. You doubtless have anticipated the company of the lovely blonde lady, the physician, you have been seeing."

"No. Not tonight. Unfortunately."

"I am sad to hear it. But the night is still young. Moq'tar City lies at your feet. Go now. And may this New Year bring you and all of us good health, peace and prosperity."

Bobby took a deep breath and exhaled slowly. "From your lips to God's ears."

Two

A mbassador N. Ronald Ellis held the telephone receiver to his ear with his left hand and poured a Scotch with his right. Settled in at his desk at the Embassy—he'd gotten to bed by two-thirty and finished breakfast only fifteen minutes earlier—he found himself occupied with yet another phone call from Deputy Assistant Secretary of State for Near Eastern Affairs Cardwell. And it was what time in Washington? Nine-thirty? At night? On New Year's Eve? He lifted his glass. Okay then.

Cardwell, growing increasingly uneasy about Sheikh Yusuf's presumed succession to the throne, had stepped away from a dinner he was hosting at his home. His anxiety mirrored that of the people above him. They wanted a firm answer to the question, When would the Sultan sign the papers? Thus Cardwell's calls kept coming despite the Ambassador's assurances that the succession papers would be signed, and that occasional acts of violence posed little threat—make that *no* threat—to Moq'tar's relationship with the U.S.

"It'll be a done deal in twenty-four hours," the Ambassador responded. "Tomorrow, Yusuf is taking his father up to the mountains where the Sultan used to steal horses or camels or something when he was a kid. Soften him up then hand him a pen."

Ostensibly, Yusuf and the Sultan would be taking the Ambassador, who'd presented his credentials only a month earlier for his first posting as a diplomat, on a sightseeing tour of the Mountains of Allah, the Sultan's ancestral home. There, with majestic views of Moq'tar before them and no distractions, Sheikh Yusuf would present the succession papers for his father's oft-delayed signature.

"Colonel Gatling, the Crimmins-Idyll guy, he's coming too. Big moment. Yusuf wants a little extra security."

Cardwell yet again stressed Moq'tar's unexpected but emerging importance to the United States' strategic position in the Gulf, what with all the unrest in the Middle East, including nearby Bahrain where the Navy based the 5th Fleet.

"Sea lanes, air dominance, force projection," said the Ambassador. "It's a military thing, right?"

The Persian Gulf was fraught with danger, Cardwell continued. If anything happened to the Sultan, legal processes would have to be in place to assure a seamless, peaceful transfer of power that would maintain America's dominance of the Moq'tari government. "It's a partnership, Ron. It's critical that Americans look favorably on Moq'tar. And it's just as critical that Moq'taris take a positive view of Americans."

"Not to worry. The new guy who checked into the Embassy after Christmas, he should help. I mean, that's why they sent him, right?" He opened a desk drawer and withdrew a small mirror. A bachelor in his early forties and five years older than Sheikh Yusuf, he'd made a night of it at the New Year's Eve party hosted by the Embassy. So had Yusuf, his special guest. The Ambassador hadn't fully recovered. His eyes were red. Patches of whiskers somehow missed by his electric razor dotted his cheeks and chin. No matter. He still displayed the ruddy face of an outdoorsman with a full head of glistening black hair brushed straight back in the style of Michael Douglas as Gordon Gekko in the first *Wall Street* movie. Although new to diplomacy, he gave the impression of a man as comfortable navigating the halls of power as skiing in Aspen or sailing the waters off California and Hawaii.

Why would anyone think differently? A Silicon Valley entrepreneur who'd turned a bottle of Scotch with two Indian doctoral students from Stanford into a fortune, he'd made hefty contributions to the president's campaign—and to his opponent's. Now he would establish a reputation as more than a businessman. The future could put him in London, Paris, Rome, Tokyo or

Beijing. Moscow or Buenos Aires wouldn't be chopped liver, either. And who knew? Possibly a major post in Washington. The White House even. Meanwhile, he'd babysit Yusuf, make his mark with the powers that be and maybe uncover a few business opportunities while he was at it.

"So anyway, Ron, Happy New Year," said Cardwell. "And see to it those goddam papers get signed tomorrow. I can't tell you . . ."

The Ambassador held the receiver at arm's length. Couldn't Cardwell just email from now on? Then he could pass the message to someone on the Embassy staff, stretched ridiculously thin though it was. Which reminded him again of the new guy. "So anyway, Bob, don't worry about Dymme. I know how important he is, and I'll get him up to speed. Well, not me personally. I'll have Colonel Gatling sit down with him. We want Dymme to know who all the players are, right?"

Cardwell went on.

The Ambassador poured a second Scotch. Career guys at State—men who'd never bankrolled a startup or met a payroll—just didn't know when to quit. "Got it, Bob. Get back to your guests. And no sweat. You don't think anything, or anyone, could keep Yusuf off the throne if that's where the United States of America wants him? Do you?"

Sheikh Yusuf, hunched forward in his leather recliner, stared at the sixty-five-inch television hung over the credenza nestled against the far wall of his office. "*Sana Saeeda*," he mumbled. Happy New Year.

"Basketball?" asked Zoraya, his only sister and a widow before her time. Although she'd stayed at the Russian Embassy's party well past midnight matching vodkas with Ambassador Kazanovitch, she looked far better rested than Yusuf. Her makeup and hair, thanks to her foreign stylist, Monsieur Pierre, were impeccable. She'd also taken her usual care with her wardrobe having selected a stunning cobalt blue suit and matching shoes she'd picked up in Paris. She fondled the petite-nonfat-latte-touch-of-vanilla espresso she'd brought up to her brother's penthouse office suite from the Mobys coffee bar on the ground floor, open 365 days a year at Yusuf's command. A perfect wake-up and start to the New Year. "I can't believe you're not at home," she said. "What does Ameena think about your coming into the office?"

"She's still sleeping, I'm sure. Anyway, there's business to do."

"Last-minute preparations for tomorrow's trip up to the mountains with Father?"

Yusuf raised his impeccable macho-double-shot-caffe-mocha-hell-yes-whipped-cream. What was with Zoraya anyway? The trip to the mountains was *his* business.

He shifted his focus to the replay of the New Year's Eve game he'd missed between Moq'tar's national team and Tunisia. He'd learned to love hoops during his years in America. But more was involved. Basketball went with the global culture. Moq'taris had become big fans like everyone else—more evidence of their desire to share in the benefits of the global economy.

"And you will finally get Father to sign the succession papers?" asked Zoraya. "Nothing could be more important to Moq'tar's stability."

Moq'tar's center blocked a Tunisian shot.

Yusuf cheered.

Zoraya needed no words to communicate her disapproval.

Yusuf took a soothing gulp from his espresso. As if he, of all people, wasn't lasered in on the matter. He struggled to hide a small grimace. When he wanted nagging he'd go home to Ameena, his first and, much to his father's chagrin, only wife. For now, he'd let Zoraya's comment ride. No matter how often she overstepped her bounds—princesses were, after all, only for show—he could never berate her. The eleventh of his father's twelve legitimate sons, he shared the same mother only with her. Although only a year older, she acted as if *she* was his mother. Yet he truly loved her, which was more than he could say about his feelings toward his brothers.

"So?" Zoraya asked.

"I've told you, I'll make it happen. That's the point of the trip, isn't it?" Yusuf had no doubts about the next day's outcome. Or his right to rule. Not to mention his ability. He'd proven himself the only son fit to succeed to the throne—a role his father acknowledged *de facto* if not *de jure* by transferring full executive power to him over the past decade. And why not? Yusuf's brilliance, accented by a dash of shrewdness and flashes of cunning, long had established him as the Sultan's favorite. A BA in finance from the University of Texas and top position in his MBA class at Berkeley—not to mention two years as a rising star at Lehman Brothers before returning home—earned him the role as CEO of what he was painstakingly fashioning as Moq'tar, Inc.

Moreover, he'd fathered the Sultan's newest grandchild, four-year-old Little Muhammad, reassuring his father, if at one remove, of his own manhood.

Zoraya tapped her fingers on the glass-top coffee table, glanced at her nails and stopped. "By the way, I am coming along tomorrow."

"The hell you are!" snapped Yusuf.

Zoraya smiled. "I have Father's blessing to charm Ambassador Ellis. In writing."

Yusuf collected himself and shrugged. "Suit yourself. Not like I need your help." He'd made a New Year's resolution to get the papers signed and so he would. No grass would grow under the feet of Yusuf bin Muhammad bin Hamza—if grass grew in Moq'tar.

"Well then," said Zoraya. "That's settled, isn't it?"

Three

Seven hundred meters above the Gulf, Sultan Muhammad bin Hamza al-Moq'tari peered out across Moq'tar. His cliff-side perch, buffeted by a blustery wind, stood at the edge of the Throne of the Shepherds, a rocky, bowl-like cleft in the Mountains of Allah set between twin limestone peaks rising an additional two hundred meters. From below, the peaks' gentle slopes suggested the breasts of a modestly endowed woman. American Embassy employees and security personnel dismissed them as the A-cups.

The Sultan—Shepherd of His People, Wellspring of Generosity, Icon of Manhood and Guardian of the Gross Domestic Product—held aloft his fabled *saif*, the curved sword given him by his father. In early manhood, following his father's assassination, the Sultan wielded it along with the threat of the infidel English's gunboats to wreak vengeance on the murdering dogs and unite Moq'tar's three major and recurrently hostile tribes. The blood of a warrior with the heart of a lion still flowed in the Sultan's veins even if his daily blood pressure readings remained low. Let anyone disparage the Throne of the Shepherds in his presence, and they would experience his wrath. Muhammad bin Hamza al-Moq'tari ruled with an iron fist even if that fist had grown arthritic with age, which could only be guessed at as well over eighty and perhaps beyond ninety.

His white *thobe* filling like the sail of a felucca in the wind, the Sultan ignored Yusuf, the Ambassador, Colonel Gatling, and his daughter, Zoraya, standing respectfully a dozen paces behind him. He knew that they'd accompanied him on this welcome visit to his ancestral home to persuade him to sign the succession papers. Did they take him for a fool? Did they think him now weak and

womanly? And was Yusuf that ungrateful? Did he seek to hurry him
to the grave?

Both elated and depressed, the Sultan surveyed the tribal lands
he had tamed and united. A large oil field some twenty kilometers
distant occupied the western extent of the sultanate. From there,
desert sands flowed eastward dotted with small villages. The dunes
led past the international airport to Moq'tar City, the sultanate's
capital and only major urban center. The growing skyline revealed
hotel, apartment and office towers in various stages of completion.
Most dotted the Corniche, the palm-lined boulevard running along
the Gulf next to the beach. Building cranes suggestive of the minarets
of the Grand Mosque rose among them and peered down on the
greater expanse of mud-brick and British-colonial buildings that
until a few years earlier comprised a secondary seaside way station.
Just east of downtown, a massive sports arena, refinanced after the
global recession, squatted toad-like on the desert floor. Further east
more dunes stretched twenty kilometers to a border lacking any
topographical definition but imposed arbitrarily in colonial days.

The Sultan sighed. He longed for the simpler, purer past when a
man required only a tent, a horse, a saddle, a rifle, a pistol, a sword,
a knife, forty good warriors and up to four young wives at any one
time—and no more lest the law of Allah be violated—all with large
eyes and ample breasts. And a good set of binoculars. A radio would
be a welcome addition not to mention a pair of British army boots.
No doubt cigarettes and a lighter. Sheep and goats, naturally. And
gold to which the spoils of war would continually add.

How Moq'tar had changed, the Sultan thought. How *he* had
changed, assaulted without mercy by the pitiless infirmities of old
age. Now, the Shepherd of His People followed Yusuf's counsel while
rarely venturing from his palace. Yet he knew his role and all that
he represented remained vital to the nation, even if Yusuf's ceaseless
promotion of business left him confused and disturbed. For this
reason, he relented when Yusuf insisted that showing the American
Ambassador his beloved mountains this morning formed the critical
part of the day's agenda. An agenda! What had life become for the

conqueror poets wrote of honor, singers chanted of courage and mothers wailed of maidens ravished?

Yet the Sultan understood fate and its demands. Failure to maintain Washington's good graces could spur grave consequences. Should America withdraw its protection, his neighbors, dearly beloved brothers all—not to mention the ayatollahs across the Gulf—would seek to crush Moq'tar like a fig beneath the hoof of an angry camel.

Still, he maintained the courage to stand up to Washington in matters of the gravest importance. Fifty million Jews lived in America. At least. They ran everything. The younger Bush's advisors who forced him to invade Iraq were Jews. Obama was one of those African Jews who hid their identity. Still, he had kept Moq'tar Jew-free.

Yes, a few Jewish businessmen from America had apartments in Moq'tar City. But with U.S. interests in the sultanate's oil, millions of dollars in military aid and Yusuf pursuing even more investment from American banks, what could he do?

No, that was it for the Jews.

Except for several from Britain and France who imported clothing and machinery. And the Jew from Luxembourg who provided wealth-management consulting to several members of the royal family. Another from Argentina brokered *halal* beef, and how could he oppose that? And some Jew from Hong Kong, who didn't at all look Chinese, imported electronic devices. A Canadian businessman came to mind. He brought with him his own food. The Jews' dietary laws—ridiculous!

As for Israelis—by the Prophet's beard, no! Except for the cardiologist who flew in monthly after the Sultan quietly visited Jerusalem. Zoraya had urged him to go to Moscow, but the Israelis offered a procedure that promised not only to extend his life for years but also to enable him to pleasure his newest wife, an Italian beauty considerably younger than Zoraya. He had only to take his blue pills.

But beyond the physician, the systems consultant Yusuf engaged for the government and a few others involved in financial software, electronic security, communications systems, drip irrigation, livestock husbandry, hotel management and currency exchange, not a single Israeli polluted Moq'tar. The Shepherd of his People guarded his nation's purity with ferocious dedication.

Bobby limped towards the Sultan. The cold—the temperature had dropped into the lower forties Fahrenheit—penetrated his right knee like a knife. "Excellency," he called, raising his voice to overcome the wind growing increasingly tenacious and accommodate the Sultan's near deafness without being disrespectful. He stopped out of range of the Sultan's *saif.*

"Let's get to it, Colonel," urged the Ambassador. "Bring the Sultan over. It's not getting any warmer, and his Excellency isn't getting any younger."

Bobby retreated a step. "Mr. Ambassador . . ."

The Ambassador raised his right thumb in a sign of confidence. The Colonel had been in country for almost a year. The locals seemed to trust him. Like powerful men everywhere, the Ambassador knew how to delegate. He would bide his time—at least, for the next five minutes.

Bobby looked to Sheikh Yusuf.

Yusuf looked down at his dust-covered shoe tops.

Zoraya motioned Bobby forward. She would have taken the papers herself—they remained in Yusuf's rhinoceros-hide computer case—but even *she* had limits. Not that as the Sultan's sole legitimate daughter she couldn't wrap her father around her little finger when she tossed her head back, flipped her scandalously loose black hair and charmed him with smile that outshone those of his many previous wives, each an incomparable beauty and none more so than her mother.

The wind blew harder.

The Ambassador pressed his hands to his sides to keep his suit coat in place.

A gust lifted the hem of the Sultan's *thobe,* exposing the bare backs of his calves. A second gust raised the *thobe's* skirt higher. It offered a glimpse of the royal backside bereft of drawers the Sultan had removed before leaving his dressing room.

Yusuf and the Ambassador turned away.

Bobby held his ground.

Zoraya, undaunted by three-inch heels, sprinted towards the Sultan. Her uncovered hair fluttered like a war banner at the head of a cavalry charge. Could the flesh of his flesh—even woman's flesh—leave her father uncovered? If no man would protect her family's honor, then Zoraya bint Muhammad most certainly would.

The Sultan turned. His beard gleamed whiter than the shell of the single egg served him for breakfast at the conclusion of the dawn *Fajr* prayer and left uneaten. A thought struggled to coalesce in his mind then dissipated like camel spittle on scorched desert sand. He pointed to his crotch. "I will make water now."

Bobby retreated to the Ambassador, Yusuf and Zoraya. Huddled together, they sought a break from the wind on the leeward side of the royal limousine, a bulletproof Bentley stretched almost to the length of three healthy milch camels. It had taken them from the capital along the Shepherd of His People Freeway and up the Ram's Intestines, the winding, treacherous single lane of road climbing to the Throne of the Shepherds.

Bobby pondered the question of Yusuf's succession. When in the future the Sultan died, how would Yusuf *not* ascend to the throne? Yusuf's surviving brothers had long conceded Yusuf's selection by their father. That included Yasaar, the eldest, who left Moq'tar for Europe thirty years earlier to live the life of a Continental sportsman and entertain a series of beautiful women in his Geneva townhouse.

Yusuf stroked a fold in the blue *thobe* he wore like a Halloween costume to please his father. He preferred western clothing as did his wife, Ameena. "Colonel, this could take awhile," he warned. "My father's prostate and all."

Bobby nodded. At fifty-two and graying, he stayed in better shape then most soldiers half his age but still possessed a familiarity with the older male body's inevitable weaknesses.

Yusuf held up his computer case and withdrew his laptop.

"More video games?" asked Zoraya. "Is that why you call on me to keep your laptop and all your other devices working?"

Yusuf grinned at the Ambassador. "My sister has a master's in computer science from the Moscow Power Institute. She speaks Russian."

Zoraya turned to Bobby. "As do you, Colonel."

"But you know all that," Yusuf added.

Bobby nodded then looked back at the Sultan, still standing expectantly in the hope of emptying his distressed bladder.

"Anyway," Yusuf addressed Zoraya, "it's a PowerPoint I thought I'd show Ambassador Ellis. A business thing. You wouldn't get it."

Zoraya stared.

Yusuf replaced the laptop.

The Ambassador's pants legs fluttered. He turned his jacket collar up. "Not that I'm not fascinated." He found moments like this awkward.

Another burst of wind hinted at a coming gale.

"Long story short, Mr. Ellis," said Yusuf, "you can see all of Moq'tar from here."

The Ambassador gazed out to the horizon. "No offense, but we have counties in the States that're bigger."

Yusuf emitted an amiable chuckle. "But we still have room for growth. So let me intrigue you with just two words. *Warrior World*."

The Ambassador glanced at Bobby and back. "You going Al Qaeda?"

"Think Disneyland," Yusuf explained. "Only with Saladin instead of Mickey Mouse."

"And Saladin would be who or what?" the Ambassador asked.

"Down there on the dunes," Yusuf continued, "we'll celebrate the Muslim conquests of Arabia, Syria, Persia, North Africa, Spain and India. Hundreds of men on horseback recreating historic battles and then selling soft drinks and sweets from their saddles."

The Ambassador scratched his head.

Yusuf faced the A-cups. "And here will arise Arctic World, future home of the Winter Olympics."

The Ambassador patted Yusuf on the back. "Damn, Moq'tar could keep American companies busy for years." He withdrew his hand and raised his arm across his face to shield his mouth from airborne grit. "You'll need people who know people."

Yusuf returned the pat. "Friends take care of friends, Mr. Ambassador."

A dull boom sounded above the wind.

Heads turned.

Yusuf squinted at the sky. "F-15 out of Al Udeid in Qatar I guess."

"Goddam, no!" Bobby cried.

Yusuf directed his gaze lower. "Oh shit!"

A fireball rose from the oil fields.

"*Allahu Akhbar!*" roared the Sultan. He waved his *saif* overhead. "Traitors!" he growled. "May a hundred camels trample their testicles!"

Yusuf rushed forward.

Bobby followed.

The wind pushed against them, swirling like a defiant stallion.

An Arab Lear disdainful of the elements, his heart bursting with the sweet lust for revenge, Sultan Muhammad bin Hamza al-Moq'tari released a torrential gush of urine in defiance of the cowards who dared challenge his authority and besmirch his honor.

Yusuf reached out for his father's right shoulder. "Dad, I have an important document . . ."

The wind tore the papers from Yusuf's hand. They swept rapidly across the A-cups like giant snowflakes in a clear blue sky.

Paying no heed, the Shepherd of His People, the front of his *thobe* soaked and clinging to his thighs, raised his *saif* to the heavens, toppled backward and entered Paradise.

Yanaayir

| January |

Four

Sheikh Yasaar bin Muhammad contemplated the grave clawed out of the rocky ground. How inelegant he considered the whole business of death in the world he'd left so long before. A shroud instead of a casket, the body facing towards Mecca. Three handfuls of dirt poured over the body by each mourner while reciting a verse from the Quran. Assurances, wailed and whispered, that his father would enter Paradise and enjoy however-many virgins for eternity. Not that such a fantasy lacked appeal.

Then there was the callous haste to be rid of the old man. Europeans took time to explore their grief, to mourn their loss. Not Moq'taris.

Yasaar nonetheless understood his duty as the eldest son of Sultan Muhammad bin Hamza al-Moq'tari, Shepherd of His People and so forth. He would have rushed back from skiing in Grenoble even if Yusuf hadn't sent a private jet. True, he'd long held religion in abeyance, having settled somewhere between agnosticism and atheism shortly after his circumcision at thirteen. However, one had appearances to maintain not to mention the protection of income from an assortment of family business interests virtually held hostage by a certain little brother. Yusuf had recently convinced their father to make him the trustee of Yasaar's assets with complete and irrevocable authority. And what did that snot-nosed little MBA understand of princely lifestyles and the expenses required to maintain them?

Added to that, Yasaar knew his own grief to be genuine if not theatrical in nature. Misunderstood as he was, his love for his father had never flagged.

Yusuf merely feigned love. Yasaar had no doubts that little brother viewed the old man's burial as an opportunity to secure political capital. Yusuf saw everything in terms of a balance sheet, whether fiscal or political. Obviously he sought to preempt criticism from conservative elements in the Assembly of Righteous Elders—men opposed to the sultanate's liberal economic and social policies, and now empowered by the constitution to elect the next Sultan. The Elders expected—indeed, demanded—adherence to Muslim law. The dead were to be buried within twenty-four hours if possible—preferably on the day of death, which this was not. Playing to the crowd as it were, Yusuf had spared no expense to bring the far-flung family together for a timely funeral.

But who said Yusuf's education and experiences living in America qualified him to hold the family's purse strings and set the nation's course?

As a man of the world, Yasaar could not easily be fooled. He knew more about Yusuf's shortcomings than his little brother could ever imagine, including his many failures to get their father's signature on the succession papers, the botched attempt on the previous day having been only the latest. A well-paid source within the palace had kept Yasaar abreast of both his father's health and his conversations with Yusuf. Moreover, he would continue to receive much reliable information from well-placed sources outside the palace.

Yasaar glanced at the grieving Yusuf over whom General bin Jabaar hovered as if to ward off the demons of death. The rest of his brothers, save the two who occupied their own modest graves nearby, stood at a short but tactful distance from the presumed heir to the throne. Of the contingent living abroad, the optometrist in London, the taxidermist in Frankfurt and the accountant in Abu Dhabi all had been provided charter flights home. Only Samir begged off, claiming he could not escape Los Angeles. Something about his new slasher film being behind schedule and over budget.

Zoraya, refusing her place with the women and heeding neither Yasaar's urging nor anyone else's, clung to Yusuf.

Yasaar stroked the collar of his wool-cashmere overcoat and sighed. The rocky ground threatened to deface his expensive Italian slip-ons. He hadn't even thought of wearing the wondrously comfortable—and obscenely expensive—pair of bespoke calfskin shoes he'd had made in London. He'd reluctantly foregone purchasing another pair given the unreasonable limitations on his cash flow imposed by Yusuf in response to his steadily mounting credit card balances. Thankfully, he had friends with deep pockets. They understood the importance of his maintaining an impressive appearance in Moq'tar.

More frustrating was the idea of Yusuf on the throne—a usurper at America's beck and call. Only a fool would consider him less of a patriot for living abroad. He'd long reflected on the issues facing his homeland and concluded that a Sultan Yusuf would prove as perilous to Moq'tar's fortunes as to his own.

Even Yusuf's behavior as a child had displeased Yasaar. He'd had ample opportunity to observe baby brother before leaving for his first university stint in Paris and during occasional holidays at home. Moreover, Yasaar made no effort to hide his disdain. Yusuf's bookishness and refusal to engage in physical play save shooting a basketball disgusted him. Yasaar taunted him unceasingly, assailing Yusuf as fit only to wear Zoraya's old dresses and work in the kitchen. Confirming his accusations, Yusuf failed to respond with anything like the determined fury emblematic of their warrior heritage. Now, Yasaar held an even lower opinion of Yusuf. Who else bore responsibility for the old man's shameful emasculation? Without question, the Shepherd of His People had produced a far worthier son.

Yasaar stepped back and watched General bin Jabaar lead Yusuf to the royal limousine. His soul curdled. Of all the family, only the eldest son of Muhammad bin Hamza al-Moq'tari understood how imminently his country risked suffering a grave injustice—a dark stain upon its honor. Only *he* seemed to comprehend that life without honor was no life at all.

Fate, however, did not necessarily dictate Moq'tar's ruin. The succession now lay in the Assembly's hands. Little brother's future was anything but assured.

Yasaar recalled the remark of an American arms dealer putting Nine-Eleven in perspective over drinks in a Bangkok brothel. God closes one door only to open another.

Five

$\mathcal{B}$obby nudged his Beretta, along with the KA-BAR serrated desert knife normally strapped to his right ankle, under the passenger seat of Makeen al Salami's silver Lexus RX 350. The challenge before him required words. Moreover Bobby, in spite of his role as senior security advisor reporting directly to Sheikh Yusuf, was still an American and thus an object of suspicion. Carrying weapons into Sheikh Fadl bin Jibril's home wouldn't cut it.

Bobby had requested the audience to help resolve a delicate dilemma confronting Makeen, the one man in Moq'tar he could come close to calling a buddy. Makeen's younger brother, Taahir, had been accused of deflowering a girl. Bobby hoped that by reasoning with Fadl, the head of their clan and ultimately responsible for the dishonor done to the girl's family, he might avert violence that, added to the intermittent acts of terrorism plaguing Moq'tar, could destabilize the sultanate and threaten Yusuf's election to the throne.

True, Bobby had no formal authorization to speak with Fadl. But his professional relationship with Qasim bin Jabaar opened doors even if those who stood behind them received him only out of anxious curiosity and the desire to avoid unwelcome scrutiny.

At the same time, the audience with Fadl offered no guaranty of success. But Bobby saw no other option if he was to play his role in smoothing Yusuf's path to the throne. That in turn would maintain Moq'tar's positive relationship with the USofA. He also had other loyalties to consider. He owed Allen Crimmins big-time for making him Crimmins-Idyll's top man in the sultanate and a well-paid one at that. Retirement had not gone well.

29

He'd enlisted out of high school and spent four years with the Eighty-Second Airborne before winning his gold bars at Officer Candidate School at Fort Benning. Making his mark in Special Forces, he'd risen to lieutenant colonel only to find further promotion blocked due to his penchant for speaking bluntly and a Pentagon more attuned to officers' political skills than merit. In all, his career produced a combat infantryman's badge, a drawer full of medals, a bad knee and two failed marriages.

His return to civilian life, unfortunately, posed a bigger dilemma than any he'd faced in Colombia, the Philippines, the Balkans, Iraq or Afghanistan. Settled in a condo in Virginia Beach—a few retired SEAL buddies continually ribbed him that he'd invaded Navy turf—he wrote policy papers for military and world affairs journals. Unlike many authors, he'd had his feet not only on the ground but also in the mud. He offered reasonable academic credentials, too—an MA in Russian history from Georgetown. But four years after leaving the Army, he'd sold only a handful of articles and failed to appreciably enhance his retirement pay.

Now Bobby would ask Sheikh Fadl to put a lid on brewing tensions while banking a favor Makeen might someday repay. Equally important, he would use the opportunity to assess the powerful Fadl's loyalty to Yusuf, the clearly preferred son of the late Sultan to whom Fadl had sworn eternal allegiance—a term defined in the Middle East as an understanding of convenience subject to abrogation by either party without notice. Whether Fadl would speak openly remained to be seen.

Leaving the SUV's warmth that comforted his aching knee, Bobby stepped onto the earthen surface of a large courtyard surrounded by ten-foot walls topped with razor wire.

Makeen, also unarmed, came around from the driver's side. A relative of Fadl's, he understood the delicacy of the situation made more complex by mutual business interests.

A short, menacing man—a lit cigarette dangling from his lips—approached Bobby. Barely five feet, he displayed impressively broad shoulders and a walk suggesting not only strength and fearlessness but also an agile grace.

Bobby nodded.

The little man held out his right hand palm up and flicked his fingers as if coaxing flight from a reticent fledgling.

Bobby raised his arms.

The little man looked up into Bobby's eyes and turned his palm over.

Bobby bent forward. He'd danced this dance before.

The little man patted Bobby's shoulders then the back of his neck.

Bobby straightened.

The little man moved his hands down Bobby's sides to his waist and then his legs then blew a puff of smoke up into his face. "You can go."

Makeen stepped forward. He ran the Muscle Club where Bobby worked out. A head and then some shorter, Makeen benched two sixty-five and loved shooting the shit over a pitcher of beer or, even more to Bobby's taste, a bottle of Pikesville Supreme straight rye whiskey.

On the downside, the Muscle Club served as a cover for Makeen's real business—moving heroin from Central Asia into the Gulf and on to Europe or the Far East. The Sultan and Sheikh Yusuf looked the other way. Anything that hyped the economy could be rationalized.

Bobby had no intention of rocking the boat. A man in Makeen's position could prove as good a source of information as he was good company.

The little man waved Makeen on without touching him.

Bobby tried to disguise his astonishment. No trained professional would let anyone pass without a search. Where power and money were involved, betrayal was a compelling temptation. In the Middle East, it was a way of life.

Bobby and Makeen started across the courtyard.

A boy of twelve or thirteen in a green sweater and pressed khakis appeared at the massive front door. He motioned the visitors forward.

They walked slowly in deference to Bobby's knee.

The little man followed.

The house's three-story exterior displayed peeling paint and patches of stone where stucco or plaster had fallen away. Rebar rose from the roof where a fourth floor was being added. Sheikh Fadl obviously wasn't concerned about showing off a McMansion in *Architectural Digest*.

The boy led them down a dim hallway and into a room lit by two narrow windows. The Sheikh sat on a camel-colored leather recliner. His back towards Bobby and Makeen, he faced a TV at least six feet wide.

A young man, perhaps thirty, wearing a dark gray, pinstriped suit jacket mismatched to checked slacks in a lighter gray sat in an elaborately carved chair painted gold. Similar chairs flanked him on either side. They would have been at home in the Palace of Versailles except for their plastic seat covers.

Bobby assumed the man to be the plaintiff.

Opposite, three gray-bearded elders in baggy sweaters ranging from sand to horseshit brown stood in front of a white sofa. Fully enveloped in plastic, it might have recently returned from the dry cleaner.

Sheikh Fadl cocked his head.

The graybeards sat. The plastic seat cover crinkled like static on a field radio.

The boy circled in front of the Sheikh, kissed Fadl's right hand then joined the little man near the doorway.

Makeen approached.

Bobby followed.

The Sheikh rose. He appeared to be as old, if not as frail, as the late Sultan with whom he had spent his boyhood. His untrimmed white beard spilled over the lapels of a nondescript sport coat under which he wore a mustard-colored cardigan sweater with two missing buttons. More impressive, gold rings encrusted with diamonds, rubies and emeralds commanded a place on each finger.

The Sheikh made no effort to look directly at his guests. Filmy, unfocused eyes revealed his lack of sight.

"*Ahlan wa sahlan*," Makeen greeted Fadl. He touched his right hand to his host's right shoulder—the locus of power for his sword arm—in an act of submission.

"*Ahlan.* My brother's presence honors my humble house," the Sheikh responded in English to put Bobby at ease. "May all men in our clan love each other as brothers." He motioned to Makeen to sit in the far chair then extended his right hand in Bobby's general direction. "And Colonel Gatling. *As-salaamu aleikhum.*"

Bobby placed his hand in the Sheikh's and held it gently. Arabs equated a strong grip with hostility. "*Wa aleikhum as-salaam,* Sheikh," he answered formally. "I'm honored."

The Sheikh motioned Bobby to the chair at his immediate right then eased back into his recliner.

"Ulaanbaatar," Sheikh Fadl called out.

"What is the capital of Mongolia?" the boy responded behind him. "World capitals for forty."

The Sheikh smiled. His mouth revealed as many gaps as teeth. "Well done, my son." He turned to Bobby. "Do you watch *Jeopardy!*, Colonel? It is an American television game show."

"I know of it, Sheikh, but I don't watch TV all that much. At night sometimes."

"Of course. You are a busy man. A *serious* man."

Bobby planted his feet flat on the floor despite the discomfort in his knee. An accidental display of the sole of his shoe would seriously insult his host who had other eyes to see for him and, Bobby suspected, a deeper understanding of everything that happened in his presence than his sighted advisors and sycophants.

The Sheikh motioned to the coffee table. It held small bottles of water, a cluster of tiny grapes and a block of hard, unidentifiable cheese along with a small knife. The meagerness of the offering suggested the Sheikh's displeasure with the matter before him.

Bobby, as a gracious guest, reached for a grape.

"I hope this New Year finds your family in good health, Colonel," Sheikh Fadl commented. "They stay behind in America?"

Bobby betrayed no rush to get to the matter at hand. The formalities associated with hospitality took precedence. "I have a son and his wife there."

"You have no wife yourself?"

"I've had two. Not anymore."

Sheikh Fadl's eyes expressed a blend of sadness and bewilderment. "Your son. You are so distant from him." His sightless eyes suddenly expressed great pride. "Some day, my son, Osama . . . not named for the one who brought trouble . . . will appear on *Jeopardy!* In America. He will represent the Arab people. *Insh'allah* he will win much money and glory. Every son is a blessing from Allah." He raised his hands, his palms up as if praying. "May Allah grant you a new wife and many sons."

A small ache twisted in Bobby's heart. He had no particular interest in a new wife, although women still attracted him. On the other hand, his lack of a relationship with Bobby, Jr. troubled him deeply.

The plaintiff, a moderately distant relative of Makeen's named Natheem, rocked forward. "The Sheikh has three current wives and twenty-seven children," he offered in the English of a university graduate with superior grades in philosophy or cultural anthropology unable to translate his education into commercial use. "*Usra.* Family. It is a man's true wealth." He turned towards Makeen. "The first duty of a man is to protect his family."

Sheikh Fadl's eyelids descended.

Natheem drew a strand of blue worry beads from his coat pocket.

The Sheikh motioned towards Natheem. "A family has been dishonored." He rested both hands in his lap and sat in silent contemplation.

Bobby placed his right hand on his still aching knee and rubbed softly.

Fadl drew in a long, deep breath, exhaled slowly and opened his eyes. "I would ask Natheem and Makeen to speak, but the details of this matter have already come before me. My decision is required.

But I have not heard from *you*, Colonel Gatling. Out of respect for your reputation as a warrior and your service to Moq'tar, I grant you this opportunity."

"*Shukran*," said Bobby. Thank you.

Fadl held his hands out. "But you will be brief. *Jeopardy!* will be broadcast in, I believe, no more than ten minutes. I could record it, but that would, how Americans say, take the edge off."

Bobby leaned forward. "I ask simply for mercy for Makeen's brother, for Taahir. He is young and their mother's only other son. I know that dishonoring Natheem's sister dishonors Natheem, his family, his clan and *you*. I know also that losing her virginity greatly limits the girl's marriage prospects."

"Limits?" Natheem burst out. "Were my father alive . . ." Acknowledging his affront to the Sheikh, he lowered his eyes.

"With all due respect," Bobby continued, "I understand that the girl was willing."

"Not so!" Natheem shot back.

"And she was no virgin."

Natheem grabbed the cheese knife and shot to his feet.

Bobby shifted his weight, grabbed the arms of his chair for leverage and kicked his right heel into Natheem's left knee. Rising, he pulled Natheem's knife hand down and hammered his right fist into Natheem's elbow.

The knife clattered against the coffee table.

The little man wrapped his right arm tightly around Natheem's neck.

Two gunmen burst through the door.

"Peace is restored," said Fadl calmly. "Thank you, Colonel. And you, Khalil."

The little man released his grip.

The gunmen retreated.

Natheem gasped for breath as he retook his seat.

Bobby's heart beat in his ears like a barrage of mortar rounds. The adrenalin rush, at least for the moment, had cleared the pain from his knee.

The Sheikh clasped his hands together. "Such is the passion that afflicts a man whose family is dishonored. As to the matter of the girl, Colonel Gatling, how do you propose that justice be done?"

Bobby had a case to make. Demanding the boy's life would encourage a blood feud and endless acts of revenge. Added to that, Makeen operated under the Sheikh's protection. In turn, Fadl received a hefty percentage of Makeen's revenues with which to pay his gunmen. The arrangement made them allies. It also made them potential competitors.

"What purpose," asked Bobby, "would it serve to compromise all you have built together?" He rose and touched his right hand to the Sheikh's right shoulder. "For the sake of peace and mutual wellbeing, I ask you to resolve this matter without a blood penalty."

Fadl patted Bobby's hand as if he was comforting an upset grandchild. "Sit."

Natheem paled. He stroked his worry beads with the desperate fury of a man lost in the wilderness attempting to start a fire with two sticks on a rainy evening.

"Your words ring true, Colonel," the Sheikh conceded. "As a man of peace, I will do this." He held his arms out towards Makeen. "For the success of our mutual interests, I will do this."

The three greybeards nodded. The rustling of the sofa's plastic covering punctuated their assent.

Bobby plunged in, following up on the momentum he'd achieved. "And Sheikh Yusuf? He can count on your support?"

Fadl placed his right hand over his heart. "Such a question has no bearing on my decision. But know that Sultan Muhammad, for whom I mourn, was a brother to me."

"Thank you, Sheik."

"Of course," remarked Fadl, "Sheikh Yasaar is the first-born of his father and a man, one may suggest, perhaps misunderstood."

Bobby struggled to avoid reacting to Fadl's lack of commitment.

Resolution swept over Fadl's face. "As to my judgment, Makeen and his entire family will visit Natheem's family to offer apology. They also will present two lambs, three-dozen chickens, a flat-screen television no larger than two-thirds the size of my own and ten thousand American dollars so that Natheem's family may regain its honor."

Natheem's color returned.

"For his offense today," Fadl continued, "Natheem will pay me ten thousand American dollars. Meat and televisions Allah has blessed me with."

Natheem pressed on his worry beads.

"As for Taahir, no harm will come to him." He tilted his head in the direction of Makeen. "Six months from today, he will marry a proper woman chosen by his elders. Until then, he will not see or speak with any woman in our clan except for his mother, grandmothers and aunts. This is my judgment. This is the will of Allah."

The graybeards rose.

Makeen stood and embraced Fadl.

Natheem attempted to stand but collapsed against his chair.

The Sheikh's young son ran up to the recliner.

"Greenbacks," Sheikh Fadl called to his son.

"What is an American slang word for the almighty U.S. dollar?" the boy responded. "And now, Father, time for *Jeopardy!*"

Six

Secluded in the small but functional bedroom of his apartment, Langley Dymme, the Embassy's new cultural affairs officer, rocked slightly forward on his right foot while keeping his upper body aligned with his trailing left leg. His right arm extended gently, palm up. His left arm reached ahead parallel to the floor, palm facing out. He had long been a devotee of the Wu style of tai chi, appreciative of its small, subtle movements and focus on balance to promote healthier organs and energy flow.

An artist at heart, Dymme remained attuned to his physical wellbeing. The same age as the Ambassador, he resembled a retired linebacker thickened by the absence of his once-Spartan training regimen. Such was the consequence of being bound to a desk with increasing frequency, lifting nothing heavier than a cell phone and running only as far as the break room. Not that Dymme considered himself particularly overweight. Plenty of muscle underlay that little extra padding. Like any man his age, he'd just matured.

Attempting to accommodate to his new surroundings, Dymme bore a growth of splotchy blonde beard destined to make no impression in a land where beards once were not only universal but also celebrated. No one, however, could accuse Langley Dymme of failing to give his all for the United States of America.

A ringing cell phone brought Grasp Bird's Tail to a premature conclusion. Duty called. The Sultan's death—not to mention the bombing that led to it—placed Sheikh Yusuf's government in something of a precarious position. Moq'taris, as best as Dymme could tell, seemed a bit jittery. That would translate to uncertainties about America and the role it played in the sultanate. For obvious reasons, a subtle tension suffused the Embassy, as well. The bell had rung. The contest for the throne was on. Only Yusuf had stepped forward as a candidate, but America's horse in the race had not burst out of the gate as expected. The Assembly of Righteous Elders seemed determined to debate the favorite son's merits—and faults—for some time to come.

In an hour Colonel Gatling would provide a security briefing over dinner at the Shepherd Palace Hotel. Dymme, whose shoulders bore weighty responsibilities if America's image was not only to be maintained but also uplifted, had expected to meet with a senior member of the Embassy staff following his perfunctory chitchat with Ambassador Ellis. The public affairs officer, burdened by double duty as press officer, provided no more than a quick handshake the day Dymme arrived. A bit sheepish about the brevity of their encounter, he passed along a file folder stuffed with maps, a printout from Wikipedia, a chamber of commerce brochure and menus from local restaurants. A few actually looked promising.

Dymme glanced at his bed. He'd laid out a navy blazer purchased in Nairobi fifteen, perhaps twenty, pounds earlier accompanied by a maroon knit tie. The blazer would identify him as a responsible employee of the United States while the tie would imply that he was something more than a government functionary.

He winced. The knit tie was wrong. It would peg him not as an individual with a true creative spirit but as an oddball. A loose cannon. A man subject to scrutiny. He had no desire for Colonel Gatling—or anyone—to pry into his business in Moq'tar. Why should he? As a professional, he knew his responsibilities and undertook them with exemplary skill. To reduce potential obstacles to his work, he'd long made "go along to get along" his mantra. That settled the business. He would wear a conventional if somewhat old-fashioned tie with muted stripes of red, blue and gold. Langley Dymme defined team player.

Dymme let Bach's Sonata [no. 1] in G minor for violin and harpsichord elevate him to a higher level of spiritual harmony as he prepared for his shower. He prided himself on possessing the soul of an artist with the vision of a cinematic auteur. In moments of self-reflection or engaged in serious conversation, a good red wine at hand, he defined himself not so much as another Scorcese or Spielberg, although he responded to their work, but more as a Frank Capra. On certain days a John Ford. While he loved contemporary film, he revered the classics of the late thirties through the fifties. As to a career in film, his time would come.

For now, the mission for which he would publicly be known and, he hoped, celebrated—a mission he embraced—was daunting but doable. He would stimulate a flourishing arts scene in Moq'tar by offering examples of America's greatest cultural accomplishments reflecting his superior education and fastidious taste. And, of course, assist the Ambassador in any way circumstances might dictate.

At dinner this evening, the Colonel would find him an attentive listener conceding he had much to learn. You couldn't take anything for granted on an assignment like this. Because experience had taught Dymme that what you didn't know could kill you.

Bobby pulled his steel-gray metallic GMC Yukon Denali into the ground floor of the new garage at the north end of the Corniche's "Krazy Kilometer" shopping district. He drove towards the pedestrian exit near the far end and took a parking spot large enough for a Conestoga wagon. He intended to walk to his early dinner with Langley Dymme. Not that he understood why the Ambassador had called on him to meet with the new cultural affairs man. But he was in no position to protest let alone argue.

At least there was an upside. The stroll offered a feet-on-the-ground view of Moq'tar City's most visited area during a time of troubling uncertainty. That's what good security was all about—taking the offensive rather than waiting for something to happen. You anticipated attempts at disruption in order to prevent them. Getting behind a steering wheel served a purpose, but it often diminished your perspective just as staying sheltered in an up-armored Humvee distanced troops from the harsh realities of places like Fallujah or Kandahar. You stood the best chance of acquiring truly useful information, including updating your sense of the public mood, when the soles of your shoes hit the sidewalk—or what passed for a sidewalk.

Bobby locked the truck and took off. He was barely out on the street when a low rumble sounded. A jolt shook the garage as if a small vehicle had crashed into it or possibly an earthquake had struck.

He swiveled his head but saw nothing.

Then he looked up.

A thin, dark gray cloud wafted skyward.

Ignoring an elevated heart rate and a throbbing knee, he double-timed to the blast site—Rockin' Daoud's, "The Gulf's Largest Music Retailer . . . Someday." Shattered guitars and shredded drum sets littered the smoke-filled store. The keys of a synthesizer lay scattered like empty casings from a .50-caliber machine gun. Several police struggled to keep onlookers, some dazed by the blast, at bay.

Bobby ordered the police, including those who continued to arrive, to disperse the growing knot of spectators drawn to the scene in spite of the inherent danger. The bad guys might have planted a second, more powerful bomb. To maximize casualties, they'd detonate it when additional first-responders and the crowd reached critical mass.

He glanced in the direction of the Royal Shepherd Hotel. Dymme would have to wait. Undertaking an accounting of what happened dictated his first order of business.

On the credit side, the device seemed relatively small. It shattered windows within a radius of a block or so while producing only minor injuries to two of Rockin' Daoud's clerks and a young male customer with hair uncharacteristically down to his shoulders. He'd come by seeking repairs to an amplifier. He'd be getting a new model.

On the debit side, one more explosion, no matter how modest, said little for Bobby's work. Just as troubling, he wondered if the bomb hadn't at all been designed to bring about massive destruction and accompanying deaths. Rather than displaying ineptitude, the bad guys might be disturbingly sophisticated, seeking to keep Moq'tar on edge without provoking a more intense response from the government—and American intervention. At least not yet.

A hand tapped his shoulder.

"Bobby, I am surprised to find you here," said Qasim bin Jabaar.

"Why should that be?"

"Please do not misunderstand. I simply meant that you have your dinner appointment with your Mr. Dymme, if I remember our phone conversation this morning."

"I don't recall mentioning it."

"Ah, but you did. How else would I know?"

"It can wait. Getting the investigation off on the right foot can't. I can have an FBI team here tomorrow."

Bin Jabaar gently grasped Bobby's elbow. "We have been through this before, *habibi*. I agree that the investigation requires specialists, but the Ministry has them thanks to the training Crimmins-Idyll has provided." He led Bobby out of the store and onto the sidewalk. Police confined the crowd of onlookers to the Gulf side of the Corniche. "Your dinner is, I am sure, of great importance to your Mr. Dymme and, need I say, to your Ambassador."

Bobby regretted having somehow mentioned the dinner. Bin Jabaar's refusal to accept FBI assistance aroused more than regret. Moq'tari investigators had come a long way, but they'd also started way behind the curve. He didn't come close to believing that they would make any more progress than they had with past bombings. His only shot would be to go over bin Jabaar's head to Sheikh Yusuf. That, unfortunately, could put a major kink in his relationship with bin Jabaar and possibly offend the Sheikh at a time of understandable insecurity.

"General!" called a voice from behind a hastily strung barrier of yellow plastic tape on which were printed the English words BACK-STAGE PASS REQUIRED.

Bin Jabaar held his right hand aloft. "Television. I shall have to answer many questions repeated endlessly. Such are the burdens one bears to promote and defend a free media."

"This isn't going to speed Sheikh Yusuf's succession to the throne," said Bobby.

Bin Jabaar patted Bobby on the back. "I would not be so pessimistic. The government is strong. The Assembly only exercises its constitutional privileges. It will come around. Moq'tar is new to this business of free elections. Let us not forget the delay in approving the younger Mr. Bush's first presidential victory. Hanging chads, as I recall."

Bobby bit his lip.

A policeman approached bin Jabaar.

"Your dinner," bin Jabaar reminded Bobby. "The Ministry shall make you proud, *habibi*. I promise you."

Bobby's fingernails dug into his palms. While this wasn't it, Bobby sensed that the time would come when he and Qasim would go toe-to-toe.

Irked by bin Jabaar's dismissal, Bobby strode rapidly down the Corniche, outpacing Moq'taris who, if nervous about recent developments, approached life at a slower tempo. He was late—a disturbing situation for a man who held punctuality and precision as major values. Even if the task on which he was now embarking should never have been assigned. Crimmins-Idyll's senior security advisor briefing a cultural attaché? What was the Ambassador thinking?

Bobby slowed. The continuing January chill played hell with his knee—the knee penetrated years earlier by an AK round in northern Iraq in circumstances often awkward to explain.

Newly promoted to major, Bobby commanded three Special Forces A-teams instructing Kurdish forces and making friends for the USofA while the no-fly zone kept Saddam at bay. He and a Peshmerga colonel were driving back to Erbil. The colonel had to piss.

No problem.

They pulled off the road outside a small village. Mid-stream, popping and not unfamiliar noises sounded in the distance. AK rounds.

No problem.

They hadn't come under fire. The locals shot off their weapons to celebrate weddings. And funerals. And the arrival of new video games. Like the Arabs they hated, the Kurds punched holes in the clouds to let everyone know they had balls and knew how to party.

The colonel dropped. Blood oozed from his head.

Problem.

Before Bobby could tuck in and zip up, a round pinged his knee. Down he went, a sorry example of a primary law of physics the local schools had failed to teach. What goes up must come down. Somewhere.

The knee was the least of his challenges in Moq'tar. He'd been pondering another negative. The people behind the bombings might target Americans next. Given all the cultural events supposedly being planned, Dymme would be one of the USofA's most visible representatives—and thus one of its most compromised. So maybe that explained the Ambassador's choosing him to brief the new man.

Only where did that leave Bobby?

If the bombing at Rockin' Daoud's had upset Moq'taris, they seemed to be making every effort to hide it when Bobby made his way to the Royal Shepherd. Local businessmen and their foreign counterparts, all in expensive dark suits, scurried from new glass office towers towards their favorite bars. Housewives popped into stores for last-minute shopping before retreating home to prepare dinner. Most were bareheaded. Some wore scarves. A few veiled themselves with *niqabs,* discouraged but not banned by the government.

Outside storefronts selling everything from iPhones to running shoes to frozen yogurt, clusters of young men sporting identical jeans and jackets of American pro basketball teams gathered beneath blue clouds of cigarette smoke. Uniformed schoolgirls hefting enormous backpacks eyed the boys while chirping endlessly as they enjoyed precious moments of adolescent freedom.

Everything seemed normal as Bobby passed the Shepherd of His People Mall with a single pronounced exception. Above the palm-lined main entry, a house-size Moq'tari flag with a green crescent imposed over three stripes of red, white and blue flew at half-staff.

Nothing changed as Bobby approached the Shepherd Palace. Men attending a regional Lion's Club convention streamed in and out through a sculpted arch formed by two giant ram's horns plated in gold. The horns rose twenty-five feet to frame the marble-and-glass façade leading to the hotel's lobby.

Unknown to the visitors, the entry served as a huge metal detector. Forget bringing in a weapon or metal-sheathed explosive. Hotel security in a below-ground control room could tell not only if you were carrying coins in your pocket but what country those coins came from, whose face was on them and in which year they were minted.

The doorman, dressed in a London designer's take on a traditional Arab warrior's get-up complete with a sword that couldn't have cut through a wedding cake, nodded at Bobby and signaled the all-clear.

Bobby strolled through the lobby beneath three palm-shaped crystal chandeliers suspended from a fifty-foot ceiling. A local English-language newspaper columnist dubbed the trio, each the size of a small oak, a reprise of the Hanging Gardens of Babylon—if Babylon was a casino on the Las Vegas Strip.

By now, Bobby looked forward to finding out what Langley Dymme was all about. He considered that the Ambassador might be yanking his chain, but Mr. Ellis had no need to demonstrate who ran the show in Moq'tar. Bobby had spent a career locked in the chain of command. After dinner, he'd check on the investigation at Rockin' Daoud's. Then he'd go to the Muscle Club for a workout. Makeen had given him a key in gratitude for getting Taahir off the hook. Hitting the gym after closing enabled Bobby to avoid watching the locals pose and preen.

Getting off the escalator at the mezzanine bar, Bobby turned to gather another perspective. He leaned forward. His eye caught a small, muscled man making his way through the conventioneers and less boisterous hotel guests. He looked very much like the little man he'd encountered at Sheikh Fadl's house. If he was, what was he doing here?

• • •

Dymme heard a deep voice call his name as he sat with a glass of excellent Merlot contemplating the merits of Sydney Pollack's *Three Days of the Condor.* He looked up and nodded. For whatever the reason—he'd never considered himself standoffish—his schoolmates at Exeter referred to him only by his last name. The practice followed him to Yale, accompanied him during his confessedly disjointed year at USC film school and found its way back to New Haven for grad school. Like a parasite, it stayed with him during his government career, as well.

"Colonel Gatling, I presume." He rose and offered his hand.

Bobby started. Dymme's hand was almost as large, its grip as powerful.

"You're late," said Dymme. He had no intention of offending the Colonel, but he had never shrunk from calling a spade a spade or a bad film a bad film.

"I was interrupted."

"The bomb at Rockin' Daoud's."

Bobby's tilted his head.

"The Embassy texted."

Bobby sat. "The beard. You didn't have it in Singapore." He'd done his homework. Every mission, no matter how insignificant, demanded preparation.

Dymme ran his hand resignedly over what he hoped might prove a more distinguishing feature than the thinning blonde hair that fell across his forehead. "In Singapore, they can hang you for going more than one day without shaving."

Bobby rubbed his knee.

"That's a joke, Colonel."

"Quiet place, Singapore," Bobby returned. "You spent time in Manila, as well."

"You, too. All over the Philippines actually."

"And before that?"

"Bogotá. But not when you were there. Tracking down narco-guerillas in the Colombian jungle must have been a tough go." Dymme put his glass down. "Your time in Russia as assistant Army attaché, that must have been interesting."

Bobby caught himself holding his breath. Had the Ambassador provided Dymme with his C.V.? But no way would he be the first to blink. "It's what we do," he shot back.

A waiter in a black shirt and green tie approached.

"Rye," said Bobby. "Pikesville Supreme. Neat." He pointed to Dymme's glass. "Another?"

"Why not?"

The waiter hurried off.

"Walked over here from the bombing, did you?" Dymme asked.

The waiter returned.

"You must have some pull around here," said Dymme. "He evidently saw you coming before I did."

Bobby raised his glass. "*L'chaim!*"

Dymme stared.

"A Jewish toast," Bobby explained. "Yiddish. I used to hear it from an old Special Forces buddy, Crazy Greenberg."

Dymme smiled. "No. That's not it."

Bobby peered into Dymme's eyes. If they were the windows to men's souls, Dymme had the shades drawn.

"So what was your family's name before they changed it?" Dymme whispered.

Bobby put his glass down. Where had Dymme uncovered this piece of information? "Gotlinsky."

Bobby's father, tormented by the end stages of pancreatic cancer, had told him they were Jewish after his return from Afghanistan so Bobby would have him buried in a Jewish cemetery. Five months later, Bobby buried his mother alongside him. What his father revealed barely sketched their lives. His parents survived the Holocaust separately, met in Pittsburgh, married and moved to McKeesport to open a TV/appliance store. Enough already.

What Bobby knew from experience was that the Gatlings lived as "just Americans." No church. No Easter baskets. No Christmas tree. Bobby's ex-wives, secular Protestants, made a big thing of

Christmas—particularly Sandi. How could they deprive Bobby, Jr.?

Bobby hadn't exactly played Santa Claus. He'd return from overseas and life would be good for a while. But he'd miss the camaraderie. The adrenalin rushes. They spent only two Christmases together.

Payback came three days after he arrived in the Balkans. LeeAnne, his second wife, emailed that she'd hit the road with an insurance salesman heading for fame in Nashville. They hadn't had even a single Christmas.

Dymme scratched his beard. "Does Sheikh Yusuf know?"

"Should he?" Bobby responded. Not that he thought it would matter. Bobby had learned from a casual and perhaps unintended conversation that Yusuf could say, "Some of my best friends . . ."

Dymme chuckled. "They say Jews always answer a question with a question."

"Do they?"

Dymme shrugged. "Gotlinsky," he said softly. "Kirk Douglas was Issur Danielovitch. Tony Curtis was Bernie Schwartz. I like *Spartacus* as far as epics go."

Bobby downed his whiskey.

"I'm not rubbing you the wrong way, am I, Colonel?" Dymme asked.

"You? A hearts-and-minds guy?" Bobby reached into his worn gray, weatherproof jacket—he hadn't seen the point of dressing for the meeting—and withdrew a cigar. From another pocket he extracted a silver lighter bearing the Special Forces logo—three gold lightning bolts flashing across a gold sword set on a green, arrowhead-shaped background. "Mind?"

Dymme shook his head while giving thought to how he might light and frame Bobby were he shooting a film. His passion for the cinematic overcame him at the oddest moments. He held a master's in American art and film history with a concentration on film. That his instructors at USC failed to grasp the promise of his writing and directing talents had driven him to frenzied rages and a return to Yale. Hollywood had not, he maintained, heard the last of him.

Bobby lit the cigar with deliberation. He wondered if Dymme was playing some kind of mind game, searching for information beyond what Bobby had been asked to give. He could play that game as well. "I'm a little surprised you came to Moq'tar directly from Singapore without a home stay back in the States."

Dymme rocked his head back slightly to suggest that his situation was a bit unusual. "Let's just say, Colonel, that the State Department is very concerned with America's image here."

"And your wife?"

"I guess we both do our homework, don't we? Margaret's in Connecticut."

Bobby drew on his cigar. It was time to shift the balance in a conversation that exhibited no direction. "Let's talk about you being a public face of the United States."

"It's all about the image you project," Dymme responded. He planned to launch a film festival at the end of April. The just-completed Shepherd of the Silver Screen Theater offered a fabulous venue—a modern icon that would serve as the Grauman's Chinese Theater of the Gulf. He'd open the festival with heartwarming classics from directors like Capra and Fleming. John Ford westerns. Movies that showed what America and Americans were *really* about. *It's a Wonderful Life. Stagecoach. The Wizard of Oz. An American in Paris. The Maltese Falcon. Casablanca,* for sure.

"Maybe *The Godfather*," Bobby suggested.

Dymme clapped his hands together. "'I believe in America!' Great opening line." He looked down into his wine. "But gangsters, Colonel? The Mafia? Don't you think that'd strike the wrong note?"

Bobby pushed his chair back. "Not necessarily."

Dymme rose. "I guess we're not in Kansas anymore, are we, Toto?"

Bobby and Dymme trailed after the host at the Lone Star Steak 'n' Chop—an Indian from Mumbai wearing a leather vest and matching chaps, red bandanna and five-gallon hat—to an isolated corner booth covered in cowhide. Their footsteps floated soundlessly in half an inch of sawdust.

Around them, dozens of animated conversations buzzed beneath neon signs hustling Lone Star and Pearl beer. Six Texas-size televisions replayed classic Dallas Cowboys victories. The restaurant had reinvented itself as an exotic American cultural phenomenon offering some of Japan's finest beef. This month, at least, it was the place to be for serious dining.

They sat. Bobby glanced up at the nearest television. He liked football as much as anyone.

Dymme, a man of the people when need be, followed suit.

The image on the screen shifted from an attempted forty-five-yard field goal to three gray-haired men shaking fists at each other.

A banner at the bottom of the screen explained in Arabic and English, LIVE: ASSEMBLY DEBATES SUCCESSION.

The Lone Star Steak 'n' Chop went silent.

One of the men on the screen wore a dark suit with a white shirt and a blue tie. He was clean-shaven. The other two, bearded, wore *thobes*. Senior representatives of Moq'tar's major tribes, the troika served as speakers of the Assembly so that no tribe could claim an advantage. Like every member of the Assembly under the new constitution, they no longer held office for life but for a restricted term of thirty years.

The picture shifted to a section of chairs at the speakers' left surrounded by a blue velvet rope. Thirteen tribal representatives of the Bani Azrak—the Sons of Blue—stood shaking their own fists, canes, daggers and swords like football fans waving foam fingers. Members of Yusuf's tribe—most in suits, a few in *thobes* with blue trim—they supported his succession.

The camera panned to the center section. Thirteen animated elders of the Bani Ahmar—the Sons of Red—clustered within a red velvet rope. Nearly half wore business suits. The rest wore *thobes* with red trim. They brandished fists, canes, daggers and swords to both their right and left. Some supported Yusuf. Others held reservations.

The camera continued to the speakers' right. Thirteen members of the Bani Abyad—the Sons of White—conferred heatedly within a white velvet rope. All wore white *thobes* with white trim and a green crescent over the heart. Like their fellow elders, they flourished fists, canes, daggers and swords while threatening to break out of the rope's confining boundaries. They opposed Yusuf and had sufficient votes to keep the succession on permanent hold. On the other hand, they lacked the votes to elect anyone else.

The TVs went black. A white title proclaimed, TECHNICAL DIFFICULTY.

Football returned.

Conversations resumed.

Bobby ordered a t-bone steak, fries and a side of coleslaw.

Dymme broke off a piece of lukewarm Texas toast—a thick slice of barely browned white bread baked by Koreans who also provided croissants and pastries to a local convenience store chain. "I'll have what he's having," he instructed their waiter. He held up his wine glass. "And another of these."

Bobby glanced around the room and startled. He thought he'd glimpsed Ilana Svadbova, the striking blonde who ran a women's clinic for the Ministry of Health. They'd met several times before making a connection. Strictly physical. They were adults. Neither sought a soul mate. She had a husband in Prague. But guilt kicked in. Not hers. His. They broke things off. Bobby had relatively few options given that American women at the Embassy were all married and Moq'tari women were off limits for practical reasons.

But it wasn't Ilana. She was hardly the Lone Star type. Besides, she'd been dodging him over the last month or so, which relieved his guilt if not his frustration.

"That little display on TV," said Dymme. "Tribal politics, I take it. I can figure out the big picture, Colonel, but you're the one on top of the details."

Bobby pointed a long finger at Dymme's chin. "Are we here so you can learn what I know or *find out* what I know?"

"Is there a difference?"

Bobby had no doubt that there was. But the Ambassador had given him his marching orders, and Bobby wasn't about to provoke a call to Washington, which would lead to a call to Alexandria and Allen Crimmins' office. The background was simple in the complicated way of the Middle East.

Centuries earlier, Moq'tar's three major tribes fought for the honor of adopting green—the color of Islam—as their own. After bloodying each other sufficiently, they arrived at a truce. Each took a different color—red for courage, white for purity and blue, the most difficult dye to manufacture and thus the most expensive, for wealth. Within a year, the truce broke down. The tribes lived in a constant state of hostility and intermittent warfare.

The late Sultan, head of the Bani Azrak, imposed a workable level of tribal cooperation through flattery, bribery, calls to faith and a campaign of violence modeled on those of Attila the Hun.

Now, disagreements about the merits and means of embracing the twenty-first century delayed, even risked, Sheikh Yusuf's succession. Assembly approval required a seventy-five percent majority, a constitutional acknowledgment of the sultanate's minority interests, which each of the major tribes—not to mention the unrepresented minor ones—could claim.

The constitution also empowered the Elders to select any candidate for the throne. This provided every Moq'tari boy, no matter how humble his origins, the opportunity, like Abe Lincoln, to grow up to be Sultan. Of course, no one in the State Department or the White House had seriously believed that such a vote would ever have to be taken or the constitutional draft, requiring approval by Moq'taris exercising their democratic rights, would never have left the Beltway.

"Political correctness," said Dymme. "Things were a lot simpler when John Wayne and Henry Fonda made *Fort Apache* in forty-eight."

America's heightened interest in Moq'tar—and Moq'tari politics—reflected Central Command's need for a defensible Fort Apache in the Gulf. But America's wasn't the only interest in Moq'tar. Al Qaeda, even if weakened, continued threatening to destabilize the region. The Saudis and Iran competed for influence. China maintained its insatiable thirst for oil. And the Russians, anything but resigned to yielding world-power status, had their own designs on their not-so-near-but-not-so-far "near abroad" if only to frustrate the U.S.

Dymme lowered his empty wine glass. "So what's the Princess all about? She's quite the looker. Couldn't she be a successor?"

Bobby took a toothpick from a container shaped like an armadillo. "No Margaret Thatchers here."

The waiter brought a dessert tray.

Bobby shook his head and pulled out his credit card.

"We should split it," Dymme offered.

"Expense account. Besides, it's Crimmins-Idyll policy. They re-bill Washington and tack on a hefty admin fee."

Bobby signed the credit card slip and stood. For a moment, both knees hesitated to support him. He grasped the table.

The host tipped his hat. "Y'all come again, Colonel sahib."

As Bobby tucked away his receipt, he noticed a man in a double-breasted charcoal suit and a pink shirt open at the collar crossing the hotel lobby. Two large companions who looked like they played for the Cowboys escorted him. Bobby froze like a bird dog on point.

Dymme stopped short. "What?"

"That's the Sultan's oldest son, Yasaar."

"Wasn't he supposed to fly back to Switzerland after the funeral?"

"I was told he had."

Dymme ran his right hand along the front of his neck. "I'd say you were misinformed."

Seven

The Ambassador and Yusuf stood shoulder-to-shoulder behind Yusuf's desk. They peered down through the massive wall of windows at the Great Hall where the Assembly of Righteous Elders met.

"The reason I asked to see you," said the Ambassador, "is that Washington wants to know . . . we *need* to know . . . what the hell's going on with those madmen down there." He wasn't about to pull his punches. He hadn't made his mark on Silicon Valley and presidential politics by skirting delicately around issues. If Yusuf hadn't learned enough in the U.S. to understand that, maybe the White House and State had him all wrong. "And no offense, but how could you not get those damn papers signed before we went up to the mountains?"

Yusuf's face flushed. His heart fluttered. How dared the Ambassador confront him—the unofficially designated Sultan of Moq'tar—in his own office? Not that he hadn't tried regularly to get Dad's signature.

Just a few months earlier he'd attempted to hand his father the prescribed papers. But the late Sultan was preoccupied—miffed that an expensive horse he'd run in Dubai came up lame fifty meters from the finish line and had to be put down. Yusuf had been forced to retreat from a furious outburst of *saif*-waving anger. The papers could wait, his father insisted. The sultanate could wait. For the sake of Allah, this was a horse!

"So what's with your brother, Yasaar?" the Ambassador mentioned. "We thought he was back in Geneva. Now they tell me he's dug in at the Shepherd Palace."

"Hardly a concern."

54

A bully when they were children, Yasaar now struck Yusuf as nothing more than an irritant, a bitter man envious of Yusuf's accomplishments and the power their father had yielded to him. Yasaar would grow bored soon enough and fly back to Geneva or Monaco or the Costa del Sol—anywhere he could find solace among the unproductive rich who comforted each other with the same lament that if only they called the shots . . .

Yusuf turned to his desk and studied a gold-framed family portrait taken on a brief vacation the previous September. The photo revealed a much younger, seemingly carefree—if important—man. Ameena looked beautiful as always. On her lap she held four-year-old Little Muhammad, as handsome a boy as there was in the sultanate—or the whole Gulf. Lovely six-year-old Maryam, who looked just like Yusuf's mother—Ameena insisted that Maryam looked exactly like *her* mother—stood at Ameena's side.

He ran his eyes over his desk. His breath caught. Casually, he turned over a confidential report submitted by the Minister of Energy. True, it was written in Arabic, but it was not like Yusuf to be careless—even with someone like the Ambassador.

Of course, the Americans would soon complete their own updated study of Moq'tar's northern oil field. They'd discover that reserves were no greater than previously estimated and perhaps smaller. Considerably smaller. That unfortunate conclusion certainly validated his strategy of diversified economic development.

On the upside, a preliminary and very secret Chinese assessment estimated that the minimally producing field to the south held reserves twice and perhaps three times that of the northern field. The depth of the oil posed a significant challenge, but Beijing might soon be ready to enter discussions leading to an agreement that could pump billions of dollars into Moq'tar's treasury over the long term—if there was to be a long term.

"Helluva view," commented the Ambassador seeking to cut the tension. He was a diplomat after all. And Yusuf *was* going to be Moq'tar's head of state. Soon. Eventually. Hopefully.

"Thanks," returned Yusuf. He was proud of his office—the twelfth-floor penthouse of a post-modern building shaped like a bullet and sheathed in glass. The ministries of Trade, Finance, Tax and Native Arts filled the floors below. A branch of the Royal Bank of Moq'tar, a small café offering an organic salad bar and a Mobys coffee shop—they could be found all over the city and in the villages, as well—occupied the ground floor.

He'd chosen one of London's leading avant-garde architects to design the building. It defined Moq'tar as an up-and-comer in the Gulf in spite of references to an engorged penis sporting a condom and the nickname "Camel's Dick." Even bad publicity, went common knowledge, was good.

Yusuf motioned the Ambassador to a leather sofa matching his recliner.

"Nice set-up," the Ambassador remarked. "I probably should have come by earlier." His eyes wandered over small white cartons sitting on a glass-topped coffee table.

"Want some Chinese?" Yusuf asked. He surveyed the remains of lunch, delivered by the Breath of the Dragon, one of the Shepherd Palace's eight restaurants. He loved Chinese food. In grad school, he and Artie Kantrowitz had eaten Chinese virtually every Sunday night—a near-sacred Kantrowitz tradition. Often, they drove to San Francisco's Chinatown to stuff themselves at a little place on Washington Street, a narrow brick building with a second-floor dining room, where they lapped up bowls of noodles delivered via a dumbwaiter.

The Ambassador sighed. "Too bad. Had lunch at the Embassy."

"Tea?"

"Pass."

"Something with a little more kick?"

"Now we're getting somewhere!"

Yusuf slid open the paneled door of the low credenza beneath his TV and pulled out two glasses. "Name your poison."

"Good ol' American Scotch sounds right. Touch of ice."

"Works for me," said Yusuf. He poured the drinks, sat and raised his glass. "*L'chaim!*"

"Say what?"

"'To life!' My best friend at Berkeley taught it to me."

"To the eternal friendship of the American and Moq'tari peoples," the Ambassador toasted in return. It seemed like the right thing to say.

Yusuf nodded and sipped. "*Mumtaaz!*"

The Ambassador looked at his glass as if something had been put in his drink.

"Excellent!" said Yusuf. "It means excellent!"

The Ambassador took a second sip. "*Mumtaaz!*" He smiled. He was getting the hang of this Arabic stuff. His face turned somber. He sighed. "Can we talk? I've got a lot of responsibility here."

"Absolutely," Yusuf returned. He understood that the Ambassador was under pressure. But what about *him*? No question, he'd come up with some way to break the logjam in the Assembly. He just needed everyone—Ameena, Zoraya and most of all Washington—to back off. "I hear you're a hoops fan."

"Hey, America invented basketball, right?"

Yusuf turned on the TV and found the previous day's pro basketball highlights. He loved the way players from around the world filled the League's rosters. Who would have thought that a seven-foot-six Chinese center or a six-ten Israeli would have been among them? But they were. Even an Iranian had made it. He liked that about the League. Like him, they didn't think old. They thought bold.

"Looks like your new arena's just about finished," the Ambassador commented.

"We're pitching the Asian championships. They held them in Doha in 2005, but that doesn't mean they can't come back to the Gulf. And there's the 2022 World Cup in Qatar. Well, maybe. No reason we can't hold some of the matches here. Hell, we'll build a new stadium."

The Ambassador took a long sip of Scotch. "Well, I guess we have more in common than most people realize. Anyway, the thing is, Joe . . . Can I call you that?"

"Yes. I'd like to think we have that kind of relationship, Mr. Ambassador."

"Ron."

"Ron it is."

"Joe," the Ambassador urged, "let's cut to the chase." He leaned back. He was in control now. Washington had sent him here to ride herd over Moq'tar and keep the world safe for democracy. He wanted to do that. He *could* do that. He *would* do that. Like they said in those Mafia movies, he'd made his bones. Ambassadors who came up through the ranks at State were nothing more than career functionaries. They'd never make it in the dog-eat-dog, my-house-is-bigger-than-yours-and-my-wife-has-bigger-tits world of Silicon Valley.

Yusuf eyed a half-filled container of noodles. He might need a snack a little later. "About that demonstration two days ago. Nothing to worry about."

It was just too easy for the Ambassador, for anyone, to misjudge Moq'tari politics. The demonstration involved no more than fifty troublemakers. Possibly seventy-five. A hundred tops. The two men who were shot would both live—although one was unlikely to father any sons. Colonel Gatling hadn't been pleased, but crises—even small ones—often justified the use of force. Besides, the government immediately distributed a skillfully written press release blaming foreign agitators.

"I've gotta tell ya," said the Ambassador. "There are people . . . people above me . . . who are, well, more than a little concerned."

Yusuf suppressed a frown. Didn't American National Guard troops once kill four protestors on a college campus somewhere in Ohio back in the early seventies?

The Ambassador finished his drink. "The thing is, Joe, the media eats this shit up . . . pardon my French. Which, hey, I don't speak either. But I've still got to say it. TV, radio, the newspapers, they all ran features. Not to mention all those blogs and tweets and Facebook stuff and whatever. And don't even ask about the clips on YouTube. Someone posts a video and suddenly, whoosh, you're way behind the eight ball. A lot of people back in the States are saying, 'America out of Moq'tar.'"

"Cut and run, huh?" Yusuf heard his voice rising. He paused to compose himself. The unfortunate incident was probably the only thing ninety-nine out of a hundred Americans knew about Moq'tar. He stretched his legs and clasped his hands behind his head. "In the old days, Dad would have taken the Michael Corleone approach. Killed anyone who opposed him. Which is what he did, for the most part."

"Don't misunderstand. We can respect that."

"Today, it's more of a Tony Soprano thing. You try to reason with people, cut a deal."

"Like you did with your stepmother?"

Yusuf gave the thumbs-up sign. His attorneys had crafted the pre-nup. As long as Cristina maintained her distance she could keep the apartment in Rome, the Porsche and the generous allowance. DNA would block any attempt at extortion through a paternity suit. Yusuf pointed to the Ambassador's glass. "Refill?"

The Ambassador shook his head. "Dinner with the Russian ambassador tonight. You know how that goes."

Yusuf nodded.

"Well hell, one for the road," said the Ambassador.

The intercom intruded.

Yusuf crossed the room to his desk. "What?"

"The Princess, Excellency."

Zoraya's smile revealed brilliant, even teeth. The white, open-necked blouse beneath her teal jacket revealed much more.

"Don't get up, Mr. Ambassador," she chirruped. She approached Yusuf, who'd returned to his recliner, bent down and pecked into the air by his cheeks—right, left then right again.

Yusuf lowered his eyes. Such affection was more appropriate in private. Zoraya made a habit of taking liberties.

"I hope you don't mind the interruption," she said in a polished English evidencing her undergraduate days in London. She noticed the TV. "Baby brother, is that all you do all day . . . watch men in shorts leap over each other to stuff balls in a basket?"

59

Yusuf glowered. But gently. Whatever she said or did—and Zoraya was no shrinking violet—he could never be angry with her. They were their mother's only two children.

Zoraya remained standing, the better to show off the new slacks and jacket set she'd recently purchased at Dolce & Gabbana along with three new dresses. She looked glamorous because her role—her duty to her people—demanded it. She also felt so very hot in one of the dozen new sets of bras and panties she'd picked up at Victoria's Secret. She could have been one of their models. Her late husband had said that more than once, and he hardly had been the only one. Why he cheated on her she could never understand, but she was not one to dwell on the past. "I'm here about Yasaar," she said in Arabic. "More specifically, the dinner I am hosting in his honor tonight."

Yusuf frowned. He would have preferred to turn down Zoraya's invitation. Ameena had insisted that they go.

"You must put aside your differences, baby brother. The poor man still mourns Father. More than any of us, it would seem, from what he's told me. He simply doesn't seem the man he's always been."

The Ambassador rose. "Hey, if I'm interfering . . ."

"Just take a minute," said Yusuf.

The Ambassador sat.

"Maybe you're buying into Yasaar," Yusuf continued, "but not me. And I'll tell you this. He better head back to Geneva soon if he wants to avoid a cut in his allowance."

"I am under the impression that Father provided him with a separate trust as he did the rest of us."

Yusuf eyed a foil-wrapped packet of onion pancakes. "He did. But he gave me a few discretionary powers as co-trustee to keep him from blowing it all. Do you know what his ski trips alone cost? And he already lives in Switzerland."

"Eight o'clock then," said Zoraya. She turned to the Ambassador. "Which reminds me, Mr. Ambassador, you are having dinner tonight with Ambassador Kazanovitch if my spies are correct."

"I wish *we* had spies that good," the Ambassador offered. He glanced at Yusuf. "Only kidding. We got bin Laden, right?"

"Yesterday Mr. Kazanovitch presented me with a very generous tin of the very best caviar. Wasn't that sweet? But forgive me. I'm prattling on. So now I will leave you two to matters of state. Or basketball. Or both if, Allah forbid, they should somehow intertwine."

Yusuf stood and led Zoraya to the door. "You're heading home to do your hair, I imagine."

"Actually, I am going to a pre-school to read stories to the children. Then I shall prepare for tomorrow's interview with Al Jazeera on women's health issues. But Monsieur Pierre shall have plenty of time to do my hair for this evening, thank you." She air-kissed Yusuf's cheeks then waved at the Ambassador. "*Ilaa al-liqaa*. Until next time."

The Ambassador stood. "Back at you."

Yusuf again returned to his recliner.

The Ambassador again sat.

They watched a series of seemingly impossible three-point baskets on the TV highlights.

"Where were we?" asked Yusuf.

"P.R. It's a mess. That's where."

"And?"

"And we've got to make the American people understand how critical Moq'tar is to U.S. security. Which means Americans better get to know something positive about Moq'tar and *like* Moq'tar. A *lot*."

A player swished a basket from the other team's foul line.

Yusuf's eyes flashed then went blank as his thoughts turned inward. He seemed on the verge of a seizure.

"You okay there, Joe?"

Yusuf leaned forward. "I just had an idea. I'm thinking we definitely *can* point American-Moq'tari relations in the right direction."

Twenty minutes later, he finished laying out his plan.

The Ambassador whistled softly. "Another jewel in the crown, huh? Slick!"

• • •

Yusuf peered across the garbage-strewn square, deserted this late at night. His attention focused on the low mud-brick-walled garage to the left of the mosque. Heavily armed men—not unlike the yet-to-be-identified terrorists whose sabotage of the oil pipeline impelled his father's awkward death—maintained positions on the other side.

A shot rang out. Yusuf flinched. He'd never become comfortable—if anyone, like Colonel Gatling for instance, could be comfortable—coming under fire.

A burst of laughter rang out above clinking glasses in the adjacent dining room. It slithered like an Arabian cat snake into Zoraya's TV room where Yusuf had made his escape.

He closed his laptop. How could he advance to level five on Warrior's Blood: Chaos in the Streets with such a commotion going on? Video games, like business, demanded focus and attention to detail. The dinner party at Zoraya's apartment hardly proved conducive to either.

He'd taken his leave under the guise of making an important phone call. Wielding power, even on an acting basis, was no cakewalk. He had no choice but to function twenty-four/seven. Let Yasaar play the clown. Yusuf was a serious man. And yet, he'd found something disturbingly different about Yasaar this evening. Not just the beginnings of a beard, so unlike him, but something more profound if not definable.

Yusuf cradled a glass of cognac—extraordinarily smooth Camus XO that Zoraya had poured from its Baccarat crystal decanter. It warmed him in spite of Yasaar, who as always continued to hold the floor.

Yasaar appeared to be finishing yet another story about his self-indulgent life in Europe to titillate the brothers who still lived in Moq'tar, as well as several cousins who filled key positions in government and business. And their wives. Customarily, the women left the men to themselves, but Zoraya insisted they remain at table. What could he say? It was her apartment.

"She didn't!" exclaimed one of the cousins.

A burst of laughter erupted.

"But that," he heard Yasaar's comment as if the volume on a sound system had been raised, "was my life before Father entered Paradise." Yusuf closed his eyes to get every word. "In confronting death, one considers what is truly important. Today . . . tonight . . . I feel nothing but shame for such transgressions."

Silence enveloped the table.

Yusuf sat stunned. Shame? Yasaar? What was that all about?

He took his drink to the large balcony overlooking Moq'tar City. Zoraya had purchased the entire top floor of the city's most luxurious apartment building, enchanted by its panoramic views stretching from the Gulf to the Mountains of Allah. In spite of Yusuf's reservations, she rejected any thought of a proper palace with grounds, stables and, of course, security walls—the kind she lived in before Nazeeh's untimely death. An apartment, she insisted, better suited her busy life given all her charitable and social commitments not to mention frequent international shopping trips. He acquiesced. Colonel Gatling devised a workable security plan. Zoraya was a happy camper. Yusuf faced one less distraction.

A hand tapped Yusuf's shoulder. He spun around.

"She really did!" said Yasaar rather somberly.

"She . . . who . . . what?" Yusuf stuttered.

"The story I just told. I'm sure you heard me in here. Or were you debasing yourself with another of your foolish video games?"

"Playboys party from sun to sun, but a Sultan's job is never done."

"Then you really *were* mulling over government affairs? Unless you were considering the election, which does not seem to be going well for you if I read the Assembly correctly."

"Actually, I thought you'd be back in Geneva," Yusuf countered. "It's the height of ski season, isn't it?"

Yasaar ran his left hand along the stubble beneath his chin.

Only now did Yusuf notice that his brother, almost Zoraya's equal as a fashionista, was the only man at the dinner party not wearing a tie.

"You're drinking *that*?" Yasaar asked.

Yusuf glanced down at his own tie—Cal blue and gold—then at his glass. "This is a cognac to die for!"

Yasaar frowned. "That poison will flush you down to Hell on Judgment Day."

Furrows of bewilderment raked Yusuf's forehead. His brother's binges were as legendary as his conquests. Now he couldn't remember Yasaar downing a drop of alcohol all evening.

"The West," said Yasaar. "The West leaves one unfulfilled. It lacks depth of soul."

The furrows in Yusuf's forehead dug deeper.

Yasaar raised his right hand. It held a scissors pointed at Yusuf's chest.

Yusuf raised his hands while realizing he had no idea how to defend himself from an attack with such an odd weapon. "Don't!" he pleaded.

Yasaar grasped Yusuf's tie at heart level, yanked down and snipped. The severed material dropped to the balcony's marble floor. "This is what I think of the culture of the unbelievers."

Yusuf clutched at the remains of his tie as if it was a lifeline tossed into a raging sea.

Yasaar released the scissors. A metallic clatter ricocheted off the cool, smooth marble surface.

Pushed too far, Yusuf found the inner fury he always brought to Warrior's Blood. "Brother or no brother!" he bellowed. The passion in his voice startled him as much as the scissors Yasaar had wielded. "I don't ever want to see you again."

Yasaar, unruffled, held his left arm out across his body and placed his left hand on Yusuf's left shoulder. "Rest assured," he said in the voice of a man totally at peace with himself, "that you have seen the last of the brother who has so aggravated you all these years. Unless our paths should cross for some reason willed by Allah."

The taut muscles around Yusuf's eyes and mouth sagged in relief. "So you're going back to Geneva for good?"

"That," Yasaar said softly, "is not exactly my meaning."

Eight

obby approached the massive, rectangular white tent erected on a yet-to-be-developed parcel bordering Moq'tar City's southern edge. Guy wires splayed out from its sides. Four poles twenty feet high supported its roof. The tent looked like something a traveling carnival might erect to host a small circus with miniature ponies and a slack-rope walker or a rental for a tabloid celebrity's welcome-home-from-rehab party. Behind it, a fifty-foot-high tower secured satellite TV and cell dishes. Off to the side and just out of site, a generator hummed.

Sheikh Yasaar was putting on quite a show, flaunting a newfound authenticity calling into question that of his government. Which was why Bobby had asked to chat. He was going behind Sheikh Yusuf's back to be sure, but with the vote in the Assembly of Righteous Elders stalled by near-round-the-clock speechmaking punctuated by intervals of raucous caucusing, he hoped to get a sense of Yasaar's intentions while delivering a back-channel message from the USofA.

A hulking bodyguard approached. The seams in his gray suit threatened to burst at the slightest provocation. He needed a shave. A touch up on the backs of his hands and across his knuckles wouldn't have hurt, either.

Bobby grinned.

The hulk held his hand out, palm up.

Bobby nodded towards his truck. As at Sheikh Fadl's, he'd disarmed.

The hulk scowled. He patted Bobby down with a less than delicate touch then motioned towards an opening in the tent.

Bobby limped from late-morning sunshine into semi-darkness.

A slimmer, better shaven man led Bobby to an ornate oriental rug dominated by varying shades of blue. Its detail suggested as many as a thousand knots per square inch with a price tag to match. His host wasn't without taste.

"The Sheikh has just awakened," said the slim man. "May I have someone bring tea and refreshments?"

"Please," Bobby answered. He had no intention of playing other than the proper guest. Having skipped breakfast and not yet eaten lunch, he hoped Yasaar's offering would be more gracious than Fadl's. Besides, he liked Moq'tari tea.

Bobby gingerly lowered himself onto one of several plump, golden silk cushions situated around a small, ornately carved wooden table. He thought he heard music playing as if he'd taken a seat in a hotel lobby. Could it really be the theme from *Lawrence of Arabia*?

He looked around. A scattering of lamps revealed that this was no car camper's tent—unless a dozen Rolls-Royces worth of campers were searching for a party. Small clusters of men—some in western clothes, others in *thobes*—sat on cushions in front of two flickering TV screens. They seemed enmeshed in conversation. Bobby figured they talked about the things all men talked about when they killed time waiting for their boss to tell them what to do next—women, cars, sports and women.

In a far corner, hanging carpets shielded what probably served as the Sheikh's bedroom. No doubt a kitchen had been put together out back with a bathroom nearby. He'd bet a month's pay it offered more comfort than a port-a-potty.

A silver tray appeared. It held two gold-rimmed glasses with handles and a gold-and-silver thermos.

A pair of blue slippers shuffled into view. Above them stood a man in a gray *thobe* with blue-hemmed sleeves. A white *kaffiyeh* covered his head. He dropped onto a cushion next to Bobby. "*As-salaamu aleikhum*, Colonel."

"*Wa aleikhum salaam*, Sheikh Yasaar."

"You honor us with your presence," said Yasaar in lightly accented English with overtones of Gulf Arabic and French. "America has recently taken a great interest in Moq'tar."

"The United States admires and respects Moq'tar."

A servant poured tea.

"We understand," said Yasaar, "that you might prefer something stronger. But in spite of appearances downtown, Colonel, that would not be the authentic Moq'tari way."

Another small tray appeared on the table, this one filled with dates and nuts.

With his right hand, Yasaar plucked a date from a small golden bowl.

Bobby did the same. The left hand was reserved for cleaning oneself after going to the bathroom.

"*Bismi Allah*," said Yasaar. "Our people bless God for the food we eat no matter how humble."

"*Bismi Allah*," echoed Bobby. He intended to keep Yasaar talking so that the Sheikh might reveal himself.

Yasaar bit off half the date with his front teeth as if they were surgical instruments. He chewed slowly then licked his lips. "Imported from Yemen. *Mumtaaz*." He threw his head back, closed his eyes, dropped the rest of the fruit into his mouth and swallowed noisily.

Bobby's stomach growled softly. He popped his date into his mouth, chewed twice and swallowed. "*Mumtaaz*," he repeated. A proper guest could not fail to show his appreciation.

"We are overjoyed," said Yasaar, "that such a friend of Moq'tar should wish to visit our humble tent." He folded his hands in his lap.

Bobby took a small handful of nuts.

Yasaar smiled.

Bobby raised a nut to his lips.

"Since returning home two weeks ago," said Yasaar, "we have developed a longing for the old, time-honored ways. Moq'taris maintain an appreciation for tradition lost on most Westerners."

Bobby knew that Yasaar had laid out only the opening gambit to a drawn-out cat-and-mouse game. Although the ritual was familiar, it frustrated him. While he would play along, sometimes a more direct approach offered a better response to the kind of challenge

Yasaar represented. The eldest brother's continued presence in Moq'tar strongly indicated his interest in the throne, making him a clear threat to Sheikh Yusuf.

Bobby determined to see how the high horse Yasaar was riding would respond to a small burr placed under its saddle. "Well, it must be good to know there's a Wal-Mart just down the road."

"Regrettably," Yasaar responded, his expression devoid of emotion, "America's commercial interests possess endlessly long tentacles. Be that as it may, our presence here makes us more accessible to our people in their time of grief and need." He raised his glass and sipped. "Moq'tari tea comforts the soul."

Bobby followed suit. The tea was sweet with touches of sage and mint. "*Mumtaaz.*"

Yasaar drew closer. Arabs, unlike Americans, did business nose to nose.

Maybe, Bobby thought, he'd provoked some straight talk.

"You shaved this morning, Colonel?"

Bobby went blank. He'd been ambushed by hostiles in countries on three continents and responded without hesitation, but the Sheikh's question came out of left field.

"So unnatural," Yasaar continued. He ran his hand over his closely trimmed beard dappled with gray. "Western men, American men, shave off their beards. Although your Special Forces grew beards in Afghanistan to cajole the local people into offering their support, no?"

Bobby cleared his head. He'd done exactly that after Nine-Eleven. "Americans are very adaptable."

"Chameleons perhaps? You, for example, speak some Arabic. And you are fluent in Russian and not a little Spanish, I believe."

"And you speak English."

"And French and Italian. Oh, and German, as well. They proved valuable in our former life."

Bobby placed his tea down on the silver tray. He'd get to the point. "You haven't shaved in a while, have you Sheikh? But I imagine you will before flying back to Geneva."

Yasaar held up his right hand and waved without turning from Bobby. "One suspects that you question the motives of our stay here, Colonel."

"In Geneva," Bobby remarked, "you were a . . . how shall I put it . . . man about town."

Yasaar pressed even closer. "And world-class skier. We were once quite content to amuse ourselves in Davos, Zermatt, St. Moritz and places of similar indulgence. Had Moq'tar a team in the Winter Olympic Games, we would have competed and, we believe, taken a medal. But Allah guides men from one path to another according to his will. Or as you Americans say, that was then and this is now."

The servant replaced the dates and nuts with a small tray of brown, formless tidbits.

Yasaar inhaled deeply. "Roasted goat testicles. A favorite of our father, may his soul dwell in Paradise at the right hand of Allah, the Compassionate, the Merciful." He lifted a piece of meat between his right thumb and index finger. "*Bismi Allah.*" He chewed slowly. His nodding head emphasized his contentment.

"*Bismi Allah,*" Bobby countered. He helped himself. There wasn't anything edible on the planet he hadn't eaten, couldn't or wouldn't. The thought brought to mind the counter-insurgency and security theorists cranking out policy papers in think tanks back in Washington, New York or California. Men who'd never carried a weapon in the jungles, mountains and deserts they wrote about. Men who held well-paid positions he was far more qualified to fill. Positions he'd been seeking in order to stay closer to home—to find his way back to Bobby, Jr. and some sort of regular life.

Yasaar sucked his fingers. He slurped loudly.

Bobby mimicked his host. Like knife fighters circling each other, they were getting into striking range. "Your new home, Sheikh. It does have us wondering about your intentions."

"You speak for America, Colonel? Or perhaps the government of Moq'tar, which would be my little brother?"

"I'm an American employee of the government of Moq'tar, Sheikh. That makes me an employee of your brother. I get paid to know what happens here."

"You are an American employee, yes. *We*, on the other hand, are a son of Moq'tar. And more, Colonel, we are the *first-born* son of Sultan Muhammad bin Hamza al-Moq'tari, may he walk in the shadow of the Prophet, peace be upon him. *Your* place is wherever your company sends you. *Our* place is here with our people on the land given to us by Allah."

"From what I see, your people are well cared for. And it's no secret that your father intended Sheikh Yusuf to succeed him."

Yasaar leaned back. "Our father was a man of the people. A man of the mountains. And of course, the desert. Yusuf is a . . . Yankee-doodle dandy. That is why our father never signed the documents that would have compelled the Assembly of Righteous Elders to approve Yusuf as the new Sultan." He stretched his arms out. The left sleeve of his *thobe* slipped off his wrist to reveal a gold Rolex that easily cost three times more than the truck Crimmins-Idyll leased for Bobby. "This is the *real* Moq'tar, Colonel. This is the Moq'tar Yusuf seeks to destroy with his embrace of capitalism and the global economy."

"And over there your boys are watching satellite TV. Al Jazeera? CNN? ESPN? The Disney Channel maybe?"

"I should think HBO, Colonel. They are showing reruns of *Rome*."

Bobby picked up another goat testicle.

"Let me tell you a story, Colonel. Every year, before Eid, the feast concluding the holy month of Ramadan, our father slaughtered a sheep with his long knife. At thirteen, each son was circumcised as is our tradition dating back to Ishmael. Our father then gave him the privilege of slaughtering the holiday sheep. We were the first, and we did not hesitate. Each year, another son followed. Even Samir, the film producer now in Hollywood, slit his sheep's throat as if he had slaughtered hundreds of animals and almost as many men. But Yusuf . . . Yusuf could not bring himself to do it. Yet somehow, this most unnatural son bewitched our father."

Bobby washed down the goat's testicle with tea. Hell, it really *was mumtaaz*. "I take this to mean you won't be returning to Geneva any time soon."

"Our people need us."

"That oil-field explosion a few weeks back. The day the Sultan died. Did they need *that*?"

Yasaar shook his head, hinting at a tipping point where calm segued to anger. "Colonel, please. We were skiing in Grenoble at the time."

Bobby put on his game face. The burr had gotten him started. Now he'd move in another direction. Sometimes you had to charge straight ahead into a difficult situation instead of dancing around it. Like attacking directly into an ambush instead of seeking cover or running. The response was counter-intuitive. It took training, repetition after repetition, to make it instinctive. He'd seen the results when indigs he'd instructed failed to follow that training. The grave offered no second chances. But when the training took hold, his boys obliterated their attackers and went home to get their medals pinned on, tell their war stories and screw the local maidens.

"Sheikh Yusuf and the United States," Bobby said, "have a lot at stake in a smooth and peaceful transition between your father and the new Sultan."

Yasaar ran his right hand down his cheek and across his chin. His beard made little noises like pieces of sandpaper scraping against each other. "Yusuf has his own ambitions. As for America . . . Have you not yet learned anything about the Middle East?"

"The bombings and the recent demonstrations in front of the Great Hall make my government, and *your* government, concerned. I ask you to consider that America can do much to promote Moq'tar's interests."

Yasaar raised his right thumb and two fingers. "Moq'tar's interests are three . . . Islam, family and tradition. But now you will excuse us. We have missed *Dhuhr*, the noon prayer. We must meditate on the will of Allah."

Bobby heard the faint music of a muezzin calling the faithful to prayer. But it seemed to come from inside the tent and very close.

Yasaar stood and pulled a cell phone out from beneath his *thobe*. "A proper ring tone. But you will excuse us. Our broker."

Bobby stood and stepped away. A sharp pain sliced through his knee. He flexed his leg and glanced across the tent. A man standing in shadow caught his attention. Short and stocky, he resembled the security chief who worked for Sheikh Fadl. The little man seemed to be popping up all over the place.

Yasaar tucked away his cell. "Colonel," he said, "Let us be frank. Moq'tar has no plans to become America's fifty-first state." His eyes narrowed. They hinted at hostility bordering on threat before widening in seeming good fellowship. He patted Bobby's right shoulder with his left hand. "Please accept our best wishes. And if we may offer some heartfelt guidance, do be careful."

Bobby's heart began to race. He'd chased, sometimes captured and not infrequently killed enemies of the USofA, but the ones he truly despised weren't necessarily the most violent but the most hypocritical. "You might find it prudent," he countered, his response more visceral than diplomatic, "to look after yourself."

Zoraya gently poured the 1982 Mouton Rothschild Ameena had presented her for installing a Blu-ray drive in her laptop then settled back on the sofa in her TV room. She thought her sister-in-law sweet—they had a pleasant relationship if not an intimate one—but so traditionally helpless.

She swirled her glass. Her palm warmed the wine to bring out its fruity aroma. She sniffed. Her nose detected spice and cedar. She sipped. Her palate delighted in the wine's full body with lush, velvety, black-fruit flavors with a hint of sweet oak. She might have waited to share such a fine wine with friends but spending a rare evening alone, she deserved to indulge herself.

The wine coursed through Zoraya's body. She felt blissfully at peace, as if she'd just shared her bed with a wonderful lover. She closed her eyes. "What I Did for Love," the song from "A Chorus Line" that she simply adored, played on her sound system. She'd become a devotee of West End and Broadway musicals during her undergraduate days and included evenings at the theater in her shopping trips to London and New York.

Placing her glass down, Zoraya turned to her laptop. Yusuf, too, depended on her. He allowed her remote access to his own laptop to install software updates, scan for viruses and troubleshoot glitches. He constantly pestered her to upgrade his memory to keep pace with all the new software he needed—including his video games—or migrate his software and all those files every time he bought a faster model. If anything ever happened to his laptop, he insisted, Moq'tar's economy—and the government—would come crashing down.

She shook her head. Her hair flounced. She stroked it. It felt clean and beautiful. No one took greater care of her hair than Zoraya bint Muhammad. With the help of Monsieur Pierre, of course.

She connected to Yusuf's laptop. With it all, she really did love him. Although she was only a year older, she'd taken upon herself the duty to help care for him when he was small—along with their nanny, of course. When he inevitably declared himself too big for a sister to watch over him, she cried for weeks. But they remained close if not always in agreement about the ways of the world.

Zoraya laughed softly. In so many ways Yusuf remained a child. He'd simply replaced his Star Wars figures and sports balls with operating budgets, bond portfolios, currency exchanges and construction projects. His files were mindboggling but not at all impenetrable.

She sipped again, fondled the wine in her mouth then swallowed. She did have to allow that her baby brother treated her well. He asked no questions after Nazeeh died, rejected the unpleasant rumors and provided a substantial allowance. Maintaining a proper home base and looking the part of a princess cost money, and her cheating bastard of a husband hadn't been worth anywhere near what he'd claimed. Given Yusuf's generosity, she continued to let him take advantage of her although he had his own paid consultant.

Nonetheless, she believed Yusuf better suited to the City in London or Wall Street, or perhaps a position in university. She held reservations about his relationship with the Americans, not to mention his complex financial involvements that she believed compromised Moq'tar's independence and the family's wellbeing.

She doubted, too, that Yusuf possessed the strength to fend off rivals both outside of the family and within. Some circles—certainly not her own—were quietly proposing Yasaar for the throne.

As to their eldest brother, she held no reservations. Until the past few weeks, he had established himself as an enchanting *raconteur* and a charming *bon vivant*—an amiable rogue one loved despite his shortcomings. But the religious elements he now seemed to court and who courted him as Yasaar 2.0 offered Moq'tar no path to a viable future.

Yusuf's computer updated, Zoraya closed her laptop. Regardless of her opinions—or perhaps because of them—it was fortunate that Yusuf entrusted her with access to all his sensitive data. She had a need to be needed. The arrangement lifted at least one burden from his shoulders while offering her a small measure of fulfillment.

That Yusuf was oblivious to all she discovered browsing his files she took for granted. He could never imagine that his sister might draw a clear picture of his complicated and rather risky financial arrangements.

Zoraya emptied her glass. Her shoulders rose and fell in resignation. She had not yet met a man who understood women.

Nine

Dymme shuffled down the hallway to an office that housed an Embassy safe for storage of personal items and small weapons. His left arm pinned two packages to his body. Plain brown paper covered each. One approximated the dimensions of a shoebox. The other was half that size.

He'd considered leaving the packages in a suitcase in his apartment. He'd also toyed with hiding them in plain sight, perhaps in a plastic bag from the supermarket down the street—a convenient place, although the wine selection left something to be desired. The ruse would almost be worthy of *The Maltese Falcon*, one of his top ten films. He'd spent any number of afternoons and evenings watching Mary Astor, Peter Lorre and Sydney Greenstreet chase after the jewel-encrusted bird only to have Humphrey Bogart wind up with a black-enameled fake.

Dymme glanced perfunctorily at now-familiar photographs of Moq'tar's natural splendor, including the A-cups. The display honored their host country but failed to mask the faded paint on the Embassy's walls. Another posting, another challenge. A little more than three weeks had passed after a dreary Christmas—not his first disappointing holiday—and he couldn't help wondering if the life he led was getting old. Life, he believed, should be more like film. You would write the screenplay of *you*, lure investors then take total control—right down to a director's cut.

He grasped the packages in his hands. He'd only be gone for a few days but why take chances? The safe in the Embassy would protect items others would surely desire. Prudence outweighed tempting but romanticized risk taking.

Turning into the office, Dymme spotted Hema, an Embassy employee who served as a floater when extra hands were needed. The position brought them into increasingly regular contact. A middle-aged and not unattractive Indian woman—Moq'tar was home to quite a few Indians, most of them merchants and low-level government functionaries—she often assisted the agricultural specialist. As if Moq'tar was going to become the date and fig capital of the Middle East! He'd been to supermarkets on New York's Upper West Side that sold more fruit in a month than Moq'tar produced in a year.

"*As-salaamu aleikhum*," Hema greeted him in an unaccented Arabic. She looked at Dymme with eyes hinting at adoration.

"*Wa aleikhum salaam. Kayf haaluki?*" How are you?

"Mr. Dymme, I didn't know you spoke Arabic. *Al-hamdu li-llah. Shukran.*" She was just fine. Her gaze shifted from Dymme's eyes to the packages. "You are going to place your pistols in the safe?"

Dymme stared as if confronted by a rude child.

"Oh, Mr. Dymme, I am so sorry. I was just making a foolish joke. You know how people say that every American at the Embassy is a CIA agent."

"Well, I don't believe they teach film appreciation at CIA headquarters back in the States."

Hema lowered her eyes.

"Hey," said Dymme, "we can all take a joke."

She smiled shyly.

"But you're not sure about me, are you?"

Hema made no answer.

Dymme shrugged. "Someone once said, 'Always keep 'em guessing.' But back to reality, I have to catch up with a stack of Fulbright applications before I head to the airport. Another part of my job."

"Mr. Dymme, I am sorry," she said in a near whisper. Her face brightened. "I have heard about your plans for the film festival. And also bringing us that modern dance company with the three initials from San Francisco. I am so excited."

Dymme nodded.

She raised her arms and twirled slowly like a ballerina more than a few years into retirement.

"Oh, your outfit . . . *jamiila*," he said. "Very beautiful, really."

"They're separates from J Jill." Hema's smile could have lit up the entire building if Moq'tar City's electrical grid ever failed.

Then the lights sputtered and went out.

Darkness descended on the windowless Breath of the Dragon.

Bobby had just lit a deeply satisfying noontime cigar after giving his lunch order to Wang Wei, his regular waiter. He liked the way Wang Wei took extra care of him. Not that he expected otherwise. Bobby provided Wang Wei with regular cash gifts disguised as tips in return for tidbits of information. Given a reasonable command of Arabic and English, Wang Wei was in a position to overhear any number of conversations involving both locals and foreigners. That's what he'd been hired to do in the first place, but Beijing didn't pay its spooks particularly well.

Bobby rose and drew his Beretta as complaints and epithets roared out in a dozen languages. He used the mini-flashlight he carried in his jacket pocket to glide past tables of disoriented patrons towards the semi-darkness of the Shepherd Palace's lobby. He had General bin Jabaar on his cell when the generator kicked in.

"Talk to me, Qasim."

"I have a man not far from you, Bobby. He thinks perhaps a transformer has blown."

"What have we lost?"

"Electricity is out all around you. We are still checking on the rest of downtown."

Bobby approached the hotel's entry. Half-a-dozen security men brandished M4s.

"All the generators have probably kicked in by now," Bobby shot back. "Let's get a complete damage assessment in ten minutes. And let's make sure this isn't a diversion."

"Slow down, Bobby. It could be a normal power failure."

"Do you really believe that, Qasim?"

"New York gets blacked out all the time, no? And as I recall, a good part of Brazil went dark in the not-so-recent past."

Bobby pushed past a small knot of Moq'taris crowding the ram's horn archway uncertain as to whether they should enter, leave or stand in place. Given the detection system's built-in fail-safe system, he'd leave them to the security men. His task was to advise bin Jabaar to place extra security on the power plant, the airport and the American Embassy. Not to mention the Camel's Dick. Protecting Sheikh Yusuf was job one.

"I do not believe you need to tell me all this, Bobby," bin Jabaar returned. "And where, may I ask, will *you* be going?"

Bobby rushed past the parking valet. "My truck's at the far end of the lot. I wanted to stretch my legs. Anyway, I'll need to do some driving to get a full picture."

"Yes, *habibi*. I expect that of you. Take care."

As Bobby paced through the parking lot, he scanned buildings to his left and right then turned his attention to the Corniche. Pedestrians seemed oblivious to the power failure. With traffic lights down, an unyielding stream of vehicles created a symphony of squealing jackrabbit starts and sudden, rubber peeling stops accompanied by a cacophony of staccato horns. Nothing out of the ordinary.

He continued walking briskly—with purpose as he defined it rather than hurriedly. Nothing would be gained by betraying undue concern. But concern weighed on him. He couldn't let go of his recent conversation with Sheikh Yasaar who, he firmly believed, posed a clear and present danger. He might even be connected to this incident or some of the recent bombings. The problem was, Qasim bin Jabaar hadn't come up with anything linking Yasaar with the terrorists, and Bobby was beginning to doubt that he would.

True, they could always cook something up. Moq'tari courts were more malleable than their American counterparts. A little creative fiction often accomplished a lot when necessity trumped principle. And the situation was growing more difficult by the day. Moq'tar struck Bobby as a truck rapidly going out of control and speeding towards a plunge off a cliff unless someone found a way to hit the brakes. And soon.

Worse, nerves were fraying not only in Washington but in Alexandria, as well. Al Jazeera and Al Arabiya fed the Arab world negative political coverage of Moq'tar on a daily basis. CNN and Fox picked up on the colorful paralysis of the Assembly of Righteous Elders and kept it flowing into homes across the American heartland. The American heartland responded appreciatively to an ongoing drama made for TV. Ratings shot up. In response, think-tank intellectuals were overheating their laptops churning out op-ed pieces for the *New York Times*, *Washington Post* and *Wall Street Journal. Time* and *Newsweek* also had climbed on the bandwagon.

Moreover, a reporter for *The Economist* had flown in and already filed two columns casting strong doubts on American intentions and capabilities. Bobby couldn't fault her. Moq'tar wasn't Iraq or Afghanistan yet, but it had all the potential to head in that direction.

As to taking Yasaar out of the game, a counter argument could be made. The law of unintended consequences had a nasty way of biting you on the ass. Sheikh Yusuf, Crimmins-Idyll and the USofA all risked being compromised and embarrassed. Bobby could cite no end of precedents. On the other hand, if the situation *did* head south, his career with Crimmins-Idyll would likely follow.

Bobby spotted his truck and pulled out his keys.

"Colonel! Colonel!" a voice called out behind him.

Bobby turned.

Wang Wei ran forward. He held up a plastic bag.

Lunch no longer stood as Bobby's first order of business. But having Shanghai Hairy Crab and rice available might come in handy. He'd have to eat eventually.

Wang Wei drew closer then stopped. His chest heaving, he presented the bag to Bobby.

Bobby reached for the cigars in his jacket. "Oh, shit!" he muttered. He'd left his cigars in the restaurant.

"Is problem with take-away, Colonel?"

Bobby pressed a ten-dollar bill into Wang Wei's empty hand. "No, this is great. Put the food on my tab." He dropped his truck keys on the ten and pointed. "The steel-gray Yukon Denali over there. Bring it around to the front and wait for me. I don't have time to waste."

Wang Wei nodded. "GMC. Nice. We build many nice trucks in China. Maybe you buy one soon."

Bobby dismissed the economic bravado—even though it might prove true—and rushed towards the hotel. He started to jog in spite of the stiffness in his knee, caught himself and slowed to a walk.

As he entered the lobby, an explosion rattled the giant ram's horns he'd just passed through. The massive chandeliers overhead chimed ominously as if a symphony percussionist had succumbed to an unrelenting muscle spasm. Then a single car horn rang out quickly joined by dozens of other bleating alarms suggesting that Moq'tar's Day of Judgment had arrived.

Ten

Upbeat if more than a little weary, the Ambassador eased out of the limousine at the side entrance to the American Embassy fronting London's Grosvenor Square. He'd arrived for a meeting that, if all went as expected, would take U.S.-Moq'tari relations to an appreciably higher level.

A U.S. Marine guard in a dress-blue uniform and white hat saluted with mechanical precision. The Ambassador nodded and rolled his shoulders. Between the airplane and the limo, he'd been doing a lot of sitting.

He'd flown with Sheikh Yusuf—who initiated the get-together—to London City Airport out east by the Docklands on a chartered Airbus A318. The choice of landing places, he assumed, made their arrival less obvious. Separate vehicles took them to the Embassy.

The Ambassador had been to London before—strictly as a tourist—but never seen the Embassy. Although he didn't consider himself to be a sentimental man, he startled when he glimpsed the gilded aluminum eagle with its thirty-five-foot wingspread perched atop the massive Chancery building. A powerful symbol of America, it maintained a rock-steady gaze—an eagle eye really—over the square looking out towards Mayfair, Soho and the West End theatres. The building, however, had been sold to a Qatari real estate company. A new Embassy would rise in Wandsworth on the Thames' south bank. Maybe, after he made his mark in Moq'tar, he'd be asked to head up the operation there.

An odd thought struck the Ambassador. It had nothing to do, he was certain, with the three or maybe four drinks he'd had on the plane. He wondered if, when the last American left the present

Embassy, the eagle would flap its metallic wings and soar away. If that happened, Dymme would want to film it.

As it happened, the Ambassador had planned on Dymme accompanying him. Sheikh Yusuf's proposal would strongly impact Moq'tari culture and the sultanate's relationship with the United States. Regrettably, higher-ups had called Dymme to some nearby emirate or kingdom or whatever on a matter considered more pressing. The Ambassador tried throwing his weight around to reverse the decision. The higher-ups shot him down.

Muffled but familiar sounds of a demonstration in the square drew the Ambassador's attention. Separated from the main entrance to the Chancery by concrete barricades, mini-mobs of what he took to be Palestinians, Pakistanis and other disaffected representatives of the greater Middle East chanted rhythmically while holding aloft placards denouncing the villain of the day. America. England. The European Union. India. Israel. Jews. Jews were the power behind all of the others, of course.

The demonstrators' words seemed nothing more than a jumble. But if the world enjoyed a bit of calm, the protestors might appear that evening on BBC, ITV, Al Arabiya and all the other television networks that sent camera crews. Mad dogs and Englishmen went out in the noonday sun. Anger tinged with hatred stoked by religious fervor and the right of free speech denied in their homelands prompted others to withstand the chilly rain of a London late-January morning.

An Embassy official in a tweed jacket stepped out of the doorway and unfurled a large black umbrella. The Ambassador waved a limp hand towards the Marine and ducked under its protective cover.

The official escorted him to the fourth floor then down a long hallway. They arrived at a large, nondescript conference room bathed in fluorescent light. It stood at the back of the building, its windows looking west towards Hyde Park.

"*Ahlan wa sahlan,*" Yusuf called out from the head of a long, rectangular table, his laptop opened in front of him. "*Kayf haaluka?*"

"I like the way that sounds," the Ambassador responded.

Two older men—clearly Americans—sat at the table with Yusuf. One, fit and tanned with blonde hair turning gray, sat ramrod straight. He gave the appearance of a serious tennis player or maybe a triathlete. He wore a dark, well-cut blue suit with the de rigueur white shirt and a red power tie—if red was the current color of power ties. His lapel bore a red-white-and-blue American-flag pin.

The other appeared to be taller but sat slumped over as if his shoulders bore the unsupportable weight of some horrid secret. Gaunt bordering on skeletal, he examined the Ambassador through gold-rimmed glasses atop a nose that resembled the beak of the eagle on the Chancery roof. His clenched jaw consisted of bony right angles. His gray suit suggested a determined preference for frugality over style.

The man in the blue suit rose and took the Ambassador's hand. "Good to see you, Ron. How's it going?"

"Nothing that a good drink couldn't help, Mr. Cardwell. Long trip, Bob. Not all that long, I guess, but . . ."

"Maybe at lunch," Cardwell responded. He nodded towards eagle-beak. "This is Mr. Ordit. Mr. Ordit, Ambassador Ellis."

Ordit nodded.

Yusuf rose and examined a table filling much of the wall to the right of the windows. It held a variety of pastries and fruit along with coffee, tea, water and soft drinks. "Actually, some Shanghai Hairy Crab and Drunken Chicken would feel good right now. Or maybe pizza."

"Anything you'd like, Sheikh," Cardwell replied. "Fish and chips?"

"How about a Hebrew National hotdog?" Yusuf replied. As heir to the throne of Moq'tar, he was entitled to a little levity, and Americans loved humor. But the proposal he intended to make was anything but frivolous, although it might initially raise eyebrows.

Cardwell started then recaptured his composure. "I'm sure we can . . ."

The door opened. The same official in the tweed jacket ushered in two men—one short and white, the other tall and black. Although physical opposites, they gave the impression of being quite comfortable with each other.

The short man, commissioner of the League, the world's premier professional basketball organization, had thinning but elegantly trimmed white hair. His well-tailored blue suit—he and Cardwell might have been uniformed teammates—attempted but ultimately failed to conceal an ample paunch. A prominent nose far thicker and blunter than Ordit's punctuated his face. A counter image of Ordit, he exuded an almost Santa-like jollity while creating an impression of no little authority, a figure not to be crossed.

The tall man wore a double-breasted charcoal suit, black shirt and yellow tie. His close-cut, graying hair provided a stately counterpoint to his dark brown skin.

The man in the tweed jacket stepped back. The door closed soundlessly.

Yusuf sprinted around the table to the short man.

The short man opened his arms and folded them around Yusuf. "What's doing, Joey? So sorry about your father."

"Mr. Kantrowitz, it's so great to see you!" Yusuf glowed as he looked around the table. "I'm sure you all know Mr. Kantrowitz's son, Artie, was my best friend at Berkeley."

Kantrowitz pinched Yusuf's left cheek between his right thumb and index finger. "He's a good boy, this Joey." He released his grip.

A red mark came up on Yusuf's coppery skin.

Cardwell blanched.

"And this," Kantrowitz said, motioning to the tall black man, "is James Buckhalter, our director of operations."

Yusuf extended his hand to Buckhalter and watched it disappear in the man's grip. "Wow, this is a thrill. I saw you in that triple-overtime game in Oakland when you played with L.A."

"My last season. My hops were gone. You find ways."

Kantrowitz lifted his arm almost vertically to grasp Buckhalter's shoulder. "James is Harvard Law, like me, and the guy who really makes us go. Like a son. Like Joey here." He approached the Ambassador. "Mr. Ellis, I presume. Daniel Kantrowitz."

The Ambassador extended his hand. "Ron."

"Our Ambassador to Moq'tar," Cardwell explained.

"Obviously," said Kantrowitz.

"I love pro basketball," said the Ambassador. He glanced at Yusuf knowingly. "Joe and me both."

Yusuf motioned for everyone to sit. "Mr. Kantrowitz . . ."

"Enough already with the Mister. Call me Dan."

"I can't. You're Artie's dad."

Kantrowitz grinned. "He's a good boy, this Joey!"

Yusuf sat. "Mr. Kantrowitz, we all appreciate your taking the time to fly in from New York . . . and you, Mr. Buckhalter . . . on such short notice."

Cardwell inched forward. He'd been briefed by the Ambassador and received Washington's blessing. "We certainly do. But Sheikh . . ."

"Call me Joe."

"But Sheikh, perhaps you would explain to Mr. Kantrowitz and Mr. Buckhalter precisely why we're all here."

Yusuf clasped his hands in front of his chest. "Well, I did leave that a little fuzzy, I suppose."

The Ambassador tugged at the lapels of his suit coat. "We wanted . . . the Sheikh wanted to discuss the matter in person without anything leaking out beforehand."

Yusuf threw a glance at the Ambassador.

"*Your* meeting," the Ambassador conceded.

"Gentlemen, everyone in this room loves professional basketball," Yusuf declared. "It's an international game, a gift from America to all the rest of us. And most of its global success can be traced to the efforts of Mr. Kantrowitz."

Kantrowitz held his hands up. "Joey, you embarrass me."

Yusuf nodded at Kantrowitz. "They don't pay Daniel Kantrowitz twelve million dollars a year . . ."

Kantrowitz rocked back as if he'd been struck. "Twelve? Way north of that, kid. How about a little respect? But enough about me."

"Well, you get my point." Yusuf held up a glass of Aqua-Pura. "May the League's success grow like the belly of a pregnant mare."

Hands scrambled for glasses.

Kantrowitz beamed. "From your lips to God's ears."

Arms reached across the table. Glasses clinked.

"This is water, huh?" asked the Ambassador.

Yusuf raised his glass higher. "And may the League truly become a global enterprise."

Kantrowitz's white eyebrows shot up. "Joey, give credit. Everyone knows the League is a leader in global merchandising. You want your favorite player's jersey in Timbuktu or a cap in . . . well . . . Moq'tar? You got it."

Yusuf drank. "Actually, Mr. Kantrowitz, I'm not talking just about merchandise. I called this meeting to talk about franchises."

Kantrowitz stroked his chin.

Buckhalter cocked his head.

Cardwell looked towards Yusuf. "If I may."

Yusuf nodded.

"We know," said Cardwell, "that for some years, the League has talked about possible expansion to Europe."

"In a conceptual way," Kantrowitz responded. "Conceptual."

"We know, too," Cardwell continued, "that the League's Board of Governors recently voted to take the plunge and award six franchises in Europe."

The Santa in Kantrowitz melted like a marshmallow in a blast furnace. "That vote was taken in the strictest confidence. No one knows, absolutely no one, or something would have appeared in the *New York Post*." Kantrowitz shot a glance at Yusuf. "Artie!"

Yusuf placed his right hand over his heart. "Mr. Kantrowitz, no one outside this room and the Board of Governors . . . and Artie . . . knows about this."

"But what," asked Buckhalter, "has this to do with you or Moq'tar?"

Kantrowitz winked. A glow suffused his cheeks as if he was everyone's favorite uncle again the focus of attention at a large family gathering. "I suspect Joey has long wanted to own a piece of a team. I suspect Joey would like us to find him points in our new European division. Which, you should know, won't play ball for three years while we work out all the details."

Yusuf shook his head. "Not points, Mr. Kantrowitz. A franchise. A whole one. And not in Madrid or Rome or Moscow or Istanbul or wherever."

"Then where?"

"Moq'tar."

Buckhalter's lips parted as if they'd been pried open.

Kantrowitz stopped him with his eyes then softly clapped his hands three times. "Joey, I love your interest. I love this game. But let's be serious. Moq'tar has a population as big as . . . what? Buffalo maybe? And Buffalo lost its team years ago."

Yusuf held his arms out. "Mr. Kantrowitz, Moq'tar is a player. We're not just a place. We're about to become a destination."

"With all due respect, Joey, Moq'tar's not even in Europe."

Yusuf held up his right index finger like a middle-school teacher clarifying a point to a class with below-average test scores. "Do the math. A League team in Moq'tar will draw basketball fans from the entire Arab world. The New York, Los Angeles and Chicago statistical metropolitan areas combined don't add up to even half of Egypt's population alone."

Kantrowitz placed his hands down on the table. "Joey, for this we flew to London? And I'm carrying a shopping list from Mrs. Kantrowitz as long as my *schlong*?"

Cardwell stood. "Mr. Kantrowitz, Mr. Buckhalter . . . Moq'tar is one of the best friends the United States has in the Middle East. In time, Moq'tar may play a critical role in the role *we* play in the region."

Both Washington and Yusuf stood in agreement. Awarding an expansion franchise would enhance the relationship between the U.S. and Moq'tar not to mention the United States' standing with the entire Muslim world. Americans—particularly those who voted—would see Moq'tar not as a nation suffering political unrest and a potential hotbed of anti-Americanism but as an ally with shared values.

"This involves more than business," Cardwell emphasized. "It's a matter of national security." He sat.

The rosy glow in Kantrowitz' cheeks turned crimson. "*Hak mir nisht ken tshaynik,*" he responded.

Cardwell went blank. "Pardon me?"

"It's Yiddish," Yusuf cut in. "Literally it has to do with a tea kettle. But what Mr. Kantrowitz means is, he'd rather we move on to a more serious conversation."

Kantrowitz smiled. "In another life Joey would be a *Yiddishe bocher* . . . a Jewish scholar."

Cardwell glanced at Ordit, who remained silent and motionless. Like his superiors, Cardwell fully supported Yusuf's plan. "I assure you, Mr. Kantrowitz and Mr. Buckhalter, nothing could be more serious."

"And no one," added the Ambassador, "could be more serious than the government of the United States of America." He folded his hands together in expectation. He understood playing hardball. All he ever asked was the opportunity to take off the gloves.

Yusuf ran his tongue around the inside of his lips. They were moving forward, but growing tension threatened to derail their progress. It was time to talk *tachlis*—the Yiddish term for nuts and bolts. "We have an arena, Mr. Kantrowitz."

And not just any arena. Workmen were putting the finishing touches on the new, state-of-the-art Shepherd of His People Center. More parking than any such structure in the world, including extra-wide spaces for the largest SUVs money could buy. Plus separate barns for horses and camels. Inside, twenty-two thousand, two hundred and twenty-two seats, each offering a television for live action, instant replays and commercials. The expected demand for tickets would make Moq'tar one of the League's top three in gate revenue.

Nothing had been left to chance. Each luxury box included a fire pit large enough for roasting a goat or sheep. Food stands along the concourse would offer truly international fare, including a major presence by the Breath of the Dragon. Of course, no one at the table needed to know that Yusuf would receive free lunches and dinners for life—his or the restaurant's, whichever ended first. Five huge clubs would each offer a full bar and dancing to live music before, during and after the game.

"Moq'taris," concluded Yusuf, "know how to party."

Kantrowitz's stillborn smile reversed course. His upper eyelids appeared almost to meet their lower counterparts. The crimson in his cheeks radiated a vengeance-seeking purple. "What the hell is going on here?" He glanced at Cardwell then at the Ambassador. "Do you people think you can tell me how to run the League? Do you really think you're more loved than we are?" He turned to Yusuf. "And *you*, Joey! Just who says you're about to become Sultan anyway? What I see on the news, it isn't pretty."

Cardwell motioned to Ordit. "Mr. Kantrowitz, this is Stanley Ordit of the Criminal Investigation Division of the United States Internal Revenue Service."

Kantrowitz shifted in his chair.

Ordit coughed into his hand then opened a gray metal attaché case and laid out a pile of manila folders with red, yellow, green and blue tabs. "Gentlemen, I have here hard-copy files on five of the League's owners, seven of its star players, two coaches . . . we're investigating a third, but we're not fully documented yet . . . and four referees."

Kantrowitz banged his fist on the table. "You don't scare me. I've faced down the heads of the players' union and our biggest TV network on the same day."

Ordit placed his hand in his attaché case and withdrew a file doubly as thick as any of the others. "And, Mr. Kantrowitz, here is one on *you*."

Eleven

Midnight having come and gone, Bobby's frustration increased with every sidelong glance at Dymme cradling the backpack he'd carried off the plane from Riyadh like a boy clinging to his first puppy. Everything seemed off kilter. Bobby couldn't connect the dots.

For starters, the Ambassador had called on his flight back from London virtually ordering him to chauffer Dymme home. But why? Piled on to that, the Embassy had taken a pass on notifying him of the Ambassador's trip in the first place. Worse, he'd been informed only several hours earlier by the Ministry of Security that Sheikh Yusuf had flown to London with the Ambassador and was about to return. Completely unacceptable.

And while he was stewing on the Ministry, Qasim bin Jabaar's boys still hadn't dug up a suspect in the bombing that destroyed his original truck and dispatched what was left of Wang Wei back to China in a handful of plastic freezer bags.

Now, Dymme sat yawning in the passenger seat. He'd brought the backpack through Moq'tari customs as a "black bag" with diplomatic immunity. Why? Lower ranking personnel served as more suitable couriers.

"Interesting trip?" Bobby asked.

"The usual. Nothing to talk about."

"Try me."

Dymme glanced at Bobby. "I appreciate the ride."

Bobby entered the Shepherd of Islam Expressway. To his right sprawled the new Royal Moq'tari Palms Golf Club—as treeless as it was flat. Palms intended to grace its fairways never made it out of

Iraq. A second order from Beirut picked up Black Scorch through what appeared to be a local vendetta.

Bobby tapped the steering wheel. He liked his new truck. It was virtually the same vehicle, although the original had leather seats, not cloth.

He eased off the gas. The fine for hitting a camel had climbed to $80,000—even for him. Sheikh Yusuf insisted on protecting Moq'tar's brand.

Bobby surveyed what he could see of the sky. Lights along the expressway obliterated many of the stars overhead. Moq'tar City's Vegas Strip approach to neon killed off most of the rest.

An eighteen-wheeler heading towards Qatar approached and passed noisily. As its taillights receded in Bobby's rear-view mirror, a pair of headlights emerged and closed to within twenty meters. The vehicle appeared to be an SUV. Traffic on this stretch of the expressway was light at this hour, but someone with a thirst or a girlfriend or both might be driving to the city.

Dymme dozed.

The SUV pulled closer.

Bobby eased down on the gas pedal. Wild camels could look out for themselves.

The SUV kept pace.

Bobby entered Moq'tar City's sleeping suburbs. Dunes yielded to new apartment buildings, townhouses, strip malls and auto dealerships in various combinations of stone, concrete, steel and glass—many still under construction. One building resembled a twisted cube. The top half of its front side faced downtown, the bottom peered out at the Gulf. A row of townhomes suggested Russia's imperial capital of St. Petersburg as envisioned by a post-modern design team in Orlando. Ahead and to the right rose slender minarets. A stubbier set of minarets came into view on the left.

Bobby slowed.

So did the SUV.

Dymme's eyes opened. "Something wrong?"

"What could be wrong?"

Dymme clutched the backpack and snored softly.

The expressway became elevated as it entered the inland side of downtown away from the posh commercial developments nearest the Corniche.

Bobby bypassed the first few downtown exits. A modest flow of vehicles crisscrossed the streets below among offices buildings, apartments and hotels. One high-rise with an aversion to straight lines and right angles might have been teleported from Barcelona, Berlin or Shanghai then left to melt beneath Moq'tar's summer sun.

Streetlights sparkled. Gaps between buildings revealed a random pattern of lots in various stages of development from rubble removal to ironwork. A maze of cranes hinted that a flock of giant one-legged storks had dropped from the sky and landed on their backs.

On the left, the Camel's Dick appeared. It shone brighter than a Christmas tree in a Dallas mall the day after Thanksgiving.

Just east of downtown, the new arena resembled a French beret left out in the rain.

Bobby exited and slowed for a red light. Two Chinese businessmen yawned sleepily in a taxi.

The SUV tailing Bobby—a white Toyota Land Cruiser similar to those used by the Ministry of Security—braked behind him. Like all cars registered in Moq'tar, it had no front license plate.

Dymme opened his eyes. "Long day."

The light turned green.

Bobby turned right onto the newly named Oasis Boulevard. Jihad Boulevard had failed to ring a bell with Washington.

The Land Cruiser followed.

Dymme shook himself awake. "I hate to tell you, Colonel, but I live farther down."

Bobby tracked the Land Cruiser in his side-view mirror. "Just checking the neighborhood."

"Kind of late, isn't it?"

"The best time."

Bobby made two rights and a left.

The Land Cruiser stayed with him.

Half-a-dozen blocks down Oasis Boulevard, Bobby pulled up in front of Dymme's building.

The Land Cruiser hung back at the corner.

"Thanks," said Dymme. He ran a hand over his eyes. "Hey, maybe you'd like to do dinner and a movie some time. My treat. Returning the favor, you know?"

Bobby lowered the window. "I'll give it some thought."

Dymme, clutching his backpack under his arm, went into the building.

Bobby rested his hand on his Beretta.

The driver in the SUV remained motionless.

Bobby counted to ten then pulled slowly away from the curb.

The Land Cruiser crept forward.

Bobby sped up.

The Land Cruiser did likewise.

Bobby felt an urge to chuckle. The driver of the Land Cruiser was quite the clown. He might as well have bolted a neon sign on the roof of his vehicle flashing TAILING THE COLONEL. If he was an assassin, he'd certainly never done this kind of work before.

In an instant, Bobby's sense of levity burst like a soap bubble. His adrenaline was flowing like whiskey at a wake. Whatever the clown's intentions or ineptitude, no way would he get to sleep for hours.

He flashed on Ilana Svadbova. If he'd just come down off his high horse, he could find better things to do at night than work out at the Muscle Club. Maybe he'd have to rethink some of his more old-fashioned notions. But the last thing Bobby needed now was to get caught up in self-reflection. Survival meant staying in the here and now.

The clown was playing a game with him. "Okay," he whispered to himself. "Let's play."

Yasaar lay back on his expansive, seductively comfortable bed. Like all the furnishings in his tent, it was worthy of a sultan.

He closed his eyes. A fine meal accompanied by a bottle of Chateau du Grand Caumont in the company of an elegant woman of subtle European charm left him drowsy. The rugs hanging around him like curtains now closed, the woman returned downtown, he would take the next few minutes to refresh. His evenings—like his days—had become increasingly hectic.

A voice called. It seemed to come not from outside his sleeping area but from within—from the foot of his bed. He opened his eyes, or at least thought he did. Was he awake? Was he dreaming? He had no idea.

At his feet stood a figure.

Yasaar attempted to cry out to his new head of security. Only gurgling sounds escaped his throat. He gasped like a man choking on a mouthful of half-chewed meat swallowed in gluttonous haste.

"Yasaar," called the figure. "It is *you*. It is *you* I have chosen."

Yasaar found himself answering without actually speaking. "Chosen? Me?"

"To maintain the glory of your fathers."

"Glory?"

"To rule Moq'tar as Sultan."

The figure drew nearer, its form and face both indistinct. Was it his father? The angel Jibril? Allah—who could not be seen—in some disguised form as he had once appeared to Abraham? Whoever it was, the figure certainly had come to comfort and encourage him, to reassure him that he had chosen the rightly guided path.

"Excellency," called a second voice.

This voice Yasaar knew—his security man. He sat up. His eyes were open now. Of that he was certain. He looked for the figure. It had vanished—if indeed there had been a figure.

"Sheikh?" the voice rang out more robustly.

Yasaar raised his hands to his face. "Is that you, Khalil?"

"Yes, Excellency. It is time to go."

Bobby took the expressway back towards the airport and exited by a public housing project consisting of two- and three-bedroom garden apartments that might have been at home in the more modest areas of Palm Springs. The neighborhood quickly gave way to warehouses and empty lots.

He stopped in front of the Muscle Club.

The Land Cruiser hung back half-a-block behind.

Bobby pulled into the alleyway between the Muscle Club and Gulf Paint, Building Supply & Linens. The gym was closed, but he could get his new truck out of harm's way by unlocking the gate Makeen had put up. Topped with razor wire, it kept prying eyes from discovering whether Makeen had parked his Lamborghini Murciélago—the pride of his fleet—in the back.

Climbing stiffly out of his truck, Bobby caressed his Beretta then reached into his pocket for the key to the padlock. While he had a pretty good take on Makeen, some things kept you wondering. Makeen's Lamborghini cost more than most people's houses back in the USofA, but the guy wouldn't spring for an automatic gate. That would have to change. Pronto. Because he couldn't come up with the key.

Bobby found himself with an uncontrollable urge to pee. He stood at Gulf Paint's wall and waited. Getting older played hell with a man's prostate—not to mention his psyche. The stream finally came in a long, slow trickle. He mumbled Eliot's famous line, "This is the way the world ends, not with a bang but with a whimper." He zipped up and climbed back into the truck.

Mussorgsky's *Boris Godunov* rang out. He clicked his cell phone on.

"Geronimo, this Little Feather," a young man announced in heavily accented English.

"I know it's you, Taahir," Bobby replied. "I see your number."

"You break security, Geronimo," Taahir scolded. "No name names on phone. Like I no say I in lobby at Shepherd Palace."

Bobby grimaced. "You just said it."

"Oops."

"Don't worry, Taahir. You're *supposed* to be in the lobby." Bobby had gotten Taahir a security post at the hotel, which served as a hub for all kinds of comings and goings among the power elite. The job represented another favor to Makeen and thus one more chit Bobby might cash if the time came.

"So I good, right? Okay then. Playboy in penthouse."

"In English, Taahir."

"Playboy . . . I no say Sheikh Yasaar's name . . . move into penthouse suite at Shepherd Palace."

Bobby twisted in his seat. "How do you know?"

"Tall woman walk into lobby with two men. One man big, other man little. Tall woman trips. Little man . . . he catch her. But bottom of *ibayah* goes up over tall woman's feet. *Big* feet. Man's shoes."

"And how do you know it was Sheikh Yasaar?"

"Little man say, 'You okay, Sheikh?' Bad security. I add two two's, get five."

"Two two's make four."

"I check with girl in office. She hot. That make five. She don't want to tell me nothing, but I promise dinner in Lone Star. I can afford. You give me money, no? Anyways, she check records. Sheikh Yusuf move into Penthouse Suite."

"For how long?"

"No checkout day. Girl so hot, Geronimo!"

Bobby looked into his side-view mirror. The Land Cruiser remained in place. "The little man . . . You know him?"

"Negative, Geronimo. He short like kid but look like cage fight man on TV. Don't work out at Muscle Club. I know *that*."

Bobby flashed on Sheikh Fadl's security chief. Maybe he'd taken another job. Or been given one.

"I done good, huh?"

Bobby checked his side-view mirror again. The Land Cruiser remained in place. He tried to pin down a likely scenario. Yasaar had given up nobly roughing it in his tent—if servants, expensive furnishings and a satellite dish meant roughing it. By doing so, he'd moved himself closer to the Assembly of Righteous Elders. But the Shepherd Palace represented everything the conservative elders professed to hate about the new Moq'tar. Why would they accept a claimant to the throne who publicly corrupted himself with the same Western indulgences they enjoyed more privately?

Unless it came down to balls.

Maybe Yasaar was hurling an in-your-face challenge at Sheikh Yusuf, the Assembly and the citizenry, too. Maybe Yasaar was through dipping his toes in the water and hinting at his candidacy. Maybe he'd decided to plunge right in.

"Stay in the lobby," said Bobby. "I'll call when I need you."

Taahir's voice revealed his smile. "You owe me one now, right?"

Bobby ended the call. If he'd come anywhere close to figuring out Yasaar's move to the Shepherd Palace, he knew why the Land Cruiser was tailing him.

The clown was Yasaar's man. The Sheikh was keeping tabs on Bobby like Bobby was keeping tabs on him. Or maybe Yasaar was sending Bobby a message to back off. Not that whoever reduced his original truck to scrap metal hadn't communicated that thought if less subtly. Most probably, both messages came from the same source.

No better way to respond, Bobby figured, than to send a message of his own. And no better time than now.

Bobby drove to the back of the Shepherd Palace. His rear-view mirror framed the Land Cruiser twenty meters behind.

The digital clock on the dashboard blinked 2:15. In a few hours, the muezzin would call to the faithful that prayer is better than sleep. Bobby would add his own version of a wake-up call: action, even if unscripted, could be better than prayer.

He slipped out of his truck and tapped his Beretta. Forget what they said in gangster movies. Killing wasn't only business, although Dymme could probably lecture endlessly on that subject. This was *personal*. His life was on the line.

He knocked on the door to the hotel's service entrance.

It opened.

"Geronimo!" Taahir burst out. "I go with you?"

Bobby shook his head. "Stay here. Someone's coming. Leave the door open. Then get back to the lobby. And don't say a thing."

Bobby crossed the kitchen where cooks chatted while waiting to fill room-service orders. He opened a swinging door leading to an alcove a dozen feet square and pressed the button between two service elevators.

The elevator door to his left slid open.

He looked toward the kitchen as he stepped in. A narrow glass panel in the door he'd passed through revealed a head jerking back.

The elevator rose. Bobby drew his Beretta. He'd disarm the clown upstairs and march him down the hall. Then he'd deal with Yasaar, who'd have at least one man and probably two outside his suite. Of course, a joker might come into play. One of Yasaar's goons could have established an observation position in the penthouse alcove. He felt like Gary Cooper in *High Noon.*

The elevator door slid open.

Bobby bounded out, aimed left then right then across the alcove. No one awaited him.

A hum announced the ascent of the second elevator.

Bobby spun around. His heart pounded. Maybe James Bond faced danger with the same calm he displayed ordering a martini, but that was the movies.

The elevator stopped.

Bobby raised his weapon.

The door opened. A Moq'tari Ichabod Crane almost as tall as Bobby stepped out. A long nose descended beneath narrow-set eyes exposing a semi-vacant stare. He wore a knee-length black-leather jacket with sleeves ending abruptly several inches above his wrists. A white cord ran from his left ear down across his heart before tucking itself into an inside pocket. He nodded rhythmically.

But his mission seemed anything but friendly. At his side, the clown's hand gripped a Colt .45—the same M1911 Bobby had carried in Desert Storm.

"Freeze!" Bobby commanded.

As the clown took an awkward step back, a dapper man in a navy overcoat burst through the door from the hallway and raised a Beretta of his own. "Freeze!" he ordered Bobby.

The clown pointed his .45 at the dapper man. "Freeze!" he echoed in English.

"Qasim!" Bobby barked.

The clown kept his gun targeted at bin Jabaar. "Uncle?"

Bobby lowered his weapon.

Bin Jabaar raised an eyebrow.

The clown let his .45 dangle by his side. "I did not recognize you, Uncle, sir," he said in Arabic.

"You think I sleep in my uniform?" bin Jabaar countered. He lowered his weapon and approached Bobby. "My wife's sister's son," he whispered. "I could tell you stories. One way or the other, I will have to rid myself of him."

The clown struggled to slip his gun into a holster beneath his jacket and adjusted his earbuds.

"So why was he following me?" asked Bobby.

"*I* assigned Abdul to watch over you beginning early this evening. We are, all of us, vulnerable."

The clown saluted. "Abdul bin Abdullah bin Azzaam, Lieutenant, Moq'tari security forces, sir. I am sorry I missed your lecture on firing discipline last month, sir. An unfortunate incident, sir."

Bobby holstered his Beretta. "And *you*, Qasim. What the hell are *you* doing here?"

Bin Jabaar stepped back. "I might ask the same of *you, habibi.*"

"I'm told Sheikh Yasaar has taken one of the penthouse suites."

"*Both* suites," said bin Jabaar. He held his overcoat open and fanned himself. "You scared me half to death."

Bobby peered into bin Jabaar's eyes. "Now it's your turn."

"I have just interviewed Sheikh Yasaar. To clarify matters."

"I have questions of my own."

"Given the hour, I believe the Sheikh has answered enough questions."

"Not from *me* he hasn't."

Bin Jabaar studied the clown, shook his head then turned back to Bobby. "I understand your presence here. Sheikh Yusuf is not happy. Washington, and this includes your Ambassador, is not happy. As a result, your superiors at Crimmins-Idyll are not happy. And if it makes you happy, *I* am not happy."

"Well, next to Wang Wei, who took one for me in my truck, I just might be the unhappiest guy of all."

Bin Jabaar raised his right hand to Bobby's left shoulder and squeezed gently. "Bobby, I acknowledge an unexpectedly complex political situation. However, if Sheikh Yasaar had returned to Geneva, one or more other candidates for the throne may well have come forward. Such a scenario is still possible."

"The guy behind all the unrest Moq'tar's been suffering through, Qasim . . . It's obviously Yasaar."

"I know this has been a difficult period for you," Bin Jabaar offered. "Not that you haven't faced greater challenges, of course." He stepped closer. His nose nearly tucked itself under Bobby's chin. "As to the destruction of your truck and the unfortunate loss of life that accompanied it, a proper investigation requires forensic expertise beyond a knowledge of creating and detonating explosive devices. Let my people do the technical work for which they have been trained."

"And your people have what to show for that training?"

"Bobby, it has only been a few days. We are making every effort." Bin Jabaar stepped back and clasped his hands together. "I *can* tell you *this*. Confronting Sheikh Yasaar . . . threatening him, perhaps instigating a violent altercation with his bodyguards . . . will serve only to create a nasty international incident."

"*You* confronted Yasaar."

Bin Jabaar shook his head. "*Spoke* with, not confronted. Furthermore, I did so at the Sheikh's request. He wished to explain that he wants nothing more than to be a legitimate candidate in a peaceful democratic election."

"And he had to do this in the middle of the night?"

"The Sheikh's schedule is not my own, Bobby. I would much prefer to be home in bed with my wife. That is, if she and the girls were not skiing in Davos. We ski Switzerland every year. Davos, Zermatt, St. Moritz. Obviously, I could not get away. As it is, I suspect my wife thinks I am up to no good. I will surely hear about my supposed misadventures when she returns." He shrugged. "But what is a husband to do?"

"I'm not sold, Qasim."

"Bobby, I understand that Sheikh Yasaar's desire to, as Americans say, throw his hat in the ring, may delay Sheikh Yusuf's succession."

"Or worse."

"Regardless, Sheikh Yasaar's appeal to the nation in general and the Assembly in particular is not illegal. If Moq'taris see an American interfering with this election, many will embrace Yasaar if only to demonstrate their independence. America demands a democracy here. It has one. Now it must live with it."

The Lieutenant's head began to nod.

"The music . . . Off!" bin Jabaar commanded with a touch of resignation. He stepped towards the elevator and pressed the button.

"Okay then," said Bobby. "Let's call it a night."

"Ah, something we can agree upon." Bin Jabaar turned towards Bobby. "I should be distressed, however, if this matter came between us in any way. Promise me that you will, as they also say in America, call off the dogs."

"I don't know if I can do that, Qasim," Bobby shot back. "I really don't."

Fibraayir

| February |

Twelve

Zoraya entered Yusuf's office as if she were parading on a catwalk. An ankle-length ermine coat set off the sheen of her thick, black, shampoo-model hair.

Ambassador Ellis and an Asian man in a black suit wearing glasses with thick black frames leaped up from the sofa they shared.

"You're early," said Yusuf.

"Oh," Zoraya uttered with a flutter of her mascara-model eyelashes. "Mr. Ambassador, I am *so* sorry to interrupt."

"Zoraya, this is Mr. Shen," Yusuf explained in English.

The Asian man nodded.

"Mr. Shen represents the People's Wealth & Happiness Bank of Shanghai."

"And Khartoum, Lagos, Caracas . . . London and New York, naturally," Zoraya remarked.

Mr. Shen pressed his hands to his sides. "It is my honor, Princess."

Zoraya let her coat glide off her shoulders.

The Ambassador caught it and tossed it over the back of the sofa next to Yusuf's recliner.

Zoraya twirled like a kindergartener to display a silver metallic dress exposing more than her royal knees. She'd topped it off with a gold suit jacket left unbuttoned. "A new designer from Australia," she warbled.

The Ambassador whistled.

Zoraya blew an air kiss at the Ambassador then air-kissed Yusuf in the vicinity of either cheek. "Actually, I *am* ahead of schedule, baby brother."

Zoraya championed efficiency. Her schedule demanded it. The *Gulf Daily News* would photograph her that afternoon for a fashion spread. Tomorrow she would attend to numerous details before hosting a major charity event that evening concurrent with the opening of a new Russian nightclub.

"All the proceeds," she informed the Ambassador, "will go to the new cancer wing at the Shepherd of His People Hospital."

"Looking forward," the Ambassador responded. "I bet Mr. Shen will have a check for you, too."

Yusuf led the Ambassador and Mr. Shen to the door.

"*Ilaa al-liqaa*," Zoraya sang out.

"Be seeing you, Ron," Yusuf said with a wink.

Yusuf closed the door and turned to Zoraya. "Aren't you exposing yourself a bit too much?"

"If you mean my activities, don't be silly. Who would harm *me*? Besides, I relented when you insisted that Colonel Gatling watch over me tomorrow evening. Ambassador Kazanovitch would be heartbroken were I not present at my own event. His government has provided the hospital with a very substantial donation. And thank you for *your* check."

Yusuf fell back into his recliner. "Hungry?"

Zoraya perched on the near sofa.

The remains of a small feast from the Breath of the Dragon littered the coffee table.

"Honestly, baby brother, if a fatal coronary hit you tomorrow, no one would be surprised. But thank you, I already had a salad."

"So?"

"*You* asked *me* to come see *you*."

Yusuf nodded. "Lots on my mind." He extracted a small dumpling from a white carton and deposited it on his gold-rimmed plate. Satisfied, he held up the TV remote and turned on Moq'tar TV's broadcast of the day's meeting of the Assembly of Righteous Elders. "C-Span's carrying the debate now. We've become the Middle East's showcase of democracy."

"Boooring. It is the same argument every day. Even more predictable than the weather in July."

A loud cry arose from the television.

Yusuf froze.

"What in the name of the Prophet is that?" asked Zoraya. Her voice registered a level of shock that might have been prompted only by two women wearing the same shoes at a formal gathering.

There on TV in front of the world, the chief of the Bani Abyad, a man Yusuf's age whose own father had died rather mysteriously in Beirut the year before—the usual pundits denounced the Mossad, but Yusuf had reasons to suspect overexertion in the arms of a Ukrainian prostitute—sat astride a white horse trotting up and down the aisles of the Assembly hall.

Fists within the sections filled by the Bani Azrak and Bani Ahmar shook in a mix of anger and support.

The representatives of the Bani Abyad stood with looks of jubilation. To a man they chanted, "Yasaar! Yasaar! Yasaar!"

"So he's cut a deal with them!" Zoraya exclaimed.

The chanting switched to "*Allahu Akhbar!*" God is great!

"Our damn brother," said Yusuf, "is trying to embarrass me."

The white horse turned, galloped down the aisle and disappeared through the double doors leading out of the chamber.

The shouting stopped as if throats had been cut. The Elders from all three tribes stood mute and motionless.

Acknowledging a sudden deficiency of drama in a medium that demanded it, Moq'tar TV cut to a commercial plugging a new pita bread with a date mix-in.

Yusuf clicked the TV off and flung the remote at the sofa to his right. It hit the back cushion, rebounded onto the coffee table and knocked over a near-empty carton of fried rice.

"Father would be furious," said Zoraya. She clenched her jaw with a courageous disregard for the tiny wrinkles forming at the corners of her mouth and eyes. "He hated foolish debates in the Assembly that lead to nothing but more debates. He was wise to ignore them and do as he wished."

"Look," Yusuf protested, "no one dislikes all this crap in the Assembly more than me. And someone better have brought a shovel." He hoisted the dumpling.

Zoraya stared in frustration as if she'd scolded a mischievous boy caught sneaking biscuits before dinner only to find fresh crumbs on his face.

"If Yasaar hadn't decided to stay here," said Yusuf, "the Assembly would have already made me Sultan. You know that."

Zoraya patted Yusuf's free hand. Her mother would never have considered doing that with one of *her* brothers. But this was a different time, and she was a different woman. No man's demure companion, she had her own agenda. Advancing the best interests of her country held a place right on top of the list. "Listen to my voice, Yusuf. You must be the man our father was."

Yusuf swallowed the dumpling whole. He wondered if he'd have time to get on the elliptical. "And do what precisely?"

"Go before the Assembly. Demand that they confirm you. Show them you are strong."

"Two words . . . No signed document." Yusuf raised his right hand, counted on his fingers and shrugged. "Another two words . . . Not allowed."

Moq'tar's constitution forbade any candidate for succession from addressing the Assembly within the Great Hall until Election Day without a formal invitation. The Assembly hadn't issued one to either brother.

Zoraya shook her head. "Other options remain available."

"Send the Elders home and arrest those who won't go? Then declare myself Sultan?"

"At last, little brother, I believe we understand each other."

"That's not the way democracy works."

"Democracy?" Zoraya gently patted her cheeks. She believed democracy a greatly overrated concept supported by those who manipulated it to their own ends. What more did Moq'taris desire than to awaken mornings to non-fat yoghurt topped with fresh fruit and a rich espresso, days of profitable business and plentiful shopping, and evenings spent peacefully in front of their televisions or partying at their favorite clubs. "Without a strong hand there can be no Moq'tar as we truly wish to know it."

Yusuf looked at her in puppy-eyed disbelief. "Without democracy, we lose America's support."

"America! America! Were I you . . ."

A hint of fire sparked in Yusuf's eyes. "You'd poison all the Elders like you did Nazeeh?"

Zoraya's eyes hinted at tears but remained dry. "My late husband developed a sudden heart problem and died unexpectedly shortly after. You saw his death certificate. I was crushed . . . in my way."

Yusuf held up his hands as if to block a punch. "Hey, he had it coming. The son-of-a-bitch cheated on you on however many continents there are on this planet." He shrugged. "It's a guy thing."

"Perhaps *I* should be Sultana. Perhaps the women of Moq'tar would have fewer guy things to worry about."

Yusuf giggled. "As if."

Zoraya regained her feminine composure. "As to Yasaar's claim to Father's throne, I find it regrettable. Yet he also is my brother, and I love him. But you know that it is *you*, Yusuf, who has my heart."

Yusuf pecked Zoraya on the cheek. "And *you* should know that I've come up with a game plan to put me on the throne. Actually, it's a done deal."

"This is why you called me here? And why, I take it, you met with Ambassador Ellis and Mr. Shen?"

Yusuf sat. "You're pretty smart. For a woman. But this is way too complicated for you. And yes. They're involved."

Zoraya ran her tongue along her upper lip, reached into her Gucci purse and withdrew a jeweled Tiffany compact. She scrutinized the staying power of the new French lipstick recommended by Monsieur Pierre. She studied her eyes as well. Would they reveal that she knew, if not every last detail, a great deal about what Yusuf had planned? Satisfied, she slipped the compact back into her purse. "And what you call your game plan. It has what to do with, as they say in the States, little old *me?*"

Yusuf reclined and clasped his hands behind his head. The lower buttons on his white shirt strained against his belly. He laid out the game plan. At least the broad strokes. What more could a woman handle? "I won't kid you," he concluded. "I'm the hero in all this, but I can't look like I'm being distracted. The Assembly and the people have to see me staying focused on leading the country. We . . . I . . . need a public face."

"And that would be me?"

Yusuf winked.

Zoraya raised a carefully groomed eyebrow. "If you believe that I will take part in this foolishness, you have been possessed by a *jinni* or an evil *marid*. Perhaps *Shaitan* himself."

Yusuf stood, placed his hands on his waist and leaned over to his left and then his right. Like Zoraya, he'd have to start eating salads and cutting back on the booze if he was going to create the impression of a warrior. "Trust me, this is a great opportunity for you, too."

Zoraya examined the sapphire bracelet on her left wrist, a guilt offering from Nazeeh. His last. "And what exactly does that mean?"

Yusuf beamed. "A can't-lose investment. Not to mention a whole lot of extra income just for looking beautiful."

"How thoughtful."

"And you'll be all over the media. Worldwide. We'll get you on *Sixty Minutes.*"

The corners of Zoraya's mouth hinted at turning up. "An Oprah special perhaps?"

"I don't see why not. So go do your photo shoot and host your fundraiser tomorrow night. But whatever you've got planned for the rest of the week, cancel it. I need you to fly to London."

"Drop everything then? For this . . . game plan?"

"For Moq'tar." Yusuf reached into his pocket and held up a debit card from the Royal Bank of Moq'tar. "Fifty thousand dollars. I thought you might squeeze in a little shopping at Harrods or wherever."

Zoraya plucked the card from his hand with the skill of a practiced pickpocket. "For Father," she pledged. "What I do, I do for Father."

Sheikh Fadl's sightless eyes expressed puzzlement as if he'd been asked to read the top lines of an eye chart. "And what makes you think, Colonel Gatling, that I can find the men who planted the bomb in your truck?"

"And killed an innocent man," Bobby added.

Fadl shrugged.

"I ask this favor, Sheikh, because little in Moq'tar escapes you."

Fadl tugged gently at the end of his beard. "If it is the will of Allah that you die, you can not escape your fate."

"And what if God wants me to find the men who tried to kill me before they can try again?"

Fadl rubbed his hands gently. Like the late Sultan, he endured arthritis. "If only I could see all that I wished."

Bobby searched Fadl's face for any sign betraying his thoughts. If Fadl could play poker, it would take an exceptional opponent to uncover his tell. "Well, should your people hear something, Sheikh . . ."

Fadl placed his hands on his knees. "This is a difficult time, Colonel. It weighs on your soul."

Fadl, thought Bobby, was taunting him. No problem. They both knew how the game was played.

"The situation," said Bobby, "will calm down once Moq'tar has a Sultan."

"And you would have Sheikh Yusuf declared Sultan immediately."

"Is there any other legitimate candidate?"

"I can make no decision in such matters, Colonel. All power resides in the Assembly of Righteous Elders. This is according to the constitution America has imposed on Moq'tar."

Bobby held no illusions that Fadl revered the principles of constitutional government. The two men were entwined in an intricate dance, each listening to music from a different orchestra. But each understood that the choice of a new Sultan lay outside the Assembly. Ultimately, the power brokers who concealed themselves in the shadows—or a stronger hand with more money, guns or cunning—would bring the impasse to an end.

"Your silence," said Fadl, "reveals your discomfort."

"I was under the impression that you support Sheikh Yusuf."

"Yusuf is a worthy son of his father, may he walk with the Prophet."

"Then my impression was correct."

Fadl closed his eyes and held up his hands. "Yasaar also is his father's son and the eldest. Having lived in the West so many years, he fears someone may attempt to do him harm. He has asked for my protection. This, in memory of his father, I cannot deny him. Am I Allah that I should judge between two brothers?" He opened his eyes.

Bobby fought the illogical impulse to turn away.

"And who are *you*, Colonel," Fadl continued, "to wish me to do so?"

Bobby frowned. If Fadl could detect his displeasure, so be it. Their little chat made everything clear. Fadl would claim to hold neutral ground while Yasaar ratcheted up the pressure to weaken Yusuf. Hell, maybe Fadl would support Yasaar in attempting a coup to strengthen his own interests in spite of Yasaar's newfound devotion to traditional values. If so, they'd leave the USofA—and Bobby—hanging out to dry.

Bobby gritted his teeth. Any doubts he might have had about Yasaar's directing his failed assassination and even the whole campaign of unrest before the Sultan's death now had been obliterated like Wang Wei. Bobby Gatling had more reason than ever to back the horse running with the red, white and blue silks. All he needed to keep that horse running to victory was a plan. And after several days of serious thinking and his chat with Fadl, he believed he had one.

Hooah!

Thirteen

The pressure squeezing both Yusuf's chest and stomach continued unrelenting. He pushed his chair back from the table. His dinner—he'd felt like eating an hour earlier although a great deal of food would be available later in the evening—remained almost untouched.

"What is the matter?" asked Ameena. "Is something wrong with the lamb? It is free-range from New Zealand. Shall I speak with the cook? I was not entirely satisfied with the Pacific sea bass he prepared the other night."

"Nothing's wrong. Not hungry, that's all."

Ameena touched her hand to Yusuf's forehead. "You have no fever, but I should telephone your physician."

"I'll go lie down. I'll be fine."

"Very well then," said Ameena, her face slightly contorted with the worry known only by a wife and mother. "Perhaps a nap. But a short one. You promised we would make an appearance at Zoraya's benefit party for the hospital."

Yusuf settled onto one of the five sofas in the American-style family room he'd had designed for the palace. He spent part of every evening there after reviewing a variety of economic, political and security reports, as well as updates on the financial markets. The ten-foot television and state-of-the-art sound system offered an unmatched experience for video games. As to basketball, he might well have been seated in Madison Square Garden, the Staples Center or Oracle Arena back in Oakland. The experience was that good.

Of course, he—and Ameena—had also considered the children's needs. Little Muhammad and Maryam delighted in standing on stepstools before either of the two old-fashioned pinball machines.

They were also learning to become prodigies at nine-ball, although he had to help them bridge and stroke their cues.

Yusuf rested his head on a thick pillow covered with golden Thai silk. Something simply didn't agree with him. He'd probably overdone it at lunch again. In a minute he'd have one of the servants bring him an antacid. Or better, he'd keep his little indisposition to himself and get one from the master bathroom, although doing so required a small hike.

Whatever ailed him, it wasn't doubts about the key decision he'd made that afternoon. To be the best you had to work with the best. And the man he'd just hired to play a major role in Moq'tar's future was the best according to every report he'd reviewed.

Of course, the unexpected could always bite you in the ass. But risk and reward went hand in hand. You had to think bold, not old.

A wave of nausea arose. Yusuf shot up and dashed around the old-fashioned ice cream fountain to the bathroom.

Three feet shy of the gold-plated toilet, he splattered the marble floor with the remains of his lunch and the little he'd had of dinner.

Bobby, wearing his one good suit, swept his eyes along the driveway leading to the entry of the Club Metropol. A security team checked vehicles and made sure that only invited guests, who'd donated plenty for the privilege, entered. The club's owners, two former generals from Smolensk who may or may not have once bought a state-owned manufacturing plant during the Yeltsin years only to have it repossessed by the Putin administration, ran their own security team, as well.

Satisfied, Bobby went inside. He couldn't say he was thrilled to have to stay at the fundraiser until Princess Zoraya was ready to call it a night. He planned on taking in an early-morning urban assault drill his people had prepared for weeks. But Sheikh Yusuf, who'd just cancelled his own appearance, insisted. The Princess always drew a crowd.

As expected, the club was filling with Moq'tari government officials and business leaders, international dealmakers and a few tabloid-celebrity wannabes searching out the next new party paradise to vault themselves a step ahead of their social sets. Officials and staff of dozens of embassies also showed up looking for something different to do with their evenings.

Bobby made his way past the bar and took a seat at a small candle-lit table topped by a bottle of vodka, a glass and an ashtray. Far more comfortable than the average observation post, it offered a reasonable field of vision. Larger tables stood closer to the small stage and dance floor. Above them, a cloud of smoke hovered like a Gulf fog.

A waiter approached in a reproduction of the uniform of Tsar Nicholas II lacking only the medals. With almost delicate movements, he found room for a plate of buckwheat blini, tiny bowls of red and black caviar, a slightly larger bowl of sour cream, small spoons and several cocktail napkins. He eyed Bobby's half-filled glass of vodka. Russians didn't leave vodka in their glasses just as propriety demanded finishing an opened bottle to avoid bad luck. Tonight Bobby would have to be culturally incorrect.

"*Spasibo*," Bobby said.

"*Pozhalusto*," the waiter returned then did an about-face to serve a couple of middle-aged Nigerians in blue, loose-fitting traditional clothes. The man sported a blue-and-gold cap, the woman a red cloth head wrap matching her purse.

Bobby checked out the far end of the bar. Ambassador Ellis held his arm around the waist of a shorthaired Canadian brunette who taught a course on sexually transmitted diseases at the local nursing school. One of the Embassy's Marines, in civilian clothes, stood discretely several paces away.

Across the room, Princess Zoraya in a red cocktail dress as effective as any laser target designator drew stares of fascination and envy. Two women almost as attractive—friends who often accompanied the Princess on her nights out and, from time to time, jaunts abroad—stood near. One gripped her hand.

Guests came and went to exchange mouth-to-ear comments barely audible above a duo playing traditional folk music on an electric balalaika and an amplified, accordion-like bayan. Women displayed Cheshire-cat smiles as they studied her clothes. Men struggled to conceal their fantasies about what was underneath them.

Bobby's own fantasies alternated between the Princess and the elusive Ilana Svadbova, but he locked them away in a relatively secure mental compartment. His professional responsibilities took precedence. They constrained him to nurse his vodka instead of downing it a glass at a time while he observed the Princess light up a room blending the ornate stateliness of the Alexander Palace with a light-and-sound system evoking the Battle of Stalingrad.

A thick hand tapped Bobby on the left shoulder. "*Zdrastvooytye*, Colonel Gatling. You like party?"

Bobby remained seated. "Colonel Medvedev, good to see you," he said in Russian. Back in Virginia Beach, Bobby visited the Jewish Community Center once or twice a week to keep up his conversational Russian with several elderly refugees from the former Soviet Union. In Moq'tar City, he enjoyed occasional conversations with Medvedev, a former SPETSNAZ officer with a military background similar to his own. Following the Soviet Union's disintegration, Medvedev had found a series of better paying clients outside what little law existed then rejoined government service when Vladimir Putin came to power.

Medvedev, who polished his English with Bobby, wedged his own bottle of vodka onto the table. "You don't drink tonight, *tovarich*?" He topped off Bobby's glass and filled his own.

"I'm on duty," Bobby answered. He looked towards Zoraya.

Medvedev puckered his lips and blew a small, silent kiss. "*I am on duty.*" He raised his glass. "*Za zhenschin.*" To women. He emptied his glass.

Bobby sipped.

Medvedev took one of the blini from Bobby's plate, spooned red caviar onto it, rolled the blin and wolfed it down. "The secret to drinking vodka, my friend, is eating, no?"

Bobby spooned black caviar onto a blin and downed it.

Medvedev stiffened slightly.

Ambassador Kazanovitch approached. The thick white hair sprouting from his head reached up only to his security chief's armpit. Wavering like a stout but supple palm in a stormy wind, Kazanovitch dropped onto the table's empty seat like a puppet whose strings had been cut.

Medvedev took a small step back.

"Colonel Gatling, you are good man," Kazanovitch shouted above the music and a hundred constantly shifting conversations. His face, even in the dim light, revealed a deep pink tone resembling borscht mixed with an ample serving of sour cream. "You understand Russian soul."

"Russian culture offers much to admire."

"You are here to watch Princess?"

"Part of my job for the moment."

"Is nice job." Kazanovitch glanced at Medvedev. "Colonel Medvedev also has job." He squinted to study his watch. "In twenty minutes, Colonel takes Mrs. Kazanovitch home." He nudged Bobby with his elbow. "Then party begins." He filled his glass and raised it. "To world peace and undying friendship between two greatest nations, Russia and America. May our peoples be brothers until end of time."

"To peace," Bobby repeated. He slowly emptied his glass.

Kazanovitch's glass already stood empty on the table.

A waiter set down a small platter of boiled beef tongue and horseradish.

"Princess . . ." Kazanovitch stage whispered. "Princess is, how you say . . . One hot babe!"

Bobby nodded in polite agreement. He had no intention of putting Kazanovitch off—not after as much vodka as Kazanovitch likely had consumed. As to his own thoughts regarding the Princess's attractiveness—which were no different from those of any other man in the room—he'd keep them to himself.

Kazanovitch ran his left hand through his hair. "I tell you something, my friend. Princess also smart. She studies computer science at Moscow Power Engineering Institute for two years. She comes to Moscow to shop last summer. And summer before. Sultan, her dead father . . . He *very* smart. Young son goes to university in America, but Sultan knows Russia very important country." He lifted a slice of beef tongue with his fingers, dipped it in horseradish and ate. "Is important Moq'tar has good relationship with Russia."

"I'm sure."

The balalaika and bayan players concluded and bowed. Before they could leave the stage, Russian rock with a heavy dance beat exploded over the giant speakers.

Kazanovitch listed towards Bobby like a battle cruiser threatening to capsize. "Russia has much to offer Moq'tar," he continued. "Here they build new cancer wing for hospital thanks God and Princess Zoraya. Is Russian consultant helping. And heart disease. Russians know heart disease." He leaned even closer. "I have major heart surgery is two years and good as new. If you ever have bad heart, I get you into best hospital in Moscow. Best doctors. Best care. Nothing in United States like it."

Bobby nodded.

Kazanovitch patted Bobby's arm. A bit of horseradish stuck to Bobby's sleeve. "Because I like you, Colonel, I tell you something else. Sheikh Yusuf . . . he is not as smart as father. Am I right?"

Bobby couldn't get a handle on what Kazanovitch was fishing for, although he definitely was fishing for something. No question the Russians would leap at the chance to drive a wedge between Moq'tar and the USofA. "The Sheikh is smart enough."

Kazanovitch threw his head back and laughed. "*You* should be Ambassador, Colonel. You are best American in Moq'tar. Best." He pointed a stubby finger at Bobby's chest. "You know how far is Moq'tar from Moscow?"

"Around thirty-seven hundred kilometers."

Kazanovitch reached out and clapped Bobby on the shoulder. "Very good. *Very* good! And from Moq'tar to Washington is over eleven *thousand* kilometers."

Bobby eyed his glass. "Sounds about right."

Kazanovitch raised his hand and gave Bobby two pats on the cheek. "I say this because I like you, my friend. Moq'tar is not good place for America. And not good for *you*."

Bobby spotted the fresh graffiti on his way home from the Metropol. Painted in bright green on the wall of an old carpet warehouse and illuminated by two streetlamps, it stood at least fifteen feet across. The Moq'tari government frowned on anyone scrawling on walls. Small disorders threatened to inspire larger ones.

He pulled off the boulevard into a small parking lot with a clear view of the wall. While his Arabic wasn't nearly as good as his Russian, he had no trouble deciphering the single huge word artfully painted on the wall:

YASAAR

Fourteen

Tired but encouraged, Yasaar slipped off his thobe. Wearing only Burberry check boxer shorts and a t-shirt, he settled into one of two matching leather wing chairs in the living room of his penthouse suite. Anticipating a few moments of peace, he propped his feet up on the suspended glass top of the aquarium coffee table filled with tropical fish. He hadn't even the strength to pour himself a drink. Content nonetheless, he turned on the television.

He'd just completed negotiating with yet another delegation of would-be supporters, including two members of the Assembly who had to rush back to the Great Hall for a major televised announcement. Ordinary Moq'taris had been summoned to watch in the plaza that fronted the ornate building. He would take in the event here given that he had eyes and ears enough throughout the city.

Yasaar surveyed the living room with satisfaction. Every detail, from the shantung lampshades to the crystal ashtrays, was worthy of a hotel rivaling any on the Continent.

His eyes focused on the far end of the long, white sofa to his right. Grunting softly, he got up, shuffled towards the object of distraction and lifted a pillow. Both a smile and a frown fought to display themselves on his face. A companion that afternoon—or perhaps last evening—had left a pair of bright red silk panties.

Yasaar picked up the delicate garment and stroked the material between his thumb and forefinger. A man—a real man—no matter how devoted to tradition could not help but appreciate beautiful women.

His father had been such a man. Of course, he'd had eight wives—several regrettably barren—but never more than the

120

allowed four at a time. He could afford them. And if he dallied with the servant women, so what? They were property really. Only a passionate man could create a nation. Only another passionate man could hold it together.

He raised the panties to his face. The woman-scent intoxicated him.

He clutched the panties to his chest. Still, he could not expect most Moq'taris, including those who opposed him in the Assembly or wavered in their commitment, to understand.

He let the panties fall to the floor. He was an intelligent man. An educated man. Above all, a shrewd and calculating man. He recalled something from the Bible, a corrupted document to be sure—imagine Abraham loving Isaac more than Ishmael—but still the foundation of all revelation. To everything there is a season.

He went to the window, parted the drapes and peered out. A great many people strolled east along the Corniche in the direction of the Great Hall. They exhibited no lack of purpose. He, too, boasted a sense of purpose, single-minded and also holy. Yes, holy!

Yasaar retreated from the window. The drapes brushed back together like lips meeting in a tender kiss. The time for women had passed. It would return following the election to be sure, but now—now he would adopt a different posture. Perception was all.

He went to his bedroom for a fresh *thobe*. His next step was obvious. He would demonstrate his worthiness to the very last of the skeptics blocking his path to the throne.

As midnight approached, fifty thousand chilled bodies jammed together in the plaza before the Great Hall. The excited crowd bore resemblance to the frenzied assembly of New Year's revelers in Times Square five weeks earlier—with two exceptions. It was far smaller. And none knew exactly why they were there.

TV, radio and email announcements in Sheikh Yusuf's name, along with Facebook news feeds and tweets to his supporters, had invited them to witness an announcement of the utmost importance. In minutes, all would be revealed—here and across Moq'tar.

Around the plaza, truck-mounted lamps turned night into day. Above, a giant video screen displayed the time and a three-word graphic: GET READY, MOQ'TAR!

As perplexed as anyone, Bobby inched his way along the rear of the crowd. His right knee throbbed in the unusually damp night air.

Lieutenant bin Abdullah, his hands held in front of his chest to protect the white iPod cord at his neck, followed like a kid brother thrilled to escape his customary banishment to the other side of the playground.

"So far so good, Tall Boy," Bobby radioed up to Qasim bin Jabaar, observing almost directly overhead from a command post on the tenth floor of the Camel's Dick. Bin Jabaar remained as much in the dark as anyone else.

Two floors above, Yusuf and the Ambassador gazed out on the swollen crowd with knowing satisfaction.

Bobby might have remained with bin Jabaar to help exercise command and control, but a high-rise office with sealed windows offered little opportunity to get an accurate feel for the crowd's mood, no matter how calm things might seem. If the situation went south, he'd make his way into the building and back upstairs.

Bobby shot out his elbows to keep the good-natured men around him at a distance even if that meant buying only two or three inches of space. To his left, Lieutenant bin Abdullah, designated his lead blocker back into the Camel's Dick, did likewise. For the first time since he'd spotted the Lieutenant shadowing him, his presence actually served a purpose.

Bobby's emotions fluctuated between embarrassment and anger. He understood that the masses, their chilled breath drifting up through the glaring artificial light like smoke from a desert campfire, had no idea what this was all about. Obviously, this little drama was being played out for them.

But Yusuf had left *him* in the dark—and even Qasim. He couldn't help finding the whole business unsettling. Surprises were for birthdays and wedding anniversaries, not keeping the peace in an increasingly unstable Gulf-side wedge of sand and rock that could slip beneath the waves of chaos at any moment.

As to the night's event, two scenarios appeared likely.

Yusuf might announce he was taking power and to hell with the Assembly of Righteous Elders, the constitution and, for that matter, Washington. If so, the Ministry of Security would have to lock down not just the plaza but the entire city and key points in the countryside, including the airport—planning for which Bobby hadn't been consulted and saw no evidence.

Or Yusuf finally had brought around the Assembly of Righteous Elders, now gathered in the Great Hall. If so, money, threats or both likely were involved. Obviously, the Assembly hadn't chosen Yasaar. Had that happened, Yusuf wouldn't be throwing this little party. But Yusuf's election being the case, the opposition might well express its displeasure. A full security alert would still be necessary.

Bobby's thoughts shifted to Yasaar's response. He texted Taahir.

PLAYBOY HOME read Taahir's reply.

The text answered an important question but revealed little more. Yasaar remained holed up at the Shepherd Palace.

Bobby checked his watch, a self-illuminating H3/Traser he'd picked up before a short but critical jaunt to Baghdad, against the time on the giant video screen. Both registered eleven fifty-nine.

The crowd went silent.

Bobby looked over his shoulder.

The Lieutenant nodded like one of those bobble-head dolls they gave away at baseball games.

An image appeared on the video screen. A beer commercial played.

The crowd cheered.

Bobby had no idea what to make of it. Had he neglected another card Yusuf might be playing—one for which he wore his business hat? Could all this just be some sort of marketing promotion? If so, whoever was behind it was taking their chances. Large crowds and volatility went hand in hand.

The commercial ended.

ESPN's logo flashed on the screen.

The crowd quieted.

A series of basketball highlights from the League followed.

Oohs and aahs ascended from the crowd. Moq'tar, like the rest of the world, followed the League avidly.

The highlights dissolved to a white man with white hair and a black man at least a foot taller holding their hands on the same basketball. The sun-dappled British Parliament building served as their backdrop. So okay, they were in London. In a TV studio, obviously, since it was now nine at night in the UK. Which made it four in the afternoon in New York and one in California. Whatever this was about, the whole Western world, as well as the Middle East, was about to find out.

Scenes of another city—definitely European—appeared.

The TV cut back to the two men. A third man joined them. Over a shirt and tie, he wore a basketball jersey. MADRID spanned his chest. The man in the jersey took the basketball, shook hands with the two others and stepped aside.

Scenes of a city Bobby didn't recognize filled the screen next. A smiling man came forward in a jersey displaying MILANO, received another ball, shook hands and retreated.

Bobby, along with the puzzled crowd, watched scenes of Paris, Athens then more of London appear. A representative of each city, outfitted in a basketball jersey, followed. Obviously, the League was expanding into Europe. But what did any of this have to do with Moq'tar?

Then the screen shifted to a video clip of the Corniche bathed in the sunshine of a warm spring morning.

A roar detonated in the plaza louder than any explosion Moq'tar had yet suffered. An observer might have thought that fifty thousand Moq'tari warriors had launched a revenge-fueled attack on an enemy who had shopped with their credit cards, siphoned gas from their SUVs, displayed the soles of their feet and violated their mothers.

Shots seemingly taken from Moq'tar's official website panned the Shepherd of His People Mall, gazed up at the Camel's Dick then tilted down to the plaza in front of the Great Hall crossed by two men holding hands in traditional Arab style.

The crowd screamed themselves hoarse. Palms and even fists pounded backs, chests and shoulders.

Bobby turned to the Lieutenant.

The Lieutenant's face radiated a sense of awe as if the Prophet had returned.

Bobby thought the decibel count couldn't rise any higher. His judgment proved faulty.

Princess Zoraya appeared in the London studio. A still photo of Sheikh Yusuf materialized in the lower right corner.

"Son of a bitch!" Bobby muttered. He couldn't hear himself. First Yusuf and the Ambassador had taken off for London without his being informed and now the Princess. He was being shoved aside. What idiocy would he find out next? That Ambassador Kazanovitch had divorced his wife to marry Zoraya, arrest his brothers-in-law and proclaim Moq'tar a province of Russia?

The rest came into focus. The Princess, her hair and makeup impeccable, stepped forward draped in a white basketball jersey featuring MOQ'TAR in block letters suggesting Arabic calligraphy. A ball cap perched uncertainly on her head. A close-up revealed the logo of a cartoon shepherd in traditional robes holding a staff in his left hand and a basketball in his right.

Unreal. Moq'tar had joined the League. The royal family—at least Zoraya and Yusuf—had ponied up for a franchise.

To Bobby's right, a chant developed. "Moq'tar! Moq'tar! Moq'tar!"

More and more of the crowd joined in. They bellowed as if fifty thousand Moq'tari warriors had conquered their enemies and thoroughly avenged their honor by shopping with their enemies' credit cards, siphoning the gas from their SUVs, displaying the soles of their feet and violating their mothers—all of whom were as crotch stirring as the Princess.

"Moq'tar! Moq'tar! Moq'tar!" the chant continued, rising from piercing to earsplitting to deafening. He might have been standing on a runway while a jet took off.

No question, the sultanate was on the map. Big time. Never again would Moq'taris be overlooked or belittled.

Pushing the limits of human physiology, the crowd kept on. "Moq'tar! Moq'tar! Moq'tar!"

A counter-chant rang out to his left—not to rival but to augment it. "Zoraya! Zoraya! Zoraya!"

Bobby looked up towards Yusuf's office. Surely he could hear. But what was he thinking? Did he expect his name also to be on everyone's lips?

In spite of their constricted status, men began to dance. The plaza shook as if hordes of shoppers were stampeding towards a fifty-percent-off-sale on new Mercedes.

The picture of a beaming, semi-uniformed Zoraya, her smile more dazzling than the lamps above, gave way to the interior of the Assembly room. The Elders stared at TVs inside the hall. Some displayed fascination. Others grinned in approval. Still others registered disgust.

None turned away.

The chant of "Moq'tar! Moq'tar! Moq'tar!" began to fade.

"Zoraya! Zoraya! Zoraya!" spread and overtook it.

Bobby rubbed his knee. The Princess probably didn't know the difference between a jump ball and a jump shot, but all the royal family needed from her was money. And no question, Moq'taris adored her.

The dancing grew more animated. Men bumped into each other with abandon. They giggled like schoolboys seeing their first photo of a naked woman.

The Elders, yielding to public exposure and political probity, smiled in acknowledgment of the crowd's love for the Princess. They, too, understood the unpredictable nature of a massive gathering that lacked a visible, dominating leader. As the chanting of Zoraya's name reached a new peak, many applauded.

A Moq'tar TV helicopter hovered overhead.

The crowd saw itself on the screen. A sudden hush of self-veneration descended on the plaza.

The picture switched back to Zoraya.

The chanting erupted as if a 5oo-pound bunker buster had exploded.

On the screen, a knot of media people surrounded the Princess. And who was that standing next to her, smiling proudly and answering questions? Hell, that was Dymme! And what was *he* doing there?

All Bobby could make of it was that on one level at least, Moq'tar had arrived. The world would learn about the sultanate now. In the USofA, people who couldn't pick out Canada and Mexico on a map would go online to start planning a road trip to see their team play, take in a little desert sunshine and drink away those exotic Arabian nights.

The chanting of Zoraya's name continued unabated. The crowd seemed to be working itself into a Sufi-like state of religious ecstasy with the Princess drawing love like a black hole drew light.

Bobby edged his way to the entrance of the Camel's Dick. Riding Zoraya's coattails, Yusuf would probably see his popularity soar among the masses. But what would Yasaar do? Would the Moq'tar Shepherds, linked to American sports and corporate culture, trigger a new round of terror attacks?

Wondering if Taahir had seen any of this and what his take might be, Bobby reached for his cell.

A text message awaited him. SHEPHERDS RULE! PLAYBOY GONE.

Fifteen

Dymme, eyes closed, sat motionless attempting to summon his chi within the moment or two remaining before his ride to the airport arrived at the Embassy. Valentine's Day left him forlorn. The object of his love was so far away. Yet duty called.

Buzzing voices intruded into his cubicle—so confining he could almost touch the walls on either side with his elbows. New personnel were arriving each week to fill unoccupied positions. The Embassy might well have been invaded by a plague of locusts parroting the soundtrack of Cecil B. DeMille's *The Ten Commandments*.

Unfortunately, while designs for a new and larger building had been approved, Congress had yet to appropriate funds, which were tied in with a bridge-and-tunnel maintenance bill that remained the subject of furious debate.

Regrettably, Dymme's unanticipated task—he saw no reason for his involvement but was hardly free to protest—ate into time better spent on planning his film festival. He'd set opening night for April eighteenth, little more than two months away. Still, much remained to be done to bring the event off in style. Granted, Moq'tar wasn't Sundance or Telluride, Cannes or Toronto. But still.

Dymme focused on each breath. The buzzing receded. An island of calm—or more suitable to a posting in Moq'tar, an oasis—appeared on his psychic horizon.

Three light taps rattled on the frame of Dymme's cube. His eyes shot open. The oasis sank beneath the desert sands.

"Is it not thrilling?" asked Hema, half hidden behind one of the cube's walls.

Dymme swiveled around. His face revealed a studied politeness that masked his annoyance. Part of his job was to know what

Moq'taris—including Indian Moq'taris—were thinking. "Is *what* thrilling?"

Hema emerged. A green MOQ'TAR SHEPHERDS t-shirt covered her dress. "I purchased it at the mall." She giggled softly.

Dymme wondered if she was flirting with him.

"For the entire past week," Hema continued, "the men in my family have all forgotten politics. They speak only of basketball."

Dymme offered half a smile. "Well, that's a good thing, isn't it?"

"Oh, yes it is, Mr. Dymme! Even the women are excited. They simply love Princess Zoraya. Sheikh Yusuf, he is wonderful for also bringing the team to Moq'tar, but the Princess . . . Is there a woman anywhere in the world more beautiful except, perhaps, Shilpa Shetty? In India, Shilpa Shetty is a cinema legend. So tall! Almost one hundred-eighty centimeters they say. But Princess Zoraya . . . Could anyone be a more wonderful representative of Moq'tar?"

Dymme nodded in concession. "An Arab Sophia Loren, I'm thinking."

"And her eyes, Mr. Dymme. Perhaps a hint of Audrey Hepburn."

"Nice," said Dymme. Short of both time and patience, he stood. "Look, Hema, I have to get out of here. Someone's taking me to the airport."

"*Another* trip to London, Mr. Dymme?"

"No, not this time. We have a very special guest *arriving*."

Yusuf's chest heaved as he dribbled the basketball listlessly at the top of the circle above the foul line. The tap-tap-tapping on the maple floor echoed throughout the almost-completed arena with almost all its twenty-two-thousand-plus seats installed.

Ambassador Ellis stood below the foul line facing Yusuf, his hands on his knees. His breaths came in short spasms.

Yusuf dribbled two steps to his right and launched the approximation of a jump shot. His toes at no time lost contact with the floor.

The official League ball clanked loudly off the rim.

"Brick!" the Ambassador wheezed.

The ball bounced across the court and rolled out of bounds.

"Let's call it a game," the Ambassador offered.

Yusuf wiped his forehead with the back of his shooting hand. "What was the score, anyway?"

The Ambassador straightened and flattened his palms against the small of his back. "You win. That's all I know."

A young man in Shepherds-green warm-ups handed each man a towel and a bottle of water.

At the other end of the arena, a dozen young women in similar green warm-ups jogged onto the court.

"Nice," the Ambassador remarked.

"They'll wear the warm-ups for the reception tonight. Some Moq'taris aren't ready for what cheerleaders wear in the States."

The Ambassador wrapped his towel around his neck. "This ain't Oakland, we know that." He stared at the cheerleaders as they stretched in various positions. "You import them from somewhere or what?"

Yusuf drained his water and breathed deeply. "Royal Moq'tari Folkloric Dance Company. Once we start playing, they'll give 'em the whole show. Tonight, they'll just add to the excitement. A little tease. TV loves cheerleaders."

"Tell me about it." The Ambassador gazed up into the open windows of the one private club that had been rushed to completion. Caterers swarmed in and out carrying trays and boxes in preparation for the evening ahead. "You think we should have gone out to the airport?"

"Let Zoraya handle it. I don't want to look distracted. Besides, I'll be here tonight. *We'll* be here."

The Ambassador peered around the arena. "Lookin' good!"

They turned in unison towards the tunnel leading to what eventually would be the Shepherds' locker room. Yusuf rolled up his towel and snapped it at the Ambassador's backside. "Only one way to welcome a Hall of Famer."

• • •

Bobby glowered as the chartered *Royal Moq'tari* Airways jetliner taxied towards the terminal. Sure, he was satisfied—redeemed in a sense—to have a more critical role to play. But he was still confused.

Qasim bin Jabaar hadn't wanted him involved with Sheikh Yusuf's trip to London. Yet Yusuf asked him to watch over the Princess at the hospital benefit—an event easily secured. Then Yusuf left him hanging about the Shepherds basketball announcement—bin Jabaar also had been left in the dark on that one—as well as the Princess's London trip. Hell, Dymme never said anything about London, either.

Now, with the American hired to lead the Moq'tar Shepherds flying in, Yusuf and Qasim had thrown him a bone. Bobby was the go-to guy again. Maybe they believed their American VIP was too important to leave in the Ministry's hands. If something went wrong, fingers in Moq'tar—and in Washington—would point at *them*. To avoid that scenario they had someone at whom they could deflect criticism.

Bobby lightly touched his right knee. Whatever was going on, he had a job to do. Keeping a cool head was part of it. Maybe he'd just gotten too emotionally involved in Yusuf's stalled succession to the throne. But if Moq'tar caught a cold, important people in Washington and Alexandria would go into a sneezing fit. They'd made a major investment in Moq'tar. Careers and the power that went with them were on the line. And money. Crimmins-Idyll was no less profit-oriented than any corporation in the Fortune 500.

Positioned back from the gate to observe the entire scene, Bobby gazed out the window overlooking the jetway through which Moq'tar's special visitors would enter the terminal. Ominous slate-gray clouds roiled the sky. The ache in his right knee warned that it wouldn't just rain but rain big. Americans thought it never rained in the Gulf, but what did most of them know about this part of the world? Or about any part of the world for that matter? Now, with a winter storm about to strike, the VIPs he would escort into town could easily get caught on the expressway with a bunch of Moq'taris who drove as if *they* didn't know it rained in the Gulf, either.

Bobby turned to verify that Lieutenant bin Abdullah remained behind him.

The Lieutenant smiled as he nodded to the beat of whatever music kept him so fascinated.

One thing Bobby knew. He sure as hell didn't want to be in any vehicle the Lieutenant drove in the rain.

As the plane taxied towards the gate, a fluttering of raindrops fell on security men positioned along the tarmac to secure the aircraft. They stood in teams of two. One man held up an oversized umbrella leaving his pistol hand free and his partner ready to use his M-4. A few semi-important government figures from around the world had visited Moq'tar on his watch, but Bobby never had ratcheted up security so high—not even for Ambassador Ellis.

Standing just inside the jetway doors, Princess Zoraya, the Shepherds' newly announced CEO, checked her makeup. A bouquet of asters, blue iris and Gerbera daisies dangled upside down against her leg. The blossoms brushed the marble floor.

Dymme stood beside and slightly behind her, a red, heart-shaped box of Valentine's chocolates tucked under his arm.

Bobby would have figured the Ambassador to be here, but the Ambassador was hanging with Yusuf until everyone showed up at the new arena that evening to join invited guests and the media for the big introduction and dinner. Regardless, Bobby's mission was clear. Make sure the VIPs got safely to the penthouse suite at the Shepherd Palace formerly occupied by Sheikh Yasaar, who seemed to have gone underground—no easy task in a sultanate as small as Moq'tar.

The media pack—Moq'taris, reporters from around the Gulf, and TV crews from the U.S. and Europe along with Al Jazeera and Al Arabiya—edged forward in anticipation. Raincoats and equipment cases littered the seats and floor where they'd been dropped like so many oversize candy wrappers.

Half-a-dozen burly security men held the reporters in check. They'd been prepared to move bodies around with a smile if the pack got out of hand. A debate about the clash of civilizations might be ongoing in intellectual circles, but the media demonstrated that people everywhere exhibited the same craving for celebrity in all its trivial details.

The jetway doors opened.

Outside, lightning flashed as if the Princess had hired God to provide special effects. Or maybe God had decided to announce his own arrival instead. Hell, there was supposed to be a precedent, wasn't there?

Not to be outdone, camera lights simulated the inside of a tanning booth. A collective "Aaah" sounded.

A man in a blue blazer over a canary yellow sport shirt and a woman in a pink pants suit made their long-awaited entrance.

"Mickey! Mickey! Here, Mickey!" shouted the media. All had received thick press packets extolling his unexcelled basketball credentials.

A Moq'tari customs official stepped forward, stumbled slightly, stamped the visitors' passports and retreated.

Dymme approached. He shook the man's hand and offered a whispered, "Welcome." Then he presented the Valentine's chocolates to the woman before stepping back.

Zoraya held out the bouquet. It seemed only a little worse for wear.

The man passed the bouquet to his wife and waved to the cameras.

Bobby eyeballed Mickey Green, the Moq'tar Shepherds' initial general manager/coach. He was shorter than Bobby expected—at least two inches under six feet—but maybe that was a function of age. Bobby was grateful that he had some years to go and inches to spare. Mickey Green's hair, cut close like Bobby's, disclosed a faded red heavily mixed with gray. His deeply tanned face seemed unusual for your average redheaded Irishman, Scot, German, Russian or whatever, but then, Bobby had run into redheaded Arabs and Afghans. Who knew who'd snuck into the tent way back when?

As to the tan, Bobby figured that while Mickey Green might have spent his life in gyms and arenas, he had nothing to do the last couple of years but sit on the deck of his house in Malibu and bank the millions owed him. Not one but two League teams had fired him with years left on his contracts. Yet everyone still hailed him as a coaching genius.

Bobby gave Mickey Green credit. He probably made as much money *not* coaching a single game as Bobby collected with a year's worth of pension. Chalk it up to the luck of the Irish or whoever. As a college All-American, an Olympian, an all-star in the pros and the coach of three college and two League champions, Mickey Green always landed on his feet. Sure, he moved around every couple of years—Bobby could identify with that. But wherever he went, he stepped out into the spotlight, and people kissed his ass because he delivered. Most of the time. No question, he'd be making big money in Moq'tar. Only Muhammad would be talked about as often.

Christine Green, thirty years younger than her husband—she was pretty much the same age as the Princess—glanced down at the chocolates and bouquet filling her hands. She offered the dazzling smile of the minor blonde Hollywood actress she was. Bobby couldn't recall seeing her in a movie or TV show, but he'd gotten good intel from Dymme. Unlike the new coach, she was the palest, whitest human being he'd ever seen.

A small gold cross on a chain around Christine Green's neck drew Bobby's attention. They'd need to chat. From a security standpoint, Moq'tar had been quiet—even docile—since the announcement about the Shepherds. No way could he let a detail like the cross screw up the first visit by the man who just might be—at least temporarily—the most important figure in Moq'tar.

The media urged Mickey Green to pose with Zoraya. Delighted to oblige, he stepped towards the Princess. They looked like the sultanate's new royal couple—Donald Duck and Minnie Mouse become the new darlings of the multi-cultural world.

"And how does it feel, Princess," a voice called out, "to bring a League franchise to the Middle East and employ one of the greatest men ever to play and coach the game?"

Zoraya's smile surpassed the brilliance of the lightning that once again blazed in the heavens. "Allah has blessed me. And surely he has blessed my people."

The media ate it up.

The Princess did, too. She could have been Queen for all the fuss made over her. Shops throughout Moq'tar already sold t-shirts with her photo next to the Shepherds' logo. Moq'tari newspapers—the Arabic dailies as well as the English-language *Moq'tar Times*—had run her picture on the front page every day since the announcement. Donations poured in to her charities.

Bobby shifted his eyes to Christine Green. Shunted aside to play only a bit role, the actress seemed even paler—if that was possible. Her smile had rearranged itself so that she less displayed her perfect teeth than bared them. But damn if her all-American warmth and grace didn't bounce back as soon as one of the cameras focused on her and a reporter stepped up with a microphone.

Caught up in a moment that future historians might be tempted to compare to the Prophet's triumphant return from Medina to Mecca, the media pack pressed forward. Someone nudged the Princess. She stumbled backward slightly then regained her balance if not her composure.

Thunder crashed.

Bobby signaled.

Security politely but firmly hustled the media off. Several of his beefiest men guided the Princess, the Greens and Dymme through the terminal.

Bobby hobbled painfully in an attempt to keep up.

A sudden turn took them into a passageway leading to a service stairway back down to the tarmac. Outside, four security men holding umbrellas at perfect ninety-degree angles shielded the party from a downpour that resembled a shower turned on at full blast.

Security ushered everyone into Bobby's GMC. The royal limousine, a Hummer and several SUV's parked at the entrance to the terminal served as a ruse. Several security men then crowded their way into Lieutenant bin Abdullah's Toyota Land Cruiser.

For the first time in a long time, Bobby toyed with uncertainty. Not that the plan hadn't been totally thought out. Security agents impersonating the Princess, the Greens and Dymme would emerge from the terminal to fool anyone who thought about taking out the man who had been chosen to guide the Moq'tar Shepherds to glory.

The problem was that by the time Bobby reached the truck, he could barely walk. On a good day, driving put a moderate amount of stress on his knee. But this wasn't normal weather. And this was anything but a normal drive. What if bad guys were on to them? What if he hit the gas or the brakes wrong? If basketball had the power to achieve a truce—defined in the Middle East as each side catching its breath and preparing to beat the other to the next punch—among Moq'tar's competing factions, no way was Bobby Gatling going to screw it up. Hooah!

Bobby opened the driver's door and gingerly raised his right leg to get in. A searing pain ran through the knee. He bit his lip. The taste of blood blossomed on the tip of his tongue. Goddam the weather, he thought. Goddamn that Kurdish motherfucker who'd fired his AK into the air like a fucking child. And goddamn the dealer who only had cloth seats available instead of leather when here he was chauffeuring the Princess of Moq'tar and the most important guests the sultanate was likely to host all year.

He weighed his options. He'd shared the trials of combat with men who'd suffered serious wounds and continued to fight. If you wouldn't protect your buddies with every last ounce of strength, you didn't belong in Special Forces. But this wasn't combat. And truth be told, his days of heroism were over.

Bobby stood down.

A security man raised an umbrella over his head. It did little for his feet. They were soaked. He ignored them. He'd been in a lot worse conditions than this. "Embrace the suck," he whispered, saluting one of Special Forces' enduring mantras.

Bobby looked into the truck. Mickey Green sat damp but relaxed in the front passenger seat. The Princess and Christine Green sat in the middle row. Dymme occupied his expected place in the back.

Bobby checked out the tarmac. It remained secure. "Dymme," he called softly.

Dymme looked up. His face expressed relief to be dry on a crappy day not to mention the partial kick of sitting behind someone whom the tabloids and their unsophisticated readers might consider a movie star, even if Christine Green constituted no more than a footnote—and an obscure one at that—in the history of contemporary American film.

"Dymme," Bobby repeated. He signaled with his index figure that Dymme should come around—and now.

Dymme winked. "Sorry, ladies," he exclaimed as he climbed out.

"Is everything all right?" asked Christine Green.

"Perfect," Bobby answered. He placed the keys in Dymme's hand.

"Me?" Dymme asked. His lips moved soundlessly while his face reflected an exaggerated sense of surprise in the style of silent films.

Bobby scowled.

Dymme held the keys aloft. "Why not?" He climbed into the driver's seat and drew it forward.

Bobby limped around to Mickey Green and opened the door. "Coach, do you mind moving into the back? Standard security procedure."

Green looked up approvingly. "Looks like you played some ball, uh . . ."

"Bobby. Gatling."

"Looks like you played some ball, Bobby."

"High school," Bobby replied. "Back in Pennsylvania." He opened the rear door.

Mickey Green entered the truck by his wife, glanced at Zoraya and squeezed into the rear seat vacated by Dymme.

Bobby eased himself into the front passenger seat.

"Should we be concerned, Colonel?" Zoraya asked.

"Colonel?" Green asked in turn.

"Everything is fine, Princess," Bobby answered. "With Mr. Dymme driving, I'll have a better opportunity to check the road and stay in communication without being distracted." He tapped Dymme on the shoulder.

Dymme pulled the truck away from the back of the terminal.

The Lieutenant followed in the Land Cruiser.

"Actually," said Christine Green, "I thought we'd be in a . . . well, a different sort of car."

"Just a precaution," Bobby explained. "We'd do the same for the President of the United States. Well, if he didn't have his own bulletproof limo. For a senator or someone like that, this works very well."

"I expect so," Christine Green responded. "But we *are* in a suitable hotel, aren't we?"

"Yes, ma'am. Five stars."

Mickey Green placed his hand on his wife's shoulder. "Just another road trip, babe. Tomorrow night we'll be in Paris."

By the time they reached the expressway, Bobby felt more at ease. The rain continued to pelt them, but Dymme kept the vehicle under control, holding his speed in the slower right lane to avoid attracting attention. Traffic flowed moderately. Ahead, an eighteen-wheeler hauling flat-screen TVs and computers for the Gulf's largest electronics superstore slowed in response to the wet pavement. What were the odds of that?

Bobby called bin Jabaar on his radio. "Cheeseburger, this is French Fries. Order to go is on the way."

"Roger you, French Fries," bin Jabaar answered. "The table is set."

Mickey Green leaned forward. His chin almost touched his wife's shoulder. "You guys really talk like that?"

Bobby shifted his eyes to the side-view mirror. Lieutenant bin Abdullah held his position only three meters behind.

The eighteen-wheeler's brake lights glowed red.

Dymme tapped his brakes.

The eighteen-wheeler continued to slow.

Dymme slowed in response.

Bobby rested his hand on his Beretta. If the ruse had been discovered and the bad guys behind all the unrest in the sultanate intended to make a statement by attacking the Greens, the big rig could box them in while a vehicle with shooters pulled alongside. Another vehicle would be unable to block them from behind, however, because the Lieutenant managed to stay on their tail. Or the big rig could stop short and absorb the crash while one vehicle took the Lieutenant off the road and another attempted a kidnapping.

"Go around," Bobby said. His voice indicated a sense of urgency.

Dymme pushed down on the gas and swung the GMC to the left.

The eighteen-wheeler cut towards the left lane in front of them.

Dymme spun the steering wheel to the right, narrowly avoided rear-ending the big rig, and sped up to pass in the slow lane.

Lights flashed directly ahead. A tow-truck with an SUV on its flatbed pulled off the right shoulder and swung in front of them.

Dymme pushed the GMC and shot the gap between the right front of the eighteen-wheeler's cab and the rear of the tow-truck. They emerged into the left lane with five meters between them and the vehicle ahead. The Land Cruiser would have to fend for itself.

"*Allahu Akhbar!*" muttered Zoraya.

"Jesus Christ!" Mickey Green sputtered. "That was some helluva piece of driving, buddy."

Bobby glanced at Dymme in disbelief.

Dymme grinned.

Returning his attention to any additional potential threat, Bobby surveyed the road ahead. Finally, he turned to check his passengers. Zoraya appeared subdued but okay. Christine Green had turned an even paler shade of white for which no name might be suggested other than "corpse." The new coach, on the other hand, seemed to have enjoyed it all.

Bobby shifted his attention to Dymme. "Where the hell did you learn to do *that?*"

The Land Cruiser pulled in behind them.

Ahead, traffic revealed its normal staccato pattern as it approached downtown.

"So everything's good, right?" said Dymme. "And I'm sure, Mr. and Mrs. Green, and of course, Princess, that tonight's welcome will be a major production." He smiled into the rear-view mirror. "I mean, after this, what could go wrong?"

Sixteen

The skin on Yusuf's knuckles grew so taut it shined as he gripped the leather steering wheel of the red BMW sedan. Morning rush-hour traffic had brought the Shepherd of Islam Expressway to a virtual standstill. "What do they expect me to do?" he asked his passenger in English. "Double-deck this thing like they did I-35 in Austin years ago? Traffic there is worse now than when I went to school."

Mr. Shen sat mute.

Yusuf slipped an old favorite, Ludacris' *Runaway Love*, the disc recorded with Mary J. Blige, into the CD player. He might have played Willie Nelson—he'd become a fan and stayed one as a Texas Ex—but he wasn't sure it would strike the right chord. Then again, he could have played anything by Umm Kalthoum—maybe one of her *Diva* CDs—to offer his passenger a classical Arab musical experience. But Ludacris fit his mood.

The fingers of his right hand loosened. He tapped the wheel to the beat. Why let a little traffic upset him? A remarkably peaceful ten days had passed since Mickey Green's triumphant introduction to Moq'tar with not a word from Yasaar. The sun shone. The Gulf sparkled. He had his music. Could he be so ungrateful as to be anything but up?

And how about Zoraya? Crowds received her with adoration at every school, clinic, recreation center and coffee shop opening she attended. She might have assumed the role of Sultana if such a position could exist. But that was okay. Actually, that was better than okay. As the team's public face, Zoraya held at bay any accusations of conflict of interest or impropriety directed at him. Focused on the throne, Sheikh Yusuf merely played the role of investor along with several unidentified limited partners. The League would do all the heavy lifting on the basketball side while Moq'taris filled positions in sales and operations.

Of course, Yusuf made sure that Moq'tar saw the loving brother and sister together with great frequency to advance what he now bitterly referred to as his election campaign. Yusuf bin Muhammad bin Hamza al-Moq'tari knew the value of a photo op. Moq'tar and marketing didn't both begin with M for nothing.

And a campaign it was proving to be. The Assembly of Righteous Elders remained legislatively constipated. Debate continued endlessly. But Yusuf had no doubt that they'd soon run down like a laptop battery absent an outlet. Time was on his side. He could feel it as surely as the beat of the music. The glass was definitely half full—and more.

Traffic lightened then thinned. The city receded. Yusuf turned onto the Sultan Muhammad Freeway. His foot caressed the gas pedal. He urged the BMW on past 130 kilometers an hour then up to 150 and finally to a cruising speed of 170. Let every stray camel in the sultanate be on guard.

"I'd really let it out," Yusuf said, "but I borrowed the car from a cousin." It was the only way he could bring his passenger up to the Throne of the Shepherds without an armed escort and unwanted media attention.

"I am most impressed, Sheikh," said Shen.

The twin peaks of the Mountains of Allah—Yusuf thought of the "A-cups" and smiled—loomed ahead. He slowed to 150. "I've got everything covered. Just like with the franchise."

One couldn't go anywhere in the Middle East without running into Arabs in Moq'tar Shepherds t-shirts, jackets and caps. According to local retailers, virtually every boy under fifteen—and not a few girls—slept on Shepherds sheets and did schoolwork with a Shepherds pencil. "And," Yusuf added, "I don't have to tell you where most of that merchandise is manufactured."

Shen smiled.

"Not to mention that all those walking billboards increase the demand for season tickets along with leverage for media contracts."

• • •

Indeed, Yusuf was creating a case study that every MBA program around the globe would analyze for years. The Shepherds would produce regional TV and radio broadcasts in Arabic. Possibly in Farsi somewhere down the line. The Iranians might be Persians, but they constituted a significant and growing market. He'd find a way to accommodate the ayatollahs. They'd do webcasts, too. Of course, they'd retain all media rights so they could sell the advertising themselves.

"Astute," Shen commented.

Yusuf had even spoken to Mickey Green about fronting a fast-food chain. They'd call it Mickey G's and feature the world's best lamburgers. Green would get points. "The guy's named GM and coach not even two weeks ago," said Yusuf, "and the Arabs love him more than they ever did Arafat or Saddam . . . or even bin Laden."

Shen nodded approvingly. "*Very* astute. But I would expect no less from a fellow Berkeley alumnus."

Yusuf couldn't help but be proud. Every t-shirt, every poster, every broadcast, every box score in a newspaper from Casablanca to Yemen, Islamabad and Jakarta would sell Moq'tar. And *that* would sell what Yusuf wanted to show his passenger, because big dreams required deep pockets.

He downshifted then braked hard.

Shen rocked forward.

Yusuf began the slow maneuver upward through the Ram's Intestines. The Fierce Shepherd towered comfortably overhead. "Love the way it handles," Yusuf said. "I should pick up a couple of Beemers for myself. Assorted sizes and colors."

Moments later, he pulled out of the last hairpin turn and accelerated into the final stretch of narrow but straight road.

Ahead, before the vestigial remainder of the expressway emptied itself into the Throne of the Shepherds, a pair of white Toyota Land Cruisers blocked his way.

Yusuf hit the brakes. A trail of rubber marked the asphalt.

Two men stood before the Land Cruiser to Yusuf's right. Neither struck him as an employee of the Ministry of Security. One wore a wine-colored, quilted jacket, the other a sheepskin coat. Both needed shaves. And both held AKs.

The man in the sheepskin coat motioned Yusuf to turn around and go back.

"Have we run into a problem?" Shen asked.

"No problem." Yusuf opened the door and stepped out.

The man in the sheepskin coat approached while the man in the wine-colored jacket strode over to the BMW's passenger side and blocked the door.

"*As-salaamu aleikhum,*" the man in the sheepskin coat greeted Yusuf. His tone of voice provided Yusuf with little comfort.

Yusuf removed his sunglasses. "*Maadha taf'al?*" What are you doing?

The man shook his head. "The road is closed."

Yusuf took a breath to keep himself in check. He'd made the drive incognito to be sure, but what Moq'tari didn't know his face? Besides, neither General bin Jabaar nor Colonel Gatling had informed him about security measures in the mountains. What was there to secure? He reached for his cell phone.

The man in the sheepskin coat raised the muzzle of his AK—not high enough to threaten Yusuf's life but sufficiently to imply serious potential damage to his manhood.

Yusuf released the cell and removed his hand from his pocket.

The man in the sheepskin coat looked towards the second Land Cruiser.

The tinted passenger-side window descended part way. A hand displaying the hint of a dark gray coat sleeve emerged and waved towards the Throne of the Shepherds.

The man in the sheepskin coat lowered the AK's muzzle. "Please continue your journey."

The second Land Cruiser backed up.

Yusuf returned to the driver's seat and guided the BMW up the road. "Security," he told Shen. "No uniforms. Creates a friendlier image."

Shen smiled. "Slick!"

Yusuf's jaw dropped as he crested the hill. A huge white tent rose in front of the A-cups. Behind the tent, a tower supported a variety of communications dishes suggesting woks stored in a narrow kitchen closet.

Yasaar, in a gleaming white *thobe*, emerged from the tent flanked by two bodyguards. Half-a-dozen armed men stood at a distance. One caught Yusuf's attention. He couldn't have been more than five feet tall.

Yasaar glanced down at a cell phone in his hand, frowned then held out both arms.

"A moment, please," Yusuf remarked to Shen. He pushed the driver's door open so hard its hinges threatened to loosen.

"*Ahlan wa sahlan*, little brother," said Yasaar. He grasped Yusuf's shoulders.

Yusuf braced himself as if Yasaar would attempt to bite and sever his carotid artery.

Yasaar air-kissed first Yusuf's right cheek then his left then his right again. "What could possibly bring you up here to the haven of our family's soul?"

Yusuf stood speechless.

Yasaar grinned. "Forgive me. You have a guest. You are on a . . . business trip?" He gestured. One of his bodyguards marched off to the BMW.

Yusuf pointed towards the armed men. "What the hell is this?"

The men moved several steps closer.

"Moq'tari tradition permits every prince his own bodyguards," Yasaar answered. "We have not violated the law . . . even those you have passed intending to mock believers."

The bodyguard returned with Mr. Shen.

Yasaar started to bow then straightened himself. "*As-salaamu aleikhum.*" He shifted to English and offered his hand. "Mr. Shen, I believe. My apologies. Bowing is a *Japanese* custom. I hope it is not too late to say *gung hay fat choy*."

"This is my brother, Yasaar," Yusuf cut in. "He's . . . he's . . ."

"Taking our rightful place in our ancestral home. Our family and the Mountains of Allah are one. But you are my guest. You must have refreshment. Please enjoy tea and sweets in my tent. Mustafa will provide you a comfortable place to sit while I take a brief moment with my little brother to discuss a family matter. Then you and he can continue your business."

The first bodyguard escorted Shen into the tent. The second positioned himself two paces behind Yusuf.

Yasaar looked out over Moq'tar and the Gulf below them. "Does not the spirit of our father and all his fathers fill this place?"

"I like the way they say it in America. Bullshit."

Yasaar shook his head slowly. "Like the Americans, little brother, you have become very direct. Of course, you could be quite useful to us when we become Sultan."

"Sultan? You? As if!"

"Then let us also be direct. You were a son of father's old age, and so he spoiled you. Our brothers and we should have done away with you when you were a boy. We could have taken you out into the desert and cast you into a dry well. Or perhaps sold you to a Saudi so that you would disappear into some palace for a brief life of . . . what shall we say . . . personal service. But we did not. Now, we see that Allah, the Compassionate, the Merciful had us spare you so that you could serve *us*. In a different capacity, of course."

Yusuf held his right hand out towards the city. "Take a good look, Yasaar, because this is going to be your last. I'll have you out of Moq'tar before you can say, 'Where are those twins I ordered from Taiwan?' Or is it, 'Where are those boys from Bangkok?'"

The crow's feet at the corners of Yasaar's eyes deepened as if he was examining a brokerage statement following a severe correction in the market. "As Allah is our witness, you will never rule Moq'tar. This basketball team . . . You think you can distract the people? And the Assembly?"

"Welcome to the twenty-first century."

"Moq'tar yearns to return to the simpler days of our father and the ways of the Prophet, peace be upon him. Only our father's memory protects you."

Yusuf's chin jutted out in defiance. He had the Ministry of Security in his pocket. And the Americans. "You really think Washington will let you take the throne?"

"The Americans?" Yasaar responded. The crow's feet softened. His eyes brightened. Yusuf's naïveté amused him. "They will remember Moq'tar no longer than the latest Hollywood divorce or infidel religious leader caught in a motel with another man."

"Not to mention the Assembly of Righteous Elders," Yusuf shot back.

"Quite clearly, you cannot make them do your bidding," said Yasaar, returning the volley with ease. In his younger days, he'd also been one of Moq'tar's top-ranked tennis players. He stroked his bearded chin slowly to emphasize his brother's clean-shaven appearance. "What did Jack Nicholson say in that gangster movie? 'If you coulda, you woulda.'"

Yusuf raised his right index finger and pointed it at Yasaar's nose.

An AK bolt clicked.

Yusuf felt himself sweating. He couldn't seem to get enough air. He stared at Yasaar. The Tom Petty song, "I Won't Back Down," ran through his head. Let there be no mistake. He was no weakling. In fact, he was way tougher than anyone thought. And what was Yasaar going to do? Kill him? Like Dad once eliminated a rival clan head? Not that those things didn't still happen. But he was a Berkeley MBA for Allah's sake. And now he was pissed. The momentary discomfort abated. "Don't get too settled up here," he advised. "Someone just may have to call in the cavalry."

Yusuf guided Shen's attention from the PowerPoint on his laptop to the dunes below.

"Really, this is most impressive, Sheikh," said Shen. "If you would email me your presentation, I will forward it to my superiors in Shanghai. In strictest confidence, of course."

"Done," said Yusuf.

They returned to the BMW.

Yusuf opened the passenger door for Shen, closed it behind him then turned his head sharply like a startled hawk.

A white Land Cruiser like those that had earlier intercepted Yusuf followed by a Humvee with a mounted .50 caliber machine gun raced towards him and stopped suddenly. General bin Jabaar emerged. He ran forward as if he intended to throw Yusuf to the ground to protect him from enemy fire. "Sheikh, what are you doing here?" he asked as he saluted.

"Do I owe you an explanation, General?"

Bin Jabaar lowered his hand and tugged uneasily at the lapels of his elegant dark gray overcoat. "Traveling alone, unprotected . . ."

"And how did you know I was here?"

"I was near the airport when one of Sheikh Yasaar's men called after you were unfortunately stopped on the road . . ." Bin Jabaar glanced at the BMW. "With your guest."

"A roadblock, General?"

"My deepest apologies. I had just been informed that Sheikh Yasaar had taken up residence here."

"With armed men?"

"The Throne of the Shepherds belongs to your family, Sheikh. Tradition gives your brother every right to be here and to hire private security."

"As they say in the States, General, I am not a happy camper."

"With all due respect, the situation favors *you*. Sheikh Yasaar has not only taken himself out of the city but out of sight. Moq'tar remains quiet."

"But why is my brother *here*?"

"Perhaps he fears enemies. The road is easy to defend."

"*Yasaar* is the enemy."

A gust of wind knifed its way through the A-cups.

Yusuf shivered.

Bin Jabaar turned his collar up. "Your brother poses no threat in the mountains, Sheikh. But I will place men here to watch him day and night."

"Do that, General."

Bin Jabaar rubbed his hands together. "It is only a matter of time. The Assembly of Righteous Elders will make you Sultan, and Moq'tar will enter a glorious new age. But now, please allow us to escort you back to Moq'tar City." He saluted again.

Yusuf slipped behind the wheel of the BMW.

Bin Jabaar started for the Land Cruiser then turned back.

Yusuf lowered his window.

"If you please, Sheikh," said bin Jabaar, "take care going through the Ram's Intestines. Loss of control can be fatal."

Zoraya, her figure set off by a plum jacket over an off-white, scoop-neck blouse and black slacks, motioned Bobby to sit in one of the elegant arm chairs surrounding her office's antique carved Ming coffee table. "You are not uncomfortable being alone with me, are you, Colonel?" she asked.

"No, ma'am," Bobby replied. For the first time, he found something positive about passing fifty. Twenty years earlier—even ten—he'd have struggled hopelessly to conceal an erection that wouldn't quit. Now, sitting in the Princess's office, he managed to keep himself under control. Not that he could discount the threat of a sudden surge of testosterone.

"I do appreciate your asking to see me."

Bobby cleared his throat. In spite of the Princess's reputation as a fiercely independent woman, he really shouldn't have been sitting across from her without another man in their presence. The Princess's admin—a woman almost as attractive—had shown him in then retreated to her own desk. Two security men stood sentry in the hallway beyond. All that separated him from the Princess was an elegant table topped by a large bottle of mineral water, two crystal goblets and a pile of pencil drawings. If this were Saudi, the risk of her being stoned or beheaded would be significant. Maybe for him, too. No one, however, had succeeded in deflecting the Princess's resolve to march to her own drummer. Which was why he was here.

"I want to express my concern for your safety," said Bobby.

Zoraya opened the bottle.

"Aksinya," said Bobby.

"You know it?"

"Very popular in Russia."

"Ambassador Kazanovitch," she responded. "He loves to send me gifts." She poured sparkling water into the two goblets and handed one to Bobby. "As to my safety, Colonel Gatling, I am not concerned. You and General bin Jabaar have taken all sorts of precautions I could not begin to imagine. Nor, frankly, can I imagine why anyone would wish to harm a simple woman like myself."

Bobby hefted the goblet. It had real weight. He wondered if it was also a present from Ambassador Kazanovitch. "To begin with, Princess, you're a member of the royal family. More to the point, everyone knows how close you are to Sheikh Yusuf. Added to that, your activities keep you constantly exposed, and this is a very challenging time."

Zoraya raised her goblet to her lips, sipped then returned it to the table. "Moq'tar seems quite peaceful to me at the moment. And while I do not wish to be immodest, the people think well of me."

Bobby set his goblet down. "Another reason I'm concerned. People in the spotlight draw attention. A *woman* in the spotlight here in the Gulf . . . There are certain elements, political and religious . . ."

"I repeat, Colonel," Zoraya cut in, "of what importance is a mere woman? As you are certainly aware, far more attention is being paid to the *men* in my family. I assure you that Moq'tar will be even calmer once the Assembly chooses a new Sultan."

"Sooner, hopefully, rather than later."

Zoraya clasped her hands together. "May I ask you a question, Colonel?"

Bobby leaned forward.

"Who do you think my father's successor will be? You are far more acquainted with these matters than am I."

"Only the Assembly of Righteous Elders knows, Princess. Or *will* know."

Zoraya picked up a drawing from the top of the pile on the table. "Well said, Colonel. I myself have no idea given developments of late."

"I just want to make sure . . ."

"I will follow instructions and be a good girl, if that makes you feel better."

Bobby's cheeks flushed. He felt as awkward as a high school kid who'd snagged a date with a cheerleader then found himself wondering what to do next. "I apologize if I've offended you, Princess."

Zoraya smiled. "You have not offended me at all."

Bobby fought back the threat of a testosterone surge.

Zoraya held the drawing out. "I should really prefer that we talk about other things, Colonel."

Bobby took the drawing and examined it. A rough but competent sketch showed a group of buildings surrounding a large plaza. It might have been a plan for a college campus or a business park.

"My brother Yusuf has a vision for Moq'tar," said Zoraya.

"Your brother Yasaar also has a vision. A nation run by God."

"Yasaar believes that God has spoken to him as the angel Jibril spoke to the Prophet, peace be upon him. I regret that God has not confided his message to *me*, although Yasaar would think that only natural. Nonetheless, I also have a vision."

"And that would be what?"

"Security. Order. Peace."

"I'm sorry, but that doesn't sound any different from what either of your brothers proposes."

Zoraya exhibited the half-smile of a schoolteacher whose student has glimpsed the outlines of a truth but failed to penetrate it. "Colonel, all people want the same things. We may, however, disagree on the methods and means for attaining them."

Bobby held up the drawing.

"A lesser vision," Zoraya sighed. "A daydream really, although your Mr. Dymme agrees that it provides a more practical approach to Moq'tar's prosperity than offered by either of my brothers."

"And this is . . ."

"A motion picture production complex."

"Bollywood West or something like that?"

Zoraya's eyes transitioned from playful to earnest. The population of the Arab world was large and growing rapidly. Moreover, its most dynamic demographic was under thirty years of age, and young people loved movies. "Why should Cairo be the center of Arab film production, particularly with all the unrest there? Why not state-of-the-art facilities *here*?"

"I'm sure Sheikh Yusuf would be quite interested."

"Perhaps," said Zoraya. She took the drawing and placed it face down on the others. "He will develop Moq'tar's economy as he sees fit should he be selected by the Assembly. My baby brother is the businessman in the family. I do, however, worry about the difficulties he faces. The world is changing so rapidly."

"Yes, it is, Princess. But please understand that Moq'tar has a close friend in the United States, one the sultanate can model itself after in many ways."

Zoraya leaned forward. The top of her blouse fell away revealing a hint of her breasts.

Bobby picked up his goblet.

Zoraya pressed her right hand over her heart and sat up.

Bobby sipped and set the goblet down.

"Colonel, I am only a woman. I do not wish to offend *you*, but I cannot help questioning whether democracy, whatever its form, suits Moq'tar."

Bobby attempted to flex his right leg without showing his discomfort—physical or intellectual. "Well, I'm only a soldier, Princess. An ex-soldier. But I'd suggest that democracy presents many advantages."

"And yet democracy often paralyzes America. You elect a president then vilify him. You call for new representatives, but your political parties refuse to reach agreement with each other or with your president. The people grow angry and frustrated, and the election cycle begins again. It is filled with brave promises full of sound and fury, as Shakespeare wrote, and signifying nothing. Don't

SLICK!

you think it takes a strong man . . . a strong *person* . . . to govern effectively?"

Bobby glanced at Zoraya's eyes then looked down. He had no doubt that in any discussion—which he would not let unfold—she would more than hold her own. Worse, he feared that he might, in spite of himself, end up agreeing with some of what she had to say.

Over the past weeks he'd begun to wonder if his work in Moq'tar represented nothing more than a fool's errand. Moq'tar clearly wasn't following the American democratic model or the British or the French, and that was probably all for the good. He loved the USofA and acknowledged the brilliance of the founding fathers. But when it came to government in a world of so many different and often complex cultures, one size couldn't possibly fit all.

On the other hand, Moq'tari-style democracy left much to be desired. Without stability, a self-styled democracy tended to mix ballots, bombs and blood indiscriminately. When Yusuf succeeded to the throne—Bobby's commitment remained unwavering—Moq'tar might well evolve. Then again, it might not. After Iraq and Afghanistan, what did anyone in Washington really expect?

Zoraya stood. "I shouldn't keep you, Colonel. But let me assure you that I will be as cooperative with the Ministry of Security, and you, as possible."

"We'll look after you, Princess."

"I am sure you will." She extended her hand.

Bobby hesitated then took it.

Zoraya squeezed lightly and released her grip. "And Colonel, do look after yourself, as well."

153

Seventeen

Yusuf sat grim-faced at his desk. He thrust his laptop towards the Ambassador. "General bin Jabaar saw this earlier, Ron. So did Colonel Gatling. I could have emailed the link to you, but I thought it better if we talked this over in the flesh. Just you and me."

"I love YouTube," said the Ambassador. "Lots of funny stuff and some great chick videos."

Yusuf clicked PLAY.

The Ambassador watched an old man being guided along a rocky path in a desolate area at some considerable elevation above the Gulf. It almost seemed as if the scene was shot up at the Throne of the Shepherds right where he'd been in early January. In fact, he was sure it was.

The video cut to Yasaar, who proudly displayed a jeweled *saif.*

The old man shuffled towards Yasaar. Upon reaching him, he held his right hand out and slid it up Yasaar's chest until it rested on Yasaar's right shoulder. Then he let his hand descend down Yasaar's right arm, gripped his hand and slowly raised it above their heads.

The sword blade glittered in the mid-winter sun.

"So Yasaar just got an endorsement from some old guy," said the Ambassador.

"Not just *any* old guy. That's Sheikh Fadl bin Jibril!" Yusuf protested. The tenor of his voice wavered between an aggrieved complaint and a helpless whine. "What do we do now?"

• • •

The Ambassador, his back to Bobby, peered out a large window. Open shutters revealed assorted palms—some tall and stately, others squat and bushy—dappled by late-afternoon sunlight and shadow. Strategically clustered, the palms blocked any view of his office from the street a floor below. "Yasaar," he snapped. "We're taking him out of the picture."

Bobby lowered himself into a wooden chair, its leather seat the color of the Army's old olive-drab fatigues. He faced the Ambassador's carrier-size desk. "Out of the picture, sir?" That would be defined in what way?"

The Ambassador turned and swiveled his executive chair back and forth as if aiming a .50 caliber machine gun at a moving target. "This standoff in the Assembly of whatever the hell they think they are. It could drag on for months. Or they could elect the wrong man."

"Democracy can get messy, sir."

The Ambassador abandoned his imagined weaponry and picked up a foot-high plastic shepherd with a staff in its left hand and a basketball in its right. "Not on my watch, it doesn't! Decisions have been made. Yasaar leaves the country. Soon."

"Sir, Sheikh Yusuf hasn't mentioned anything about deporting his brother. Besides, it would be a complex legal matter. It could take months, and there's no guarantee the courts would go along."

"Who's talking lawyers? Or courts?"

Bobby's eyes shifted to the American flag in the corner. Atop the pole, a golden eagle perched on a golden globe held fast in its talons. Below, the cloth hung limp. With stars and stripes folded in on each other, the flag bore only a distorted resemblance to the image Americans associated with it. "And Sheikh Yusuf approves?"

"He'll thank us when Yasaar's history."

Bobby bit his lip.

The Ambassador spun around. "Drink?"

Bobby looked at his watch.

"Don't tell me you've never had a drink before five o'clock, Colonel."

There wasn't an hour in the day when Bobby hadn't had a drink, but that was no business of the Ambassador. And if a drink provided a more collegial tone to their conversation, how could he refuse? "Very kind of you, sir."

The Ambassador put the plastic shepherd down, squatted with a grunt and opened a door in the credenza below the window. He removed a bottle of Scotch and set it and two glasses on the desk. "Will this do?"

Bobby would have preferred rye. Since retirement, he'd increasingly become a creature of habit. But Special Forces put a premium on flexibility. "Scotch, sir. Absolutely, sir."

The Ambassador poured drinks. "You know what the difference is . . . the *real* difference . . . between people like you and people like me, Colonel Gatling?"

Bobby stroked his glass with his thumb. He'd heard the same harangue any number of times as if lines had been memorized from a script: Strategic thinkers like the Ambassador sent operatives like Bobby off to some shit hole. The operatives ate what the locals ate, slept how the locals slept and wiped their asses like the locals did. If the operatives got lucky, they fucked some of the local women, however *that* was done. The problem was, by the time they figured out which hand to hold their dicks in while they pissed, they assumed they knew how America should conduct its foreign policy. But they were merely functionaries. Their sole mission was to do as they were told and let the people who saw the big picture make the big decisions.

Bobby made no effort to counter the argument. Any case he might make would hold up only at the end of a bar with a few sympathetic ears to bend. In Moq'tar, the Ambassador was the USofA incarnate. Moreover, one phone call to Alexandria and Bobby's contract with Crimmins-Idyll would go up in flames—along with his reputation. Then what? Work as a security guard at Suntrust Bank?

The Ambassador's face softened like ice cream under a summer sun. "I hope you understand how delicate this situation is. And complicated. Complicated in ways a guy like you wouldn't understand. Long story short, commandos go up to the mountains,

SLICK!

snatch Yasaar and put him on a plane back to Switzerland. Or any place else for that matter. If the bastard objects to the travel arrangements, they toss his coffin into the cargo hold. Either way, we knock some sense into, or scare the shit out of, the goddamn Assembly of Righteous Elders."

Bobby stared into his drink.

The Ambassador mimed shooting a free throw. "So what do you recommend?"

Bobby rested his hand on his right knee. An operation to snatch Yasaar would prove satisfying personally, but it represented a political minefield. He took the Ambassador through a reality check like a parent explaining to a child why he shouldn't wave a metal baseball bat in a thunderstorm. A night operation with helicopters would probably be required. But a force from Centcom would draw obvious attention to America's heavy hand. Ditto a CIA team.

"What about Crimmins-Idyll?" the Ambassador asked.

"Crimmins-Idyll could get it done, sir, but contractors involved in another nation's internal affairs would hardly reflect well on Washington."

The Ambassador frowned. "Like we never had contractors in Iraq and Afghanistan, right?" He sat. "But your objections. I've been one step ahead of you all the way."

"Which I assume, sir, is why I'm here."

The Ambassador winked. "Big picture . . . You round up your best people from the Ministry of Security and find a bright young officer to lead them. Put together a plan, train them fast and get out of the way. Then it's all a Moq'tari deal. Uncle Sam's hands are clean. Or clean enough."

"And if something goes wrong, sir? Back in nineteen-eighty, an American operation with elite forces lost eight men and two aircraft when we failed to rescue our Embassy staff in Tehran."

The Ambassador shook his head. "Doesn't ring a bell."

Bobby finished his drink and put his glass down. "And General bin Jabaar, sir?"

"What about him?"

"I would have expected him to be here with us. We'll be using his men. And he may have objections about our interfering in the election."

The Ambassador cocked his head in amazement. "Why would he do that? Because he wants this crisis to continue? Is he a patriot or what? And don't forget who funds his budget." He clasped his hands behind his neck. "Like I said, it's complicated. That includes the General. But you leave him to me. In three days, you show me a plan signed off by bin Jabaar. Training, you've got a week. End of story."

Bobby emptied his glass. "With all due respect, sir, I'd feel better if this had come from Sheikh Yusuf. It's *his* country."

The Ambassador pivoted towards the window and studied the palms' lengthening shadows. "Not if *Yasaar* gets elected. Big picture . . . Setting up a proper democracy in the sovereign Sultanate of Moq'tar is way too important to leave to Moq'taris. Drive home safely."

Bobby stood.

The Ambassador poured another Scotch, swiveled to face Bobby and raised his glass. "To freedom!"

Bobby turned to leave.

"And Colonel."

Bobby performed an abrupt about face.

"If you don't believe you can make this happen, I've got somebody else who can."

Eighteen

ymme watched Bobby unlock the door to his apartment. The lock seemed rather basic—little challenge for anyone with even rudimentary burglar's skills. He found it hard to reconcile with the Colonel's professional position.

"It's not the Shepherd Palace," Bobby said, "but it's home."

Dymme spotted a coffee table and set down two plastic bags from Monsoon Palace filled with Punjabi Lamb Curry, Tandoori Chicken, Prawns Masala and warm nan.

Bobby deposited the six-pack of Kingfisher, India's most popular beer, Dymme had also brought. Dymme hadn't been able to carry it.

"I have a couple of DVDs," Dymme remarked. "Didn't know if you had a Blu-ray player. Sultan of Hollywood has a damn good selection in English."

Dymme figured he owed the Colonel for the briefing dinner back in January. And for the ride home from the airport when he'd returned from Riyadh. "What's better than two Americans far from home kicking back with dinner and a movie, and getting to know each other?" The loneliness factor came into play, as well. Dymme hadn't made any friends yet. He'd always been a bit standoffish. That was his nature.

Of course, there was this whole mess about the succession. Their little get-together offered a convenient opportunity to find out what the Colonel was thinking. And what he was doing. Dymme wanted to know about things like that. It was part of his job.

That the Colonel was a little rough around the edges had seemed evident to Dymme as he drove up to the apartment building. Over the past several years, developers had presented Moq'tar City with generally garish but not infrequently vibrant new architecture. Even the moonlight, however, failed to hide the drabness of the building's seven-story, faded-yellow concrete façade. The design hinted at earlier origins Dymme could only equate with an attempt to create a Mediterranean seaside motif from the perspective of the former East Germany.

Slowing at the entry to the ground-level garage, Dymme had pulled past a white Toyota Land Cruiser parked under a streetlight. He let a casting-agent glance linger over a man sitting behind the wheel. A white cord descended from the driver's ear. He filed the man's presence away in the back of his mind and rang the intercom.

"Who?" the Colonel asked. The small speaker made his voice tinny, almost comical.

"Me. Dymme. I could use a little help."

"Help?"

"Hurt my elbow. The left one. Nothing serious."

"What are you driving?"

"A Jeep. Green."

"Popular color around here. Guest parking's to the right."

"So can you . . ."

A buzzer sounded. The gate rose.

Dymme entered into the bowels of the garage. Who knew where the evening would lead?

Dymme remained standing as Bobby went into the kitchen for utensils and, hopefully, napkins of some sort. His eyes swept across the small living room. Where a man lay down his head revealed a lot. And Langley Dymme had a director's eye for telling detail.

The apartment seemed pleasant enough if a man had monkish tastes. The cheap tile floor matched that of the poorly lit hallway. Two dumbbells, black and lusterless, crouched like wary animals in a corner by a small window covered by mini blinds. Several of the blinds' slats bent at odd angles like the teeth of an orthodontically challenged teenager.

A small bookcase stood beneath the window. Along with a number of volumes, it contained a set of *matryoshka*—Russian nesting dolls.

In the middle of the room, an ersatz Scandinavian sofa and two wooden-armed chairs, all in a matching slate blue, brought to mind the waters of the Gulf on a cloudy day. A white end table held a stack of journals on military affairs and geopolitics. Three books lay next to them. Dymme bent over for a better look.

"Churchill's *The River War*," said Bobby, reappearing with plastic plates, metal forks and spoons, and paper towels. "And I'm re-reading the Army/Marines' *Counterinsurgency Field Manual*."

"And this is what?" said Dymme, picking up the third volume. "*A History of the Jews* by Paul Johnson."

Bobby stared at Dymme's left arm cradled in a black sling. "What happened?"

"It's an old injury, actually."

"Football?"

"Rugby. The violent game beloved by intellectuals. And beer lovers." Dymme patted the sling. "This was squash. I jumped to hit the ball and tore a calf muscle."

Bobby's eyebrows arched.

"It's all about how things connect," Dymme explained as if he'd ascended another step on a journey to spiritual enlightenment. "I dropped like a rock and landed on the elbow. It acts up if I strain it. Like when I drove from the airport with the Greens and Princess Zoraya. A few more days, and I'll be fine."

Bobby sat on the sofa.

Dymme took a chair offering a reasonable view of a large flat-screen television that appeared to be the apartment's lone extravagance. "Colonel, if you don't mind, you look worse than you sounded on the phone this afternoon."

"Haven't slept much," said Bobby. It was none of Dymme's business that he'd worked through the night and just finished the plan for removing Yasaar from the Throne of the Shepherds. His head felt like an inflated ox bladder turned into a flotation device. But he could use the break to wind down.

"Nothing's wrong, I hope," said Dymme. "A man in your position must deal with a lot of stress."

Bobby sensed Dymme fishing. He couldn't help wondering why he'd agreed to Dymme's offer. But he knew the answer. Something about Dymme still struck him as off. A little informal time together might help him get a handle on it.

He examined one of the DVDs. "*Seven Brides for Seven Brothers?*"

Dymme smiled. "A classic. Perfect for a couple of guys who spend their evenings alone."

Bobby thought of Ilana Svadbova, tossed the DVD on the sofa and held up the other. "*Casablanca*, huh?"

"Some critics rate *Citizen Kane* the best American movie ever. What do they know?"

"I've seen it. *Casablanca*. But what the hell, let's do it."

Dymme seemed almost to glow. "Then I'm not spilling the beans when I say the ending, when Bogart and Claude Rains walk off together into the night . . . Well, film doesn't get any better than that."

Bobby chugged half a Kingfisher.

"So what do you think, Colonel? Should we watch the film while we eat or after?"

Bobby reached for the remote. "Let's eat while we catch the nine o'clock English-language news on Moq'tar TV."

Dymme winked. "Intel, right?"

"You'd be surprised."

"Yes, I would be. The local news . . . It's nothing but auto accidents or store openings or some speaker at a chamber of commerce lunch. And now, Shepherds basketball. What can you learn from that?"

"Little things. But that's not in your line of work, is it?"

Dymme held up a piece of nan. "Tell you what, Colonel. I'll bet a bottle of Napa Valley cabernet, which a friend in San Francisco just happens to make, against whatever you want to surrender that either an accident or something about the Shepherds is on the news right now."

"Cabernet, huh?" Bobby clicked the remote. "Sure."

An American reporter sat across from an elderly woman—obviously not an Arab—in her cramped living room. A title at the bottom of the screen read SPECIAL TO MOQ'TAR TV.

A floral housedress hung loosely from the woman's bony shoulders. Her short gray hair exposed her freckled scalp. Her eyes seemed no more than shadowy depressions on either side of a nose shaped like a punctuation mark. A small mouth concealing almost invisible lips formed the period beneath it.

Bobby pointed his finger at Dymme. "I'll let you know when you can deliver the wine."

The woman held up a photo of Mickey Green during his playing days.

"Son of a bitch," Bobby whispered. He turned up the sound.

" . . . was always a good boy," boasted the old woman.

"Did you and your husband travel to see him play, Mrs. Green?"

The camera zoomed in on the old woman. "Call me Stelly. It's Estelle, but everyone calls me Stelly. Like everyone calls Michael, Mickey. When he was little, Michael had this fire engine-red hair. Like Lucille Ball. You remember Lucy? Rose Leibowitz says in front of a whole gang outside the candy store . . . Harold, rest in peace, and me, we were still in Brooklyn . . . She says, 'With that red hair, he looks like an Irishman . . . a little mick.' That was it. He was Little Mickey."

"You must be very proud of Mickey," said the reporter. "His basketball accomplishments, being an instant hero in the Middle East and having such a wonderful family."

Estelle Green pursed what could be seen of her lips. "Hero schmero. When he divorced Phyllis, and my grandchildren were still small yet . . . Like a daughter she was. His second wife, it wasn't *beshert*. You know what *beshert* means?"

The camera cut back to the bemused reporter.

"Seven, eight years ago, Michael tells me he got married again. Not *getting* married. *Got* married. A California girl. A *shiksa*, you should pardon the expression. She's on some television show, but did I ever see her on my soaps? So I wasn't at the wedding. At my age, who wants to fly?"

The interviewer cut in. "But could you tell us . . ."

"And then they have Connor. Only there's no *bris*." She put her frail hand to her mouth. "You can talk about a *bris* on TV?" She dropped her hand. "Maybe on cable, huh?"

The reporter burst out laughing then segued his response into a cough.

Estelle Green took a small white tissue from a box on the table beside her, dabbed her eyes and dropped the tissue onto her lap. "The little girl, Tanner, they have two years later. Pictures they send me . . ." She clasped her hands as if she'd caught a fly and would tear its wings off if only she had the strength. "In front of their Christmas tree."

The reporter cleared his throat.

"So what did we ever ask of Michael, anyway? Fame? Money? *Feh*. Only he should be a good Jew."

Bobby had just entered the freeway when Qasim bin Jabaar returned his urgent call.

"Where are you?" asked bin Jabaar. "Are you all right? It is almost midnight."

"I'm driving over to the Muscle Club. I saw the news. No way I'm gonna get to sleep for a while."

"You are going to the Muscle Club at this hour? We are meeting tomorrow morning. The arrangements."

"Eight o'clock. I'll be there. But how about you? Did *you* catch the news on TV?"

"Car crashes. Basketball. What is the point? But yes, one of my people called. We will talk in the morning, *habibi*. Get some sleep."

"Qasim, I wouldn't take this stuff about Mickey Green lightly. Not lightly at all."

Bobby checked his rear-view mirror as he slowed to exit the freeway. Lieutenant bin Abdullah once again shadowed him. This time, the

Lieutenant's working so late seemed a bit unusual. Certainly he could lose the Lieutenant as he did every once in a while just for fun, but then Qasim would call and bitch. He dismissed the idea. The tails were harmless. If Qasim was happy, he was happy.

Only Bobby wasn't happy at all. The Estelle Green interview would be the talk of Moq'tar, and the talk would not be positive. All he could do now was get in a good workout then prepare several scenarios to present at the Ministry of Security in the morning.

Bobby approached the Muscle Club. The amber glow of streetlights gave the neighborhood the look of sunset in a dust storm. No one else, though, was likely to appreciate his poetic inspiration. The area, as always this late at night, appeared desolate. People in homes and apartments nearby had settled in for the evening.

It didn't take a Sherlock Holmes to figure why Makeen had opened his gym here. The obvious deduction would be that converting a small warehouse in a light-industrial district cost a whole lot less than a new building in an expensive commercial-retail area. Of greater importance, little traffic and few people translated into privacy for doing his *real* business.

With the Lieutenant twenty meters behind, Bobby turned left into the narrow alleyway between the Muscle Club and Gulf Paint next door. The Lieutenant would be more than content to listen to his music in the parking lot out front while Bobby worked out.

Bobby clicked the remote. The new automatic gate swung open. Hooah!

He pulled forward and hit the remote again. The gate closed as he drove around back. Not surprisingly, he didn't see Makeen's Lamborghini. Very surprisingly, a steel-gray metallic GMC Yukon Denali identical to his own smothered Makeen's parking spot near the office door. He walked up to it and peered in.

A light shone in the office. Bobby thought about calling Makeen but pulled out his Beretta instead of his cell. Knee or no knee, he sprang from his truck and positioned himself beside the door. Gingerly, as if handling an IED that could detonate under the least amount of pressure, he placed his hand on the knob and twisted. Whoever was inside had failed to lock up behind him.

Bobby released the safety on his weapon. Then he pushed the door open, swung the Beretta's muzzle to the right down the hall towards the entry to the gym and back to the left.

The muzzle of a Beretta stared back.

Hadn't he seen this movie before?

"Geronimo!" yelled Taahir.

"What the fuck?"

Taahir lowered his weapon.

Bobby did the same. "What are you doing here without your brother? Whose truck is that?"

Taahir's smile threatened to ram his cheeks into his ears. "Is my GMC Yukon Denali. Steel-gray metallic. Leather seats. Just like yours, Geronimo."

"We're not on the radio, Taahir."

Taahir's smile dissolved like a sugar cube in hot coffee then recovered. "Sorry, boss. You like my truck?"

"You like *mine*?"

"You the man, boss. If I be like anyone, it be you. Same truck . . ." He held up his Beretta.

Bobby repressed a frown. "How did you get leather seats? They gave me cloth."

Taahir frowned without a struggle. "Cloth? You pimp ride with cloth?" He slapped himself on the forehead with his free hand. "Why I got leather?"

Bobby took a deep breath. His pulse pounded like a bass drum in a high school marching band. He nodded towards the open back door. "You forgot to lock up behind you."

Taahir raised his free hand. Again he slapped himself on the forehead.

Bobby motioned Taahir inside Makeen's office. His eyes swept the room and locked on seven brick-size packages atop Makeen's desk, each wrapped in plain brown paper. "Doesn't your brother think it's risky for you to be out with this stuff by yourself?"

Taahir tucked his Beretta into his pants. "We learn from you. Sometimes, bunch of guys attract attention. Bad people make armbush . . ."

"*Am*bush . . ."

"But you go somewhere yourself, no one think nothing. Except maybe you got woman." He gestured to the packages. "This not problem, no?"

Bobby shook his head.

Taahir opened a plastic Shepherd of His People Mall shopping bag. It bore a Moq'tar Shepherds logo and words in Arabic and English promoting the team's official mall. He placed the packages inside one at a time then turned to Bobby. "What *you* do here, boss? No sleep?"

"I'll feel better after a workout."

Clutching the handles of the bag in his left hand, Taahir raised his right arm to flex his biceps hidden within the sleeve of his parka-like coat. "I work out, too, boss. When I old, I want look like *you*."

Bobby nodded. What could he say? He'd passed the half-century mark. But he was in great shape—good enough to whip Taahir's ass in a New York minute if it ever came to that.

Taahir lowered his arm. "You know what put you sleep, boss?"

"Tell me."

"Woman."

Bobby ran his hand over his hair. No doubt he'd sleep a lot better after a workout with Ilana Svadbova.

Taahir hefted the shopping bag. "Got to go, boss. Finish business." He extended his right hand and touched the front of Bobby's right shoulder. Then he turned towards the door.

Bobby followed and retrieved his gym bag from his truck.

Taahir stepped forward. "I get cloth seats, boss. You the man!"

Bobby patted Taahir on the back and went inside. He dropped the gym bag in the hallway and strolled into the rest room. He was peeing more these days. It was a rare night he didn't make at least one trip to the bathroom. He chose the right-hand of three Western-style urinals. Moq'tar had gone way beyond traditional holes in the floor.

He flushed. A roar like the drone of angry hornets—large ones—drew his attention. The rush of the water subsided, but the roar continued. His heart raced as bursts of AK fire erupted towards the front of the building.

A horn blared.

The firing stopped.

Bobby rocketed out of the bathroom. He grabbed his Beretta and an extra clip from his gym bag then ran down the hallway. After bursting through the back door, he turned the corner of the building and sprinted down the alleyway.

Tires screeched.

The automatic gate lay open. Just past it, smoke illuminated by a street lamp spewed out from the hood and grille of Taahir's truck.

Bobby moved forward in a semi-crouch, his Beretta cocked, his finger on the trigger. At six-five, he remained a substantial target. But the kill didn't necessarily go to the man who shot first. Just as often it went to the one who stayed calm, aimed deliberately and fired under control until his opponent went down.

Taillights disappeared around the street corner to his right. The sound of the escaping vehicle faded.

He looked left. The Lieutenant's Land Cruiser stood at an angle across two parking spaces. At its rear, the Lieutenant lay motionless on the asphalt.

Bobby ran towards Taahir's truck and approached the driver's door. Glass crunched under his feet. He swung the unlocked door open.

Taahir slumped over the steering wheel. Bobby gently pulled him back.

The horn went silent.

Bobby pressed his fingers against Taahir's bloody neck. The kid was gone.

He noticed the plastic shopping bag toppled over on the passenger seat. He peered inside. All seven bricks remained.

Bobby took a step back to gather his thoughts. He was no stranger to violent death. He'd seen his share. And he'd inflicted more of it than he'd a right to be proud of. The guys who'd served in Vietnam just before his time had hidden their emotions behind the blithe catchphrase, "Sorry about that." He'd never found words that worked for him or attempted to fool himself that any would.

He ran to the Lieutenant and gingerly eased himself into a crouch over the bloody body. Maybe by some miracle he could find a sign of life. He couldn't.

He stood slowly. His eyes searched for a lingering gunman. Nothing moved. Only his breathing disrupted the stillness. He had to think now, sort out what had happened before the police arrived. Only then could he take a next step.

Maybe business competitors, or even the people Makeen and Taahir were dealing with—the drug trade wasn't a gentleman's business—decided to rip the brothers off. But then, the bricks sitting next to Taahir in plain sight remained untouched.

He considered the possibility that Taahir had been getting into the pants of a maiden whose angry father, brothers and uncles followed him here without regard to a meeting of family leaders. That one didn't stick to the wall either. Sure, the aggrieved relatives would be burning for revenge, which passed for justice in the Middle East. But they'd likely know Taahir was Makeen's brother and this was Makeen's turf. What they *wouldn't* know was what kind of firepower might be coming out of Makeen's office, even at midnight.

A small shudder erupted between Bobby's shoulder blades. The chill air had little to do with it. This wasn't rocket science. Taahir, he understood, hadn't been the target at all. The bull's-eye had been pasted squarely on the back of Bobby Gatling.

Someone blew it. The kid drove the same truck that he did. The people who sent Wang Wei to his ancestors after Bobby confronted Yasaar at his tent outside downtown had fucked up. Again.

But why now? Because he'd been pushing Qasim bin Jabaar for a more thorough investigation? He hadn't gotten anywhere with that. Or had someone leaked the idea to remove Yasaar from the country? That made more sense. But only the Ambassador and Qasim knew of it. They wouldn't even pick a team until the tactical plan was approved.

Bobby again lowered himself over the Lieutenant's body. The earbuds attached to the Lieutenant's iPod rested on the asphalt.

Unhit, the iPod remained inside his leather jacket. He held up one of the earbuds. A song by the Four Tops played—vintage Motown Bobby'd listened to as a kid. But this was no time for a trip down memory lane. He wiped the earbuds clean on his sweatshirt.

The lieutenant's right hand drew Bobby's attention. It held his .45 in a death grip. He touched the muzzle with his knuckles to avoid leaving a fingerprint. A hint of warmth registered on his skin. He bent down and sniffed. Good for the Lieutenant. At least he'd gotten off a couple of shots.

He rolled the body onto its left side. A pool of blood greeted him but nothing more. He released the Lieutenant and let him roll onto his back again then glanced around the body. The problem was simple and complex at the same time. Where were the shell casings from the rounds the Lieutenant had fired?

Bobby rose and limped towards the alleyway. Twenty feet from the Lieutenant, two overlapping groupings of AK shell casings lay scattered on the asphalt. Two shooters, Bobby figured. Each pretty much emptied a magazine into Taahir and his truck. One also managed to pump a lethal burst of half-a-dozen rounds into the Lieutenant.

He glanced towards the street. The driver probably stopped there with the motor running, ready to leave rubber. The shooters would have gotten out of the vehicle when Taahir started his engine and opened the gate. They'd have begun firing as the GMC pulled forward.

He looked back at the Lieutenant. It didn't figure. Wouldn't he have noticed their vehicle approach? Or was he so caught up in his music that he never heard them?

Bobby returned to Taahir's truck and removed the plastic shopping bag. Then he went down the alley, entered the building and stuffed the shopping bag into his gym bag. Taking out his mini-flashlight, he went back outside.

The street remained silent.

He returned to the parking lot out front and shined the light around and under the Lieutenant's body. Then he moved on to the AK casings.

Sirens sounded in the distance.

Bobby made no effort to retreat. Given the phone conversation he'd had with bin Jabaar not long before, the police would know where he'd gone. They could ask all the questions they wanted. No problem there. He'd tell them what he'd tell them. And unless they were totally incompetent—a real possibility given their inability to find a suspect in the bombing of his truck—they'd figure Bobby as the intended victim. Taahir's death would go down as collateral damage. That would take the heat off Makeen.

The sirens grew louder.

Bobby swept the beam from his flashlight across the grouping of casings nearest the Lieutenant. It hit something odd.

He squatted and winced. The pain would have to wait.

Red, white and blue flashing lights reflected off Gulf Paint's wall.

Like a field surgeon removing shrapnel, he poked carefully. The light glinted off three casings that hadn't been ejected by an AK-47. They came from the Lieutenant's .45. And they explained everything.

At three in the morning, Bobby shouldn't have been thinking about eating. He had work to do. Yet here he was digging into haloumi, falafel, hummus and kibbeh as if he'd been without food for days.

He and Makeen had been overcome by a hunger that defied both the late hour and Taahir's untimely death. After they escorted the ambulance with Taahir's body to the morgue and left someone to watch over it, they drove to an all-night Lebanese place near the new arena. Three of Makeen's men sat at the table by the door to secure the restaurant and give them privacy. Several more remained outside.

They talked. Makeen had to express his love for his brother. And his anger. And his duty.

They ate. Both put away food as if every dish they emptied could bring Taahir back to life.

Bobby lit a cigar. It was time to get down to business.

"You are sure?" Makeen asked after Bobby detailed what happened.

Bobby opened his gym bag, withdrew the plastic shopping bag and slid it across the red-and-white checked tablecloth.

Makeen peered inside and counted. "Six. I thought there were seven."

Bobby rolled the cigar between his fingertips. He had a plan in mind—a hazy plan at this stage but promising. Only now, he felt like an EOD technician trying to diffuse a complicated bomb. In many ways, the brick of heroin he'd held back represented just that.

Makeen looked into Bobby's eyes. "I do not doubt, my friend, that the seventh package will turn up. In a few days perhaps. No longer than a few weeks, I am sure."

Bobby nodded.

Makeen drew the shopping bag towards him. "This means a lot of money to us, Bobby. And you are right, I know. If they had come for Taahir, they would have taken these."

Bobby dragged on his cigar again and blew out a puff of smoke. Somehow it didn't taste right. He put it out.

Makeen sighed. "In a few hours, I must tell our mother. How do I do this?" He sipped from a bottle of mineral water. "Then we must urge the police to release Taahir's body. This will be difficult. Perhaps you can help. We must bury him as soon as possible. Allah commands this."

"My heart cries with yours, my friend. I'll see what I can do."

"And the murderers. After the three days of mourning, I must avenge my brother. You understand."

Bobby nodded in sympathy. The same man behind Taahir's death had given the orders to blow up his own truck. But there was the big picture to consider. The matter had to be handled with cool deliberation. Overheated passion, no matter how justified, risked compromising the succession. If Moq'tar fragmented into rebellion or civil war, the Ambassador might take some of the blame, but Crimmins-Idyll and more than a few people in Washington would point the finger at Bobby Gatling. "My friend, justice will be done. I ask only for patience."

Makeen made a fist then released it.

Bobby placed his hand in Makeen's. The act would be virtually unthinkable with an American. But men in the Arab world shared a different view of physical closeness. He was grateful for that now. There was much to be learned from it. "Let's start with the fact that you don't know who the killers are. And more important, who stands behind them."

Makeen made no attempt to protest.

Bobby leaned closer. "But *I* do."

"You didn't tell me you saw them."

"See the shooters? No."

"Then how?" Makeen eyed the shopping bag. "Forgive me, but how can I trust you will do this, Bobby?"

Bobby pulled three Colt .45 casings from his jacket pocket. "These, my friend, tell me everything I need to know. When the time is right, and it won't be long, justice *will* be done."

Maaris

| March |

Nineteen

The protestors, numbering over two thousand, assembled at the Grand Mosque shortly after the noontime Dhuhr prayer. All shared a single objective—terminate Mickey Green's association with the Moq'tar Shepherds.

Responding to the calls of fliers and loudspeakers flooding Moq'tar City since before dawn, many had come early to silently recite the four prescribed *rakaat* in a holy place. Some had unrolled their prayer rugs in their offices or shops before hurrying to the mosque. Still others delayed assembling until the prayer's conclusion. The muezzin's recorded *adhan* singing out from loudspeakers affixed to the nearest minaret served only as a reminder that this first day of the secular month was moving forward with great rapidity. Much business remained to be done.

No matter their level of observance, the protestors responded with unswerving dedication. Their march on the Great Hall of the Assembly represented divinely inspired improvisational theater in which the protestors would play critical roles. A Jew's leadership of Moq'tar's beloved Shepherds represented nothing less than a monstrous affront to God. The protestors would dramatize the awakening of a people to its glorious heritage and the will of Allah.

Moreover, the ad hoc Committee for the Propagation of Virtue and Opposition to Vice in Basketball and Related Sporting Endeavors pledged that the protest would be as peaceful and punctual as it would be emphatic. After delivering their message to the world, the nation's warriors for God would return to their places of business to conclude the day before going home to a hearty dinner and settling in front of their televisions to approve of themselves on the nine o'clock news.

Half an hour following *Dhuhr* the multitude reached critical mass. All was in order. Even the backs of the professionally designed homemade signs distributed by men in uniform green windbreakers thoughtfully admonished the protestors to:

WALK QUICKLY,
CHANT LOUDLY,
KEEP OFF THE FLOWERS,
SMILE!*

Leaving nothing to chance, fine print had been inserted at the bottom of each sign:

> *Participation in the march for any or all of its duration constitutes an acknowledgement of the hazards posed by all such demonstrations and a waiver of any claim to liability on the part of the Committee.

The protest's leader—a tall, thin man almost anonymous in his green windbreaker and sunglasses—held aloft a green bullhorn. In a voice displaying the enthusiasm of a career university student devoted to social reformation, he instructed the throng to extemporaneously follow him and his phalanx of green-jacketed warriors several blocks to the Corniche and onward. The ad hoc procession would begin to arrive at the Great Hall in precisely one hour. The media had already gathered there in response to digital and faxed news releases furiously launched even before the pre-dawn *Fajr* prayers.

The march began.

"Watch your step and keep moving," ordered the protest-leader's amplified voice. "Remember, this is a peaceful demonstration. Anyone who resorts to violence will suffer our wrath."

At one-fifty, adhering precisely to the schedule prepared by the Committee, the first wave reached the plaza in front of the Great Hall. Enough marchers would be in place by two o'clock to begin preliminaries. Stragglers would reinforce the crowd and strengthen the vigor of its complaint. Well before the sun set, the first green shoots of a new, pure Moq'tar would burst forth from the desiccated soil of the old. The nation would embrace true progress through its own *hijra*—a journey back fourteen centuries offering refuge in the unsullied days of the Prophet.

Bobby stood alongside bin Jabaar looking down from the tenth-floor observation post the Ministry of Security had again commandeered in the Camel's Dick. The inside of his eyelids felt like sheets of sandpaper.

After leaving Makeen around four-thirty following Taahir's murder, he'd dozed fitfully on his sofa for no more than an hour, showered, reviewed the document he'd prepared for bin Jabaar then driven to the Ministry of Security for their eight o'clock.

Bin Jabaar met him with the news. Planning for Yasaar's removal would have to wait. A brewing protest left them little time for preparation and an urgent need to marshal all the forces available to them. Bobby welcomed the opportunity in spite of his exhaustion. He was back in the loop once more. Determined to prevent any significant outburst of violence, they rushed to set security procedures in place.

Now all they could do was wait.

Four Humvees ordered by General bin Jabaar saluted the protestors with .50-caliber machine guns where the far end of the Corniche intersected the Avenue of the Righteous. Just beyond stood a mass of helmeted riot police and special security troops with visors down, shields raised, riot clubs at the ready. Gas masks rested on their thighs. Additional police held positions along the avenue. Some blocked the smaller side streets that fed into it—and led out. Three blocks up, more helmeted men guarded the entries to both the Great Hall and the Camel's Dick.

Police and troops supported by armed Humvees also sealed the Avenue of the Righteous on its far side. Should the situation get out of hand, the marchers' way into the plaza would provide their only escape route—a gauntlet the prudent among them would not wish to run.

A multitude of outraged protesters expanded across the plaza in front of the Great Hall like an oil slick spreading from a ruptured underwater wellhead.

Television trucks uplinked satellite feeds.

A chant drifted up to the top of the Camel's Dick. "Hey, hey, ho, ho. Hoops yes! Bagels no!"

Yusuf burst through the door of the command post. "General, this farce has my brother's name written all over it."

Bobby glanced at bin Jabaar.

Bin Jabaar stroked a drawn, stubbled cheek. "I have people on the ground, Sheikh. Everything is under control. And there is no sign of Sheikh Yasaar."

Yusuf peered out the window. "I've just asked Ambassador Ellis to alert Centcom to stand by for backup."

Bobby's eyebrows shot up. If he was back in the loop, it wasn't Yusuf's. The Sheikh should never have contacted the Ambassador before conferring with him. "That really isn't possible, Sheikh. And if it was, it would look like the invasion of Grenada back in 'eighty-three. The American media would go into a feeding frenzy."

"I assure you, Sheikh," said bin Jabaar, "intervention will not be necessary." His usually serene composure betrayed a bit of fraying around the edges. "The organizers have pledged their peaceful intentions. Our intelligence corroborates that pledge. Nonetheless, my people, with Colonel Gatling's assistance, are ready. We will, of course, exercise the utmost restraint. Violence will serve only to embarrass the government."

Yusuf thrust his hands into his pockets and turned to Bobby. "I'm not pleased, Colonel. I thought you and General bin Jabaar had my back. And for the record, Mickey Green is the best coach in professional basketball. What's more, he's a great guy. He autographed balls for me and for each of my children. And he waived his normal fee."

A new chant rose from the crowd. "Chop heads, not livers!"

The protest-leader mounted the steps in front of the Great Hall.

Helmeted police tightened their grips on their clubs.

The crowd buzzed expectantly. The undercurrent suggested vengeful Parisians gathered to witness Marie-Antoinette kneeling before the guillotine.

On the second floor of the Great Hall, Righteous Elders pressed their faces to the windows.

The protest-leader raised both hands towards the heavens.

From within the crowd, a resonant voice indicative of several years of theatrical training in Cairo proclaimed, "Yasaar! Yasaar! *Allahu Akhbar!*"

"My brother," Yusuf declared, "is a clear and present danger."

"I agree, Sheikh," said Bobby. "But let's not fall into a trap here."

"I, too, would affirm the folly of yielding to provocation," said bin Jabaar.

Bobby felt torn nonetheless. If all went well, the challenge from Yasaar would soon be removed. If anything, unfolding events proved the wisdom of that decision regardless of the potential risks. For the moment, finesse would serve better than brute force.

The demonstrators, encouraged by supportive voices bellowing from a dozen bullhorns, picked up the chant. "Yasaar! Yasaar! *Allahu Akhbar!* Yasaar! Yasaar! *Allahu Akhbar!*"

A line of police, clubs poised, took a step toward the crowd.

Bobby leaned towards bin Jabaar. "Your people need to back off."

Bin Jabaar studied the situation.

"Qasim," Bobby asked, "what the hell are you waiting for?"

The chanting grew more animated.

The police moved closer.

"Fall back! Fall back!" bin Jabaar ordered into his radio.

Before the order to withdraw could be acknowledged, a knot of protestors attempted to wrestle riot clubs from the hands of several police. One protestor—still smiling as instructed—swung a sign.

A policeman fell.

His comrades charged.

Clubs rained down on heads offering no more protection than a *kaffiyeh* or a New York Yankees cap.

The protestor who wielded his sign as a weapon dropped to the plaza floor. Scurrying feet trampled him.

A second protestor hoisted the sign of his fallen comrade as if playing out a scene from *Les Misérables*.

A dozen scuffles broke out.

Police advanced from all three sides of the plaza.

Several knots of protestors attempted a countercharge.

Clubs pounded heads, necks and shoulders.

Cries rose of astonishment, fear and anger.

Bodies collapsed.

"My God!" complained Yusuf. His voice cracked with alarm. "Al Jazeera will run this around the clock."

"*Restraint!*" bin Jabaar scolded his commanders on the ground.

A shot rang out in response. A second followed.

Some protestors crouched. Most, bewildered, remained standing. A few attempted to retreat towards the avenue but found themselves penned in by the crowd, the Humvees and additional security forces pressing forward up the single available route back to the Corniche.

"This is a disaster," Yusuf moaned.

"Withdraw your men," Bobby snapped.

"Now?" bin Jabaar snapped back. "Impossible. The protestors will run wild through downtown. We must use gas."

Bobby shot bin Jabaar a look of disbelief. "Qasim, what the hell are you thinking? Don't you know how this will play on TV?"

"General," Yusuf pleaded. "Colonel . . ."

"Withdraw your people to the Gulf end of the avenue," Bobby insisted, "and clear the other end." The tactic reflected common sense. Cornered people—like cornered animals—only fought more ferociously. Better that police and security personnel drive the protestors towards the elevated freeway and a path out of harm's way. Then they could disperse frightened, still angry no doubt, but none the worse for wear. Government embarrassment would be minimized. As the old basketball saying went, no harm, no foul.

Bin Jabaar shook his head. "The mob is out of control. We must restore order. Order and respect."

Yusuf pressed his hands to his cheeks. "It's your call, General. Do it. Use the gas!"

Bobby glowered at Yusuf. The Sheikh wasn't responding to a crisis, he was creating one. And bin Jabaar had set it all in motion.

Bin Jabaar raised his radio to give the order, paused then lowered it.

At the Gulf-side corner of the plaza, an M113 armored personnel carrier forced its way into the crowd then stopped. A figure emerged and walked forward.

The crowd around the M113 parted.

"Like God splitting the Red Sea to clear a path for the Israelites," Bobby mumbled to himself.

Yusuf glanced at Bobby then back down at the crowd.

Protestors and police disentangled. A wave of calm spread like ripples in a pond from the corner of the plaza across its center and out to its far sides.

The figure advanced towards the steps in front of the Great Hall and mounted them.

The protest-leader backed away.

The figure turned majestically and held out its hands toward the crowd.

Protestors and police stood together in hushed tranquility.

"I don't believe it," said Yusuf softly. "I simply don't believe it."

Without prompting, thousands of right arms shot into the air simultaneously. "Zoraya!" roared the crowd. "Zoraya! Zoraya! Zoraya!"

The Ambassador stood at his desk in shirtsleeves, his tie unknotted. He had news and it wasn't likely to be taken well. But men who shouldered grave responsibilities never wavered in their commitment to the cause of truth and justice no matter how often they had to change their position. N. Ronald Ellis served as the Ambassador of the United States of America to the Sultanate of Moq'tar. He had money behind him. More than that, he had firepower. And thus he had the right to call—and recall—the shots.

He set down three glasses of Scotch while Bobby and Qasim bin Jabaar displayed their best military posture in spite of a fatiguing day.

"How about that Princess Zoraya?" said the Ambassador to focus his guests' attention.

"The topic of conversation throughout the sultanate I am sure," bin Jabaar responded. He looked at Bobby.

"I'd think so," Bobby agreed.

"Well, and after everything they told me about the Middle East," the Ambassador remarked. His shoulders rose and fell in a shrug of amazement. He lifted his glass.

Bobby and bin Jabaar did likewise.

"*Salaam!*"—Peace!—the Ambassador toasted. His Arabic was coming on strong now.

"*Salaam!*" Bobby and bin Jabaar returned in tandem.

The Ambassador downed his drink.

Bobby and bin Jabaar followed suit.

"By the way, Colonel," the Ambassador remarked, "your eyes are as red as the flag of China. It's still red, isn't it?"

"Yes, sir," Bobby answered. He placed his empty glass on the desk alongside bin Jabaar's.

The Ambassador poured three fresh drinks. "General," he said, shifting his attention to bin Jabaar, "I appreciate your coming here. Moq'tar is *your* country. I'm only an honored guest."

"That is quite thoughtful of you, Mr. Ambassador," the General replied.

The first drink of the evening out of the way, the Ambassador sipped slowly to emphasize that rational minds were at work here. Nightfall had produced an anxious calm tempering religious intoxication with fear and exhaustion. Now, while Moq'taris sat down to dinner following the day's bizarre events, sophisticated men who understood the subtleties of international relations would give new direction to their best interests.

Bobby emptied his glass.

The Ambassador put his drink down, eased into his seat and folded his hands on his desk. It was time to get down to the nut cutting. The march and the riot made the morning news in Washington and New York. There'd been blowback. It hadn't been pretty. "The White House doesn't know what the hell's going on here, which means State is all over my backside. Again. Long story short, I'm the coach, and I'm sending in a new play. The attack on Sheikh Yasaar is off."

"Bullshit!" Bobby exploded. The hours he'd invested in planning the operation to snatch Yasaar had convinced him of the operation's necessity.

The Ambassador looked at bin Jabaar, who sat expressionless, then stared at Bobby. "You're out of line, Colonel."

"You're out of your mind!" Bobby shot back. "Sir."

The Ambassador balled his fists then released them. He wasn't a violent man. He had no need to be. In his world, money was the weapon of choice to secure the loyalty of friends, put fear in the hearts of enemies and settle old scores.

Bobby took a breath and let it out slowly. "What I'm trying to say, sir," he continued, "is that Sheikh Yusuf commented this afternoon that he believed the march was all Yasaar's doing. General bin Jabaar can vouch for that. And I absolutely agree." Regrettably, media coverage of security forces bloodying the protestors—in spite of Princess Zoraya's pacifying influence—doubtless had increased Yasaar's confidence that he could disrupt the country, appeal to the public's fears and rally the Assembly to his side. Sheikh Yusuf would never mount the throne until Yasaar was forced out of the country at the very least.

The Ambassador turned to bin Jabaar. "And you?"

Bin Jabaar twirled his glass gently in his hand. "I am sure, Mr. Ambassador, that Colonel Gatling's reaction and his unspoken suggestion of assassination represent a passionate concern for Moq'tar's stability and democratic progress. I must, nonetheless, agree with *you* just as I registered my protest in our previous conversation."

Bobby attempted to stare daggers but succeeded only in blinking with great discomfort.

Bin Jabaar laid out a simple rationale. The day's events most certainly reflected the religious concerns of the more conservative elements of Moq'tari society. Whether politics played a role was beyond anyone's determination—at least at the moment. Given Sheikh Yasaar's absence from the protest, a move against him would most likely erode trust in a government now represented, if somewhat ambiguously, by Sheikh Yusuf. This in turn would disturb others in the Gulf, both friends and those who sought to advance agendas not in Moq'tar's—or the United States'—best interests.

The Ambassador turned back to Bobby. "Colonel, I'm a forgiving kind of guy. Your little outburst . . . I can let it slide. But I have to ask, could you be taking all this a little too personally?"

"Too personally, sir? That someone tried to kill me less than twenty-four hours ago? Unquestionably the same people who turned my truck into scrap metal that ended up back in China along with a man I put behind the wheel?" He looked at bin Jabaar. "The people you can't identify, Qasim?"

Bin Jabaar rocked forward. "If you will excuse me, Mr. Ambassador, perhaps I should explain to Colonel Gatling that someone else, and not he, was killed last night. The man is . . . was . . . of uncertain character." He turned to Bobby. "And yes, he drove a truck resembling yours. We understand the implication, and we are working with that."

Bobby searched the Ambassador's eyes for some hint of sympathy. He found none.

The Ambassador took a breath, crossed his arms and rubbed his shoulders. How much tension was a man supposed to endure in this job? He released the breath and dropped his hands. "By the way, Colonel, General bin Jabaar has other news. *Important* news."

Bin Jabaar edged closer to Bobby. "We have word that the Assembly of Righteous Elders is about to call for a formal and binding vote. Assuredly by the end of the month and more probably within two weeks."

The Ambassador stood, stretched and yawned. He felt a bit better now. "Let me translate, Colonel Gatling." He lowered his chin to his chest and grunted. Thai food for lunch three days in a row was probably a mistake. "If Yasaar gets killed or disappears between now and the election, no matter how it happens, the whole world will accuse the United States of interfering with Moq'tar's political integrity. That's a no-no. Violates everything we stand for."

Bobby struggled to compose himself. "But we went over that at our last meeting. And what if Yasaar *wins*?"

The Ambassador came around the desk and sat. "Colonel, just how much confidence do you have in your government's ability to guide its friends?"

Bobby glanced towards the corner where the American flag remained folded in on itself.

"Bobby," said bin Jabaar, his voice barely above a whisper, "Moq'tari politics are far more complicated than those of America. And addressing your personal concern, that is why we have not been able to call in the FBI."

Indeed, the Ambassador had passed the call on to Sheikh Yusuf who left it to General bin Jabaar with whose decision they both agreed. The FBI's presence would inflame Moq'tari sensibilities and serve only to destabilize a tenuous situation.

Bin Jabaar reached for Bobby's arm. "May I confide in you Bobby?"

Bobby offered no response.

"I will take your silence as assent. Therefore I will propose that you have become very involved in Moq'tar's affairs. Perhaps *too* involved. This is, after all, *my* country. I love it. *Insh'allah* I will see it follow the rightly guided path."

Bobby shook his arm free of bin Jabaar's grasp. "And you don't think it's doing that now under Sheikh Yusuf?"

Bin Jabaar curled the fingers on his rejected hand as if he were holding a knife. "I like you Bobby. I hold you in great esteem. But the situation in Moq'tar is not about *you*." He looked at the Ambassador then back at Bobby. "Perhaps your work here is done. Perhaps it would be better if you, rather than Sheikh Yusuf or myself, asked Crimmins-Idyll for a new assignment. Something less stressful. Possibly, with all due respect, less dangerous."

Bobby looked down at bin Jabaar's hand then up into his eyes. If, after last night, he'd entertained any doubts at all, he had none now. His vision of how things were playing out in Moq'tar couldn't be more clear. "I see your point, Qasim," he said softly. "Things'll work out for the best. *Insh'allah.*"

Only Bobby Gatling, not God, would determine how they played out in the days to come.

Twenty

usuf felt queasy yet again. Unable to finish breakfast, he pushed away his half-eaten bowl of Grape Nuts. Lifting his eyes from the digital edition of The Wall Street Journal displayed on his laptop—as integral to his morning routine as the new, healthier nonfat, decaf latte sans whipped cream awaiting him at his office—he cast a glance at his children playing with their oatmeal then at Ameena nibbling her croissant. Only now, he couldn't focus on The Journal either. He took a breath, held it then released it. An audible sigh shot out from between his lips as if his bankers had called all the debt he'd acquired over the past year.

"Father," whined Maryam from across the table, "Muhammad hit me."

"She's only a girl!" Muhammad replied with the self-assurance befitting a young prince.

"Children!" Ameena scolded. She turned to Yusuf. "*You* are their father. Make them behave."

"Don't I have enough on my plate?" Yusuf countered.

Ameena scowled.

The children left the kitchen.

"You haven't eaten your breakfast," said Ameena.

"Not hungry. I didn't sleep well."

"And why not? The protest against Mickey Green . . ." She shook her head slowly. "The protest was a week ago. Allah be praised for Zoraya. She somehow calmed the people and prevented terrible bloodshed. This surely provided you with an opportunity to, how they say, seize the moment."

"Like *how*?"

Ameena shook her head. "And still you are unsure how to take the throne."

"I know what I'm doing."

"You are my husband. I know *you*."

Yusuf reached for his spoon and absentmindedly pushed his soggy cereal to the far side of the bowl. There were so many factors involved. So many uncertainties. But the Assembly would come around. He had to believe that.

"The election is only days away," said Ameena. "You must *do* something, Yusuf, not play Hamlet."

Here it came again. If Ameena hadn't been born into royalty and, as a woman, freed from financial and other practical concerns, she would have become a therapist and been quite at home in Berkeley or San Francisco. She knew everyone's business. Or at least, she thought she did. Including his. "Give it a rest, Ameena," he cut her off. "You're not Dr. Phil."

"You are afraid you lack the strength of your father," she declared, undeterred. "You therefore cannot make a decision about ridding Moq'tar of your brother and taking the throne. And all because that unreasonable fear paralyzes you."

Yusuf dropped the spoon into the bowl. What Ameena couldn't get into her head was that the situation had nothing to do with fear. It was about *trust*. Politics worked no differently than the markets. Trust kept the wheels turning. Without trust, everything ground to a halt. So who could he trust? Yasaar? That was a no-brainer. His ministers? He had faith in General bin Jabaar, but the General was a military man, not a politician. Ron Ellis? They were on the same wavelength, but Ron was still the U.S. Ambassador with his own set of loyalties. Colonel Gatling? He seemed to be a straight shooter, and Yusuf had to admit he'd been right about not using gas during the demonstration, but he was just a contractor, a hired hand. Maybe if something extraordinary was called for . . .

When it got down to it, he could count on Ameena. He'd never doubted that. And Zoraya. Over these last weeks she'd been a rock. She really had. But what did all this say about him as a man if the two people he trusted most were women?

Now, with the Assembly of Righteous Elders about to get off their asses, what came next? At least he'd found a new general manager for the Shepherds, a guy with solid credentials willing to stay in the background for the time being. Together, they'd exercised damage control by coming up with a quick fix for the coaching situation to restore the fans' faith in the franchise before it suffered irreversible damage. Only this time, he had the new coach coming in for an interview—he was probably having breakfast at the Shepherd Palace right now—and a little face time to make sure the fit was good before Zoraya made the announcement. Hoops aficionados might not consider the decision particularly bold, but it definitely would hold up to scrutiny.

Yet unless he came up with something fast to win the approaching election, everything he'd worked so hard to build would collapse like a tent in a sandstorm. Only where would he find an idea?

The crash of a lamp in the next room interrupted them.

"Children!" screamed Yusuf, unable to restrain his frustration. "Come in here at once!"

Little Muhammad entered the kitchen. Maryam trailed a step behind.

"It wasn't just *me!*" cried Little Muhammad. His cheeks reddened in anticipation of a swat on the backside or worse. He turned towards his sister. "It was *her*, too!"

Maryam's eyelashes fluttered like the wings of a falcon chasing its prey.

His anger passing, Yusuf beckoned the girl onto his lap. "Well," he said, "accidents will happen."

Maryam kissed him on the cheek and ran off.

Yusuf watched her skip away carefree. And then it struck him that there might be a lesson in this. But what was it?

Bobby waited as Makeen locked the door to his office. This wasn't a social call. One of Makeen's men stood outside. Another positioned himself down the hall to make sure the gym's lunchtime devotees remained attentive to their workouts. Business was business, and the Muscle Club had reopened right after the three-day mourning period for Taahir.

Bobby sat in front of Makeen's desk.

Makeen poured tea and sat opposite.

"You're sure," Bobby asked in a voice uncharacteristically subdued, "that your man with Yasaar has accurate information? He hasn't given you anything before. At least not that you've told me about."

Makeen took a deep breath then lifted his glass. "Things have changed. Trust me, Bobby. I am sure."

Bobby nodded. He feared he might have offended a friend when he needed him most. Makeen's first concern, he understood, focused on his own interests. Men who exercised any degree of power kept information—and informants—close until circumstances prompted sharing.

As to teaming with Makeen instead of going solo, several factors came into play. Not the least of which was that he'd been abandoned. After two attempts on his life, the USofA wasn't coming to his rescue for damn sure. And no one from Alexandria seemed ready to lead a cavalry charge in his direction. They'd left him with no other choice than to change the rules of engagement.

Of no little importance, Makeen also had a score to settle. And the intelligence provided by his collaborator would simplify bringing a complex matter to a satisfactory conclusion.

"Okay," said Bobby. "We're good to go when you get the word."

Makeen smiled. "Faith, my friend. And patience."

Bobby sipped his tea and smiled. As they said in the USofA, this would be for all the marbles. In a few days, one tidy little operation would enable the two of them to see justice done and Yusuf guaranteed the throne.

Yusuf dribbled forward, yielded to second thoughts and retreated behind the three-point line. Jamal McCarthy stood in the paint, a considerable—and intimidating—obstacle. Six-three and probably two-fifty-five given a decade of retirement and a less than discriminatory diet, J-Mac had established a reputation as one of The League's strongest players inch for inch and perhaps the most aggressive. A simple cost-benefit analysis dictated avoiding the Shepherds' prospective coach anywhere near the basket. Whatever last-minute contract concessions he might make through his agent, J-Mac would concede nothing on the court.

"Take it to the hole, Joe," the Ambassador called out in support, heedless of Yusuf's scouting report on the coach designate.

"Bring it on Sheikh," said J-Mac. "Let's see what you got."

Yusuf smiled. He had no fear that J-Mac would actually hurt him. Not badly anyway. But he hated the thought of being embarrassed, even in a friendly little one-on-one game. He'd take his chances shooting from beyond the arc since J-Mac made no effort to check him out there.

What he hadn't taken a chance on, he believed, was another screw-up. J-Mac had won a championship ring, been an all-star three times and, most important, converted to Islam during his rookie season. A faithful Muslim and respected basketball lifer—he'd coached two minor league champions before becoming a top assistant in the League—J-Mac boasted ample bona fides. Not to mention that they'd hit it off personally.

"No rush, Sheikh," J-Mac called out. "Ain't no twenty-four second clock."

Yusuf continued dribbling. He just needed a moment to catch his breath. Going one-on-one with even a retired League player represented a major stretch of his hoops skills not to mention a daunting test of his manhood.

J-Mac motioned Yusuf to dribble towards him. "Bring it, Sheikh."

"Nothing ventured," the Ambassador offered.

Yusuf took a deep breath. Nothing ventured, indeed. Except that Ron was standing on the sidelines. But what if? It was all about momentum. As he eased his way towards the basket, J-Mac would inevitably shift his weight forward. All it would take was one quick step to get by him. One quick step and an explosion to the basket for an easy hoop.

The explosion took place but not in the paint. Chunks of concrete, shards of glass and strips of twisted metal hurtled down from a luxury box at the opposite end of the arena. The remains of a wide-screen television found a perch atop the support for the far backboard.

Yusuf felt as if a pair of hands gripped his neck. He struggled to take short, rapid breaths.

J-Mac and the Ambassador stood shocked and speechless.

Smoke snaked across the ceiling. Vibrations from the newly installed scoreboard above the court suggested its imminent descent.

Yusuf held his right hand over his heart.

Lights throughout the building flickered then went out leaving only dim emergency lighting and exit signs as guides.

Yusuf blinked. And blinked again. The emergency lights seemed to be fading. The basketball dropped out of his hands, bounced off his right shoe and rolled away in the darkness.

"Goddam, Ambassador," J-Mac ordered, "call the cops. And get a motherfuckin' doctor."

"Daddy, it wasn't your fault," Maryam whispered. She clutched the soft Minnie Mouse doll she'd brought home from Disneyland Paris the previous fall. Minnie accompanied her almost everywhere. She even slept on her pillow at night.

"*What* wasn't my fault?" Yusuf answered softly. He still felt groggy. Besides, bedtime demanded gentle voices.

Maryam, her bedcovers up to her chin, glanced at the nightlight that kept evil spirits at bay. "The bomb the bad men set off at the new basketball place this afternoon."

Yusuf rested his hand on her cheek. "Of course, it wasn't my fault." He wondered how kids learned news like this so quickly. Maryam was too young for a PC and the Net, although one of her little friends might have heard from her parents. Maybe they'd made a mistake giving her a simple cell phone. "Very bad men did a very bad thing, but they won't hurt me. Or Mommy. Or Little Muhammad. Or you."

Maryam rubbed her cheek against Yusuf's palm.

He closed his eyes. The innocence of his daughter's little-girl scent soothed him. He felt far better sitting on the edge of her bed than he would have had he relented to Ameena's foolish insistence that he spend a few days in the hospital. The little incident he suffered after the explosion was meaningless. And how would the Elders respond to *that* if word leaked out? And word *would* leak. This was no time to show weakness.

"Will the bad men hurt Aunt Zoraya?" Maryam asked.

"No, of course not," Yusuf responded. "Aunt Zoraya hasn't done anything wrong."

Maryam looked into Yusuf's eyes. "Aunt Zoraya never does a bad thing. But even if Aunt Zoraya *did* a bad thing, no one would blame her. Everyone loves her as much as I love Minnie and the Prophet."

Yusuf withdrew his hand from Maryam's cheek and sat in silent contemplation. A father had to savor such moments. Children grew up so fast. What's more, if you paid attention to them, really studied them, you could learn so much. And now, the earlier but hazy thought Maryam had inspired gained startling clarity. "It's late," he said. He kissed Maryam on the forehead. "And you know what?"

"What, Daddy?"

"You've given me a very good idea."

Twenty-one

Bent over like an actor taking a bow but uncertain of the audience's favor, Yusuf rested his hands on his knees while his executive assistant opened the door to his office for him. How much exertion could a man expend?

He'd started the morning ebullient, having found the solution to his problems. Then things went south.

Daniel Kantrowitz had called. The League's board of governors, rocked on its heels by the Mickey Green protest, was considering revoking Moq'tar's franchise. Only the commissioner's determined support held them off. That and Yusuf's assurance that he would double—no triple—security around the arena and end Moq'tar's political turmoil within thirty days.

Then he'd gone downstairs to meet with key trade officials from Turkey. They'd failed to reach an expected agreement due to a stream of objections from their leader, a Wharton School grad. Ivy League prejudice without question.

Finally, to prove his mettle as a leader of men, he'd rejected his doctor's admonitions regarding the previous day's fainting episode at the arena and run up three flights of stairs. Or more accurately, run up one flight and staggered up the final two.

He stumbled inside. "What . . ." he wheezed.

Zoraya looked up from behind his desk. "Are you alright?"

Yusuf waved his hand.

Zoraya spun Yusuf's laptop towards him. "You asked me to meet you here, so I upgraded your memory while you were out. Then I surfed the Web while I waited. Come. Come see this."

Yusuf approached the desk. "Dresses?"

"Evening gowns, silly."

Yusuf coughed into his fist. "Had lunch?" he asked.

"I'm starving."

"You?"

"I was up early. The Academy Awards."

"Who won?"

"I have no idea. I only watch the female stars arrive to see what they are wearing."

Yusuf shrugged. "I can order in from the Breath of the Dragon."

Zoraya puffed out her cheeks as if she were about to be ill.

"Maybe salads from the café downstairs."

"Lovely." She moved to her accustomed seat on the sofa and gestured to a box wrapped in silver paper atop the coffee table. "I brought you a present."

"Not more vodka?"

"Ambassador Kazanovitch gave it to me."

Yusuf looked up. "He pays a lot of attention to you, doesn't he?"

"Kazanovitch? He fancies himself a ladies' man. With a wife like his, I think not. But he is sweet. He wants to arrange a meeting with a wealthy clothing manufacturer about designing my own signature line for women. He believes I can make Moscow a major fashion center."

Yusuf sprawled in his recliner. "It's nice to have special friends, isn't it?"

"The American Ambassador is *your* special friend."

"Ron's a good man. We need America."

Zoraya threw her head back. Her black curls fluttered softly. "Always politics. So complex. Almost as complex as fashion. Which is why I shall have to make a preemptive flight to Milan. I've discovered a wonderful new designer. Everyone in the Gulf will soon know about her."

Yusuf sat up. "Tell you what. Wait until after the election, and you can take a trip to anywhere on the government's dirham. Moscow included."

"You have never been, have you?"

"Moscow? No. Maybe I'll make a state visit."

"I shall accompany you. There are many handsome men in Moscow."

Yusuf loosened his tie. Zoraya surprised him. He'd begun to think his sister preferred the company of her women friends. "Back to your trip to Milan or wherever. You'd have a proper credit line."

Zoraya leaned over and pecked Yusuf on the cheek. "And now you require something else from me in return?"

"This election . . ." He paused. Everything Dad and he had worked so hard to accomplish lay in the balance. Admittedly, Yasaar had gathered more support than he'd thought possible. But the ballgame wasn't over. "Last week at the protest against . . . well . . ."

"Your Mr. Green."

"You practically cut Yasaar's balls off. The throne's still up for grabs."

Zoraya's lips turned up. "I'm beginning to think there is more of Father in you than I give you credit for."

"And maybe there's a little of Dad in *you*. Anyway, I've been thinking." His plan was simple yet calculated. Moq'taris loved Zoraya. They didn't *know* their princess, but they adored her. That made Zoraya an incredibly valuable asset. Yasaar didn't get it, but *he* did. "I have a role for you."

"A role? Like an actress?"

Yusuf took Zoraya's hand. "Think of women loving and envying you from here to Beverly Hills . . . in both directions."

Zoraya glowed as if she'd just been presented with an Oscar. She knew what Yusuf was about to say—and that he hadn't a clue that she could read him like an e-book.

Yusuf laid out the details. The Elders would end up making him Sultan in a heartbeat. "Because," he declared, confirming Zoraya's intuition, "what's going to bring the Assembly of Righteous Elders to the tipping point is *you*."

The Ambassador hoisted a beef rib and ran the tip of his tongue over his lips. He looked as if he was about to devour one of the exotic dancers at the city's semi-notorious Oasis Club. He was in no rush. Anticipating a great meal was half the fun. He would enjoy every bite even more since Yusuf had just called to reveal his plan. He had to hand it to Joe. The guy was one smart cookie. Practically a white man.

"Anything wrong, sir?" Dymme asked. He held aloft a forkful of baked potato. A drop of sour cream—a man had to forego his otherwise Spartan regimen from time to time—clung to his bearded chin.

"Wrong? What could be wrong, Dymme? I've eaten some damn good ribs in my day, and I'll tell you this . . . The Lone Star does ribs as good as anyone anywhere."

"This barbecued chicken deserves a bit of recognition, too, sir."

The Ambassador went in for the kill and emerged like a famished lion savoring the rewards of a difficult hunt. Sated for the moment, he placed the rib down and wiped his fingers. Sauce smeared his white napkin like a bloodstain. "Eat up on the United States of America, Dymme. This is business."

Dymme placed his fork on his plate. "Yes, Mr. Ambassador. But shouldn't we . . ."

"Shouldn't we what?"

"Lower our voices? Cover our mouths perhaps? Security, sir."

"You don't think I had one too many up in the mezzanine bar, do you?"

"I'm sure you can handle it, sir."

"I'm fan-fucking-tastic, Dymme. And do you know why?" The Ambassador gestured to his plate. "Because, Dymme, ribs like these are America's gift to help civilize the world." And the world needed civilizing. Badly. Without America, the ragheads wouldn't know what really great ribs were. Or great steak. Or even great chicken. "We'd be eating camel right now," he exclaimed.

"And drinking mare's milk," Dymme proposed.

The Ambassador coughed into his hand then turned it upside down. A piece of gristle dropped onto his plate. "You're a good man, Dymme," he said, his voice barely audible. "You're damn well going to *have* to be."

Dymme propped his chin on his left hand and concealed his mouth behind his fingers. "I understand the situation, sir," he said with an air of nonchalance. "I'll handle it."

The Ambassador stared at Dymme. He wasn't being taunted by second thoughts so much as undergoing a sobering experience with reality. He'd been informed that Dymme was a good man. One of the best. Okay. But who did Dymme think he was? James Bond? This was no movie with Dymme the director and everything happening just the way he said because he said so. The security of the United States hung in the balance. If Moq'tar went down the tubes, America's friends in the Gulf would cozy up to other friends. The Ambassador had no intention of being the sorry answer to, "Who lost Moq'tar?"

Dymme sliced a piece of chicken with the deftness of a surgeon. "This isn't, as some of the more picturesque elements of American society like to say, my first rodeo."

The Ambassador rubbed his nose. "Sure. Fine. As long as every country in this godforsaken region gets the message that we can control our allies."

Dymme stared down at his fork. "But actually, isn't that what we *don't* want, sir?"

The Ambassador pushed his plate back. Did Dymme, with his limited perspective, really think the United States gave a shit whether third-world countries loved us? Love had nothing to do with anything. It was all about respect. And countries respected the United States only when they *feared* the United States. Dymme—like Colonel Gatling for that matter—needed to pull his head out of his ass.

Dymme wiped his lips, removed the sour cream from his beard and replaced his napkin in his lap. "On another front, sir, our April film festival and the dance performances in May will present us in a very positive light."

The Ambassador frowned. "Don't you ever give it a rest?"

Dymme concealed a small sigh. His feelings weren't all that easily hurt most of the time, but the Ambassador's attitude revealed a dismaying lack of sensitivity regarding his multi-faceted professionalism. He was a Yale man not to mention a loyal American and, although he would never mention it in Hollywood, a registered Republican. He wasn't about to let the American people down in any regard. "Everything's going to be just fine, Mr. Ambassador. I can absolutely guarantee you that."

The Ambassador picked up his rib. "Then it's on you, Dymme. And remember, if the information you've got on certain people is wrong, if you fuck up and we can't nudge the election our way, this was all *your* people's idea. *My* nose is clean."

Twenty-two

The critical text message appeared just before midnight: LET'S ROLL! Bobby turned off the TV that hadn't done much to keep him company, threw on his quilted jacket and grabbed his duffle. After slipping out the door, he checked to make sure it was locked. The apartment held little of value aside from the TV and his laptop, of course, but maybe asking the building manager for a stronger lock was the right thing to do. His father's advice still lingered. He'd cautioned not to place a stumbling block before the blind. Some people would steal or do worse whatever the circumstances. Others might be deterred if kept from temptation.

He tiptoed down the hallway, bypassed the elevator and ducked into the stairwell. He practically skipped down to the basement, stiff knee be damned, then trotted out along the narrow hallway past the garage.

He emerged into the trash-strewn alley behind the building and nudged aside several clan-size boxes from Hungry Herdsman Pizza #2. He'd have to complain to the manager about the mess.

Headlights flashed.

Bobby approached a dark gray Subaru Outback and opened the door. The passenger seat had thoughtfully been pushed back. "Haven't seen this one before. Wife borrowing the Lamborghini?"

Makeen laughed. "I love Americans' sense of humor, Bobby. Americans never stop making jokes. The earth on my brother's grave is still fresh, watered by our mother's tears . . ."

Bobby shifted in his seat. "I'm sorry."

"No, no, no, Bobby. I like it. I really do. The whole Arab world is so obsessed with death. Laughter gives life."

"Life, death . . . it's all part of the same picture. You brought food?"

"A little. You are still comfortable with this, Bobby? There is risk."

Bobby glanced out the window. More than a few lights glowed in apartments along the street leading to the expressway. A modest stream of cars and taxis kept the pulse of the city beating. "Let's do this," he said. The bigger risk was doing nothing until the people who sought to kill him made their next—and possibly successful—attempt.

It was all about timing. The people behind Taahir's killing—people obviously on Yasaar's payroll—had laid low to avoid making obvious the obvious to the police. Their target had been the lead American on Yusuf's payroll, the American who had confronted Yasaar and would remain loyal to his younger brother and the interests of the USofA.

Now, with the election scheduled for tomorrow, the proverbial shit would likely hit the proverbial fan. If Yasaar won, an American's life would mean no more than it did in Iraq or Afghanistan. If he lost, Yasaar would seek revenge—this was the Middle East. His gunmen would come after him faster than Taahir made moves on a good-looking girl. Bobby wasn't about to let that happen.

"The way everything is falling into place," said Makeen, "it is the will of Allah."

"With all due respect, my friend, Allah helps those who help themselves."

Makeen turned onto the expressway and drove west.

"There's a question I've held off asking," Bobby said. He'd committed himself—committed both of them. He had to know.

"Ask it," Makeen replied.

"Your informant with Yasaar. Who is it?"

Makeen pulled into the right lane to let a truck pass. "Ordinarily, I would not say. But for you, Bobby, and considering the circumstances . . . His name is Khalil. You saw him first at Sheikh Fadl's home."

Bobby shook his head.

"Very short but very powerful. The man who now heads Sheikh Yasaar's security."

Bobby looked at Makeen with a heightened sense of respect.

"Khalil," said Makeen, "informs me that our friend, as anticipated, has gone from his office up to the mountains to prepare for tomorrow's election in the Assembly. He has given instructions to be awakened before sunrise in order to return to Moq'tar City. This . . . how you say in America . . . falls into our lap. I hope."

They approached the airport. Makeen slowed for the exit to the Sultan Muhammad Freeway.

Bobby turned on the radio and found a station playing oldies. *Goldfinger* burst out of the speakers. He pulled his cell from his jacket pocket and dialed.

"Yes? Bobby?" answered bin Jabaar. "Is that you?"

"Who else calls you this time of night, Qasim?"

"What is it? Something is wrong?"

"Nothing could be more right. I think I know who was behind that little blow-up in the parking lot at the Shepherd Palace two months ago. And for what it's worth, I think I know who killed that kid at the Muscle Club."

Makeen winced.

Bobby squeezed Makeen's shoulder.

"This is good news, Bobby," said bin Jabaar. "Very good news. Tomorrow you will tell me. It is long past midnight."

"You're in bed?"

"Tomorrow afternoon is the election, Bobby. Big day. Where else would I be? And you?"

"Just listening to the radio."

"Tomorrow then. In the evening. When everything is finished. Then we will see that justice is done."

"I think we should get together in the morning, Qasim. Early. Let's say seven."

"Not possible, Bobby."

"You're sleeping in?"

"Bobby, be serious. I am having breakfast with Ambassador Ellis to brief him on security measures for Election Day."

"A briefing without *me*, Qasim?"

"Bobby, I thought we settled that after the protest. You are now a man somewhat at his leisure."

"So maybe around eleven? Or lunch?"

"Lunch will not work. It will be too close to the election. Eleven it is. But just for a few minutes. I will call you half-an-hour earlier and tell you where. You don't know who to trust these days."

Bobby stared ahead at the six empty lanes of freeway knifing through the dunes. "Truer words, Qasim. Sleep tight."

"And you, Bobby."

Bobby dialed another number. It rang half-a-dozen times.

"*Maa?*" asked a woman's voice sleepily. What?

"*'Afwan*, Mrs. Bin Jabaar. It's Colonel Gatling. May I speak with your husband, please?"

"Colonel?"

"Gatling, yes."

"Speak with Qasim?"

"Yes."

"Qasim is not home. He is preparing for the election. You are not with him?"

"Not now, no."

"You call cell, please, Colonel. For home, you call tomorrow evening."

"*Shukran*," Bobby responded. "Sorry to bother you."

The freeway began its ascent. It quickly narrowed to four lanes. Ahead, the limestone thrusts of the Fierce Shepherd rose in the moonlight. The four lanes became two then, entering the Ram's Intestines, one.

Makeen stopped in the first of a series of turnouts hollowed out of rock so vehicles could make way or, with the exception of large trucks, change direction. He turned the engine off then rolled his window down several inches to keep the interior from fogging.

Bobby opened the passenger door and eased out. He glanced up the empty road and crossed over to the far side. The lights of Moq'tar City glistened in the distance. He looked down. Moonlight revealed part of the cliff's descent to the rocky surface five hundred feet below. Feeling frisky, he jogged back behind the sheer wall of limestone that concealed Makeen's car. The heater had dulled the ache in his knee. Now a surge of adrenaline masked the pain that normally accompanied a chilly night outside. He listened intently. The silence was so near to absolute, it almost shrieked.

"Good spot," Makeen offered.

They studied a series of outthrusts that forced the road to double back on itself half a dozen times. From here, Bobby would pick up his target before the vehicle headed into the Ram's Intestines. The driver, riding his brakes, would come in and out of view. Given the way the curve above them jutted out, Bobby would take advantage of a clear line of fire on the outside of the last downhill turn.

Not that Bobby wasn't sorry things had come to this. He liked Qasim bin Jabaar. They'd had their differences, but he respected him. Under other circumstances, he'd have accompanied him into combat without hesitation. But the casings from the Lieutenant's .45 put everything—including Bobby's being pushed out of the loop—into perspective. Qasim had thrown in with Yasaar early on.

Bobby pointed with his finger. "Boom!"

Bobby's cell alarm went off at first light. Overhead, clusters of plump white clouds ambled across the mountains like sheep heading for water.

Makeen held out a plastic container.

Bobby picked out a boiled egg, several olives and a piece of pita. "*Bismi Allah*, my friend." He opened his thermos. "Coffee?"

Makeen held up a green plastic thermos with a Shepherds logo. "Tea." He checked his cell. The signal remained strong thanks to coverage extending along the entire road leading to the Throne of the Shepherds.

Bobby reached into his jacket pocket, withdrew the three Colt. 45 casings and held them out to Makeen. "You keep these now."

Makeen studied the casings in his palm then closed his fist around them. "Your lieutenant. He was not very smart."

"Let's just say that his uncle was a lot smarter. And a lot more vicious than I would have expected."

Bobby had put the pieces together. The Lieutenant took part in Taahir's killing—the reason three .45 casings lay mixed among the AK casings in the parking lot. But having assisted the errant assassins, he posed a risk to Yasaar and his elegant hatchet man. Killing was easy when all you had to do was pull a trigger. For many men, keeping quiet posed a far bigger challenge. Bin Jabaar, who held no fondness for his nephew, obviously took to heart a Moq'tari version of the famous American warning during World War Two: Loose lips sink ships. The two AK shooters killed the Lieutenant after he approached his Land Cruiser and turned to wave or signal his approval of a job well done.

Makeen held his hand up. His cell glowed. "The General is leaving the tent."

Bobby got out of the car, reached into his duffle and withdrew an M4 assault rifle fitted with a grenade launcher. Leaving Makeen at the wheel, he positioned himself behind an outcropping of rock. He'd situated the kill zone no more than twenty meters across the chasm created by the hairpin turn above them. With a flick of his wrist, he loaded a 40-millimeter grenade and steadied himself against the limestone wall.

Above, bin Jabaar's Land Cruiser approached the Ram's Intestines.

Bobby rested his finger lightly against the trigger to avoid jerking the weapon when the target vehicle appeared in the kill zone. He'd spent decades mastering every modern weapon known to man and not a few ancient ones. Still, a voice in his head took him back to basic training at Fort Polk. "Breathe, relax, aim, slack, squeeze." Some things never changed.

The Land Cruiser disappeared into the first turn above.

Bobby slowed his breathing. His heartbeat followed.

The Land Cruiser emerged momentarily then disappeared. Bin Jabaar would next appear in his line of sight one curve up from the kill zone.

Bobby raised the M4, took in a breath and let out half.

A high-pitched squeal shattered the stillness.

207

The Land Cruiser failed to hold the curve, shot straight ahead and tore through the guardrail at the edge of the cliff. During bin Jabaar's few seconds of freefall, no one would hear him scream.

Bobby ran across the road.

Makeen joined him.

The sun rising over the Gulf lit the Land Cruiser's plummet, as elegant as the dive of an Olympic champion, until the vehicle disappeared into shadow. But no graceful plume of water greeted its contact with the unyielding surface below. A faint glow appeared from between two limestone up-thrusts. The muffled sound of an explosion followed.

Tires screeched behind them.

Bobby and Makeen turned in unison.

A green Jeep hurtled through the last twisting curve of the Ram's Intestines then accelerated on the straightened road leading to the freeway. Behind the wheel, Dymme sat focused and fulfilled.

Twenty-three

Dymme, his left arm braced in a sling, poured coffee into a Moq'tar Shepherds mug—the only clean mug he could find in the Embassy's break room. He added a generous splash of cream. This was not a morning for self-deprivation. Satisfied, he shambled to a corner table, eased the two wrapped packages he'd managed to sustain under his right arm down on the table's plastic surface and sat wearily.

Given the option, he'd have slept until noon. The Ambassador, however, had ordered all hands on deck since the election in the Assembly of Righteous Elders was only a few hours off.

Regarding the candidates, Dymme had no particular favorite. A man in his position avoided getting personally involved. Washington chose the favorite—or created circumstances in which any winner served its purpose.

Dymme stared into the mug. He had ample reason to celebrate yet another demonstration of his various, and essential, skills. But that didn't preclude a downside. He would lose virtually the entire day—a discouraging thought given that the film festival, his true passion, was fast approaching.

Although his roster of films was pretty much set, he'd started receiving requests for screenings from various Hollywood publicity flacks. They pitched new films being readied for theatrical release overseas or classics on DVD or Blu-ray packaged in elaborate boxed sets with booklets, posters and God knew what other gimmicks. If people thought geopolitics were Byzantine and cutthroat, wait until they discovered Hollywood's distribution system. He could make a movie about that for sure.

Resigned to a challenging day, Dymme blew on his coffee and sipped. Then, as if in a scene from a Fellini film, a plate with four bagels appeared in front of him.

The not-quite delicate hand that held the plate was affixed to the right arm of the smiling Hema. Her left hand held yet another Shepherds mug, undoubtedly her own. She startled. "Mr. Dymme, what happened to you?"

Dymme glanced down at his sling. "Oh, this . . . an old sports injury. A sudden strain and my elbow goes out." He studied the bagels. "Fresh?"

Hema bit her lips as if blotting a fresh coat of lipstick.

"Oh, sorry. Sit, please," said Dymme.

Hema floated down onto a chair. "Do you know the Taj Mahal bakery on Salah-al-din Street near the technical school?"

Dymme nodded, although he hadn't yet managed to make it there.

"My cousin, Subbu, owns it."

He took a bagel and squeezed. The crust was reassuringly crisp. The dough evidenced a firm yet yielding texture. He sniffed. "This is the real thing."

"Subbu bakes them for the better hotels. He knows the secret. He once worked in New York."

"Boiling first," said Dymme. He smiled in anticipation. "You don't have to be Jewish, you know."

Hema stared at Dymme's packages.

Dymme put the bagel down. "I left these in the safe, remember? To tell you the truth, I forgot all about them until this morning." He picked up the smaller package and shook it.

Hema startled again. "Mr. Dymme, it might go off!"

Dymme pulled back. He had no idea what Hema was thinking. Then he remembered her suggestion that he was a CIA agent. He placed the package in his left hand and ripped the paper off with his right.

Hema held her breath as if she was a television game show contestant waiting to learn whether she'd won an all-expenses-paid

SLICK!

trip to tour the Bollywood studios in Mumbai. "This is like a moment from *Slumdog Millionaire*," she gasped.

Dymme opened the box and held up a flash drive. "I was working on a screenplay in Singapore, and I finally wrote a new scene a few nights ago. My backup. I need to update it."

Hema released a breathy sigh of relief.

Dymme placed the flash drive down and opened the larger package. "I won't shake this one."

"Is it dangerous?" Hema asked. She lowered her eyes. "Well, of course it isn't."

Dymme opened the package to reveal a small statue of a bird encrusted in what, at first glance, appeared to be priceless jewels.

"Diamonds, emeralds and rubies, Mr. Dymme. It must be worth a fortune."

"All glass. I picked it up in the Old Souk for ten dollars. It's what the Maltese Falcon might have looked like."

Hema smiled.

"I got it for a friend."

Dymme's cell serenaded them with "Lara's Theme" from *Dr. Zhivago*. "Yes, sir," he responded. "I understand, sir. Immediately, sir."

"Is anything wrong, Mr. Dymme?"

Dymme nudged the flash drive and the falcon towards Hema. "Would you hold on to these? And no peeking at my screenplay." He stood. "A little fire to put out."

Bobby held his Beretta only inches from Corporal Wheatley's left ear above a copper-toned cheek that, had Wheatley not been a Marine, would have come into contact with a razor no more than twice a week.

"Son of a bitch, Dymme!" the Ambassador pleaded from his seat behind his desk. "Do something!"

"Colonel Gatling does seem to have the upper hand, sir," Dymme advised. He turned to Bobby. "Honestly, Colonel," he said in the dispassionate tone of a film patron ordering butterless popcorn and bottled water before seeing a new Woody Allen film,

211

"I appreciate your inviting me to this little discussion, but you've misinterpreted this morning's events."

Bobby had a very different take on the game the Ambassador and Dymme had been playing with him. He'd stormed into the Ambassador's office and slammed the door only to have Wheatley burst in behind him. Now, Wheatley stared defiant but helpless at the Ambassador's inert American flag.

Dymme stroked his sling as if it was a kitten. Maneuvering his Jeep in the Ram's Intestines had aggravated his left elbow once again. "We really were doing our best to protect you without giving the game away."

"Ingrate," the Ambassador murmured. "Besides, the goddam election is only hours away."

Bobby swung the Beretta's muzzle into the Ambassador's field of vision.

The Ambassador tucked his head between his shoulders like a turtle retreating into its shell.

"Perhaps, sir," Dymme suggested, "our discussion might focus on the broader issues rather than on individual grievances."

"I think there's room for both," Bobby responded. "And considering that we have confidential information to exchange, I suggest that Corporal Wheatley withdraw. Without heroics."

Dymme nodded.

"You can go, Wheatley," said the Ambassador. "I'll handle things."

Wheatley eyed Bobby with a mix of bravado and admiration.

"Really," the Ambassador emphasized. "It's okay." For the sake of the United States of America and all their careers—Wheatley's included—they'd move on. News of this little misunderstanding—these things happened in the best of families—would never leave the four walls surrounding them.

Wheatley saluted, strode across the room briskly to indicate that fear had never overcome him and closed the door silently behind him.

Bobby, the Beretta still poised, rounded the desk towards Dymme. "Your coat."

Dymme deployed his sling-encased hand to grasp the left lapel of his all-purpose blue blazer and urge it away from his chest.

Bobby extracted a Walther P99 from Dymme's shoulder holster. "Legs."

"Colonel, I'm not a walking armory. There's no knife around *my* ankle."

Bobby ignored Dymme's assertion and patted him down. "Okay, let's talk. This morning, you pulled into the Embassy parking lot in an Escalade."

"Jesus," the Ambassador interjected. "We've got an election coming up."

Dymme shrugged stiffly. "A rental. Someone here in the Embassy handled it. To be honest, I would have preferred a Ford Focus. The mileage. Maybe they didn't think a Focus is manly enough. But while you might be surprised to hear it from someone like me, Colonel, global warming is real, you know. Give it some thought."

Bobby resisted the urge to smack the Beretta across Dymme's face. Where did the CIA get these people? He'd thought the two of them had achieved some level of trust. But Dymme had concealed valuable intelligence since arriving in Moq'tar and left Bobby exposed. "Your Jeep is probably in Qatar getting its front end repaired. General bin Jabaar . . . well, he's beyond repair."

Dymme straightened his back. Despite his devotion to tai chi, he often failed to pay sufficient attention to good posture and the health benefits that accrued from it. "I believe we shared the same intention regarding General bin Jabaar."

"But there's lots more you *haven't* told me."

The Ambassador raised his head. "Don't," he wheezed, "tell this snake-eater anything."

Bobby swung his Beretta towards the Ambassador.

The Ambassador placed his hands over his heart.

Bobby turned back to Dymme.

The muzzle of a Smith & Wesson model 60, its barrel scarcely more than two inches long, confronted him.

"At this distance, Colonel," said Dymme, "I can perforate either ventricle of your heart. Have a preference?"

"The sling!" Bobby responded.

"You're another Inspector Clouseau," Dymme retorted.

Bobby lowered the Beretta.

Dymme dropped the Smith & Wesson to his side as an act of good faith to be followed by a statement of contrition. "Forgive me. That remark was uncalled for. We *are* on the same team. But we're losing time."

The confrontation that had just ensued, Dymme proposed, represented nothing more than the release of a little extra testosterone. It was done. He and the Ambassador, as the popular saying went, had other fish to fry. The Assembly of Righteous Elders had invited Sheikh Yasaar and Sheikh Yusuf to begin the election proceedings by addressing them at three o'clock.

"Assuming we'd all like to move forward," Dymme suggested, "shall we put our weapons away?"

Bobby withdrew the clip from his Beretta and held it towards Dymme.

"Empty!" Dymme said, his voice bordering on amazement. "I'll give you the benefit of the doubt, Colonel, and assume the same for the chamber."

Bobby displayed a grin not unlike that of the Mona Lisa.

"Marvelous performance," said Dymme. "You had me thinking you were Travis Bickle. Remember *Taxi Driver?*"

The Ambassador looked down. A wet spot covered his crotch. Remaining seated, he removed a bottle of Scotch from his credenza and bolted down a hefty swig.

Dymme tucked away his weapons. "So Colonel . . . Given the brief time available for discussion, what's troubling you?"

"What's troubling . . . You knew Qasim bin Jabaar was working for Yasaar."

Dymme flashed a microsmile. "You'll understand when I say that your intelligence, by which I mean your information, appears to be somewhat flawed. We've had bin Jabaar and Yasaar under surveillance since they had lunch last winter at one of Switzerland's most charming ski resorts. Moles, hidden cameras, tapped cell phones, email intercepts, yadda yadda. Anyway, you have it all backwards."

Bobby rocked forward and hunched over as if he was auditioning for the role of Quasimodo in *The Hunchback of Notre Dame*. "Yasaar was working for Qasim?"

Dymme flashed a broader if condescending smile. The story was simple as most such intrigues were when those involved moved past the mundane details. Bin Jabaar sought out Yasaar in Switzerland and made a convincing case that as Sultan, Yusuf would put a major squeeze on his brother's trust fund and even have it voided by the courts after their father succumbed to the final stages of colon cancer, a shot prostate, a weakened heart or all of the above.

The ironic twist—irony being not at all uncommon in such matters—revealed that the worldly bin Jabaar had close connections to Moq'tar's not insignificant religious conservatives.

Additionally, a deal with Sheikh Fadl, whose business interests they would protect—and whose competitors they would suppress—offered another powerful ally from a different but no less important segment of the political spectrum.

In tandem, bin Jabaar and Yasaar would rule a quasi-Islamic state with revenues from enterprises legal and otherwise bolstering their regime.

"And Sultan Yasaar would retain his accustomed privileges," Bobby put forward.

"That's the way things work in the real world," the Ambassador cut in. But now, he explained with professorial gravitas, Moq'tar was a whole new ballgame. Yes, Yasaar might win the election that afternoon. But without bin Jabaar, the remains of whose remains likely wouldn't be found for days, weeks or longer, he'd pose no threat to the United States. "The guy wouldn't have the balls to go Al Qaeda or Taliban on us."

"So Sultan Yasaar is acceptable to you?" Bobby asked.

The Ambassador glanced at Dymme then back at Bobby. "Imagine you're a hedge fund guy or a trader at a big bank in New York. How do you make the really big money?"

Bobby made no attempt to answer.

"You bet for and against the same position. Whatever happens, you win."

"I think we know how that works out for the rest of us," Bobby replied.

The Ambassador poured another drink. "You're the conscience of America, is that it?" He lowered his head between his knees, pulled his wastebasket forward and discharged his breakfast.

"And if Yasaar wins," asked Bobby, "what happens to Sheikh Yusuf?"

The Ambassador rose and reached for a tissue. "We'll give him asylum, obviously. What kind of country would we be if our friends couldn't depend on us?"

There was little reason for Yusuf not to land on his feet. He could end up at one of those self-same hedge funds or big banks. Or maybe a venture capital firm in Silicon Valley. Given his cachet, he might teach at Berkeley or in Austin or anywhere else for that matter. And deficit or no deficit, Washington would find sufficient funds to ease Yusuf's transition and help him maintain a reasonable semblance of the lifestyle to which he was accustomed.

"Not to worry," said Dymme. "Everything's under control."

Bobby thought of rubbing his knee again but this hurt more. The Ambassador and Dymme were in the driver's seat. If Yusuf won, America's relationship with Moq'tar would grow stronger. If Yasaar won . . .

"Trust me," said the Ambassador, "Yasaar will get in bed with Uncle Sam and take it any way we put it to him."

Dymme placed his right hand under his injured elbow. "Have you seen the films Hollywood's made about the Middle East? You know, where everything goes to shit? There's a reason the box office is always so bad, even with an Oscar winner. Americans like happy endings."

Bobby ran his tongue across the inside of his teeth. He wanted answers. He got them. Only they failed to provide much satisfaction. He checked his watch. It was nine forty-five. "So you two are just going to sit here?"

SLICK!

"Damn right!" the Ambassador shot back. He and Dymme were nothing but objective observers of the democratic process—not that Dymme's opinion counted. What mattered was that the camel jockeys would hold their election that afternoon. The winner would tuck himself into America's deep pocket.

"However, *you*, Colonel," said Dymme, "have at least a co-starring role to play."

Since Bobby had inserted himself into the unfortunate little episode with bin Jabaar, they'd put him to good use. Given the General's noticeable absence, Bobby would immediately step in and honcho Ministry security operations at the Great Hall and everywhere else in the sultanate. In one hour, the Ambassador would notify the anxious Yusuf that bin Jabaar had mysteriously disappeared but the Ministry was in the capable hands of his trusted advisor, Colonel Gatling. The news, he hoped, would raise Yusuf's spirits if not his prospects. It would also forestall a possible last-minute attempt by Yusuf to stage a coup, which would serve only to compromise the Sheikh's image and cast a pall on that of the United States.

Bobby strode towards the door.

"So?" Dymme asked. "Are you with us? Are you with your country?"

Bobby opened the door and straddled the threshold. He had no intention of abandoning the USofA. And now, the Ambassador and Dymme had given him official sanction to do nothing less than what he'd already planned as a follow-up to Qasim bin Jabaar's removal. "Looks like I've got an election to protect."

"All right everyone," Dymme called out. "Lights, camera, action!"

Twenty-four

$\mathcal{Y}$ usuf stood off to the side of his desk fidgeting with his suit coat in preparation for being targeted by the camera lens. The next few minutes would elevate him to the heights of glory or plunge him into the depths of dishonor.

"We are ready, Sheikh," the director from Moq'tar TV advised. In his late twenties, he appeared very much the contemporary media guru cum artist in jeans and a black shirt with a pale blue sweater thrown casually over his shoulders. His neatly trimmed goatee and gold-rimmed glasses attached to a gold chain created a reassuring aura of thoughtful calm at this most challenging moment.

Yusuf squared his shoulders. History summoned him. The only way to meet its demands was to charge forward balls to the wall. He would use television to make an unofficial appeal to the nation before crossing the avenue and entering the Great Hall. There, following Yasaar, he would present his official remarks to the Assembly of Righteous Elders. But what he said now would make their appearances before the Elders moot—if the strategy he believed to be nothing less than brilliant met his expectations.

"What about Yasaar?" he called across the room.

Zoraya, seated on a sofa, shifted her attention to the television. "He is still in the Grand Mosque praying *Dhuhr*." She wore a Chanel suit and a white blouse with a ruffled collar suggesting a visionary yet suitably conservative approach to her responsibilities. The corner of a matching headscarf peeked out of the Prada purse tucked against her thigh.

Monsieur Pierre fell to one knee to grapple with a rebellious curl.

"Sheikh?" the director asked, attempting to maintain control on the set without stepping on royal toes.

Yusuf waved him off. "*Dhuhr* will end in a moment. Sheikh Yasaar will come out to speak. I will address the nation when he is done." He turned to Bobby. "Still no word from General bin Jabaar?"

Bobby shook his head.

"This is weird, Colonel. Aren't you concerned?"

"Everything's secure, Sheikh. The Grand Mosque, the route to the Great Hall, the plaza and everything around it, and of course, this building. We control Moq'tari air space, and Ambassador Ellis will be the first foreign representative to arrive at your office after the election to offer his government's congratulations."

Yusuf held his hands out, palms up as if praying. *Insh'allah*, and with the crafty announcement he was about to make, the Assembly of Righteous Elders would fall right in line and elect him Sultan.

"Here he comes," Zoraya sang out.

Yusuf stepped over several lighting cables and around the ever-attentive Monsieur Pierre to stand behind Zoraya's left shoulder.

The camera in front of the Grand Mosque zoomed in on Yasaar. His white *thobe* appeared almost radiant in the mid-March sunlight. What passed for an election campaign, however, seemed to have taken its toll. Yasaar's beard appeared noticeably grayer. Deep lines formed dark crevasses splaying up from the inside edge of each eyebrow. Yet the camera embraced him like an actor long past his prime but newly adopted as a beloved icon of a vanished but fondly remembered past.

Someone thrust a microphone into Yasaar's hands.

Zoraya turned the sound up.

Yasaar addressed the assembled crowd. His remarks at first seemed tentative. Then, summoning the inner strength of his late father, he gave his words greater force. His face, haggard only a moment earlier, radiated the visage of a sage, the reassuring presence of the eldest son of the commonly, if not universally, beloved Muhammad bin Hamza al-Moq'tari.

Yasaar's comments rushed past Yusuf's ears like an IndyCar roaring pedal-to-the-metal down the back straightaway at the

Indianapolis 500. Not that Yusuf needed to hear them. He could anticipate every deceptive word. His brother would be a tough act to follow.

Yasaar concluded and waved victoriously.

Cries of *"Allahu Akhbar!"* rang out.

Encircling bodyguards escorted Yasaar to his yacht-length limousine.

Accepting full responsibility for the fate of the nation, Yusuf walked with appropriate dignity to his desk and sat.

Monsieur Pierre scuttled across the room and applied a touch of powder to Yusuf's left cheek.

Zoraya turned the TV's sound off to avoid generating feedback.

A photo of the Camel's Dick appeared on televisions across Moq'tar. A graphic announced yet another special Election Day broadcast.

The director held up three fingers and counted down. *"Thalaatha . . . 'ithnayn . . . waahid . . ."*

The camera framed Yusuf at his desk. A Moq'tari flag hung behind his right shoulder. A Shepherds logo cap rested at his right hand.

"My brothers and sisters," he began. He gulped slightly. Were his nerves betraying him?

"Today is a day of greatest importance for all of Moq'tar. The Assembly of Righteous Elders, reflecting the will of Allah, the Compassionate, the Merciful will choose a new Sultan to lead you into the future. I need not tell you that we stand at a crossroads." He paused to catch his breath. Was he speaking too fast?

"Moq'tar can continue to establish its rightful place among the great nations of the Gulf and the Arab World," he continued with measured deliberateness. "Or it can desert the way of my father, the Shepherd of His People, may he rest in Paradise. My words will be few, for Allah, the Compassionate, the Merciful will judge me by my deeds. And it is my very first deed as Sultan that I wish to tell you about." He feared he was going too slowly now. He needed to pick up the pace or appear lacking the energy and enthusiasm to be the Sultan Moq'tar wanted. If Moq'tar knew what it wanted.

"My very first deed . . ." Yusuf paused. Would this come off as nothing more than a typical campaign promise? But then, Moq'tar had never had a political campaign. Besides, he was telling the people exactly what he was going to do.

"My very first deed . . ." He'd repeated himself. Was that okay? Sure it was. He was emphasizing action.

"My very first deed will assure continuity for the throne and peace for the nation. Following a provision inspired by the constitution, the details of which need not concern you, I will appoint *in writing* Moq'tar's first-ever Vice Sultan . . . or Vice Sultana . . . we'll figure it out . . . my sister, Princess Zoraya."

"Ohmygod!" Monsieur Pierre squealed.

Yusuf's eyes shifted quickly to the left then back towards the camera. Would he come across like that old American president, Richard Nixon? He wanted to clear his throat but feared that would only reinforce a negative image.

"The Princess's beauty and grace have captured the hearts of her people," he continued. "You have demonstrated your love for her as she has for you. Should any tragedy befall me, Sultana . . . yes, Sultana Zoraya will occupy the throne until my son, Muhammad bin Yusuf, comes of age." He sniffled. Was he coming down with something? Would his nose start running with all of Moq'tar staring at him?

"Rest assured . . ." He gave in and cleared his throat. Okay, that was done. Why hadn't he sipped some tea or sucked on a cough drop before starting? "When the Assembly of Righteous Elders elects me as your new Sultan, I will stand humbly in the shadow of the Prophet, peace be upon him, to lead my flock to prosperity and glory. May Moq'tar heed the words of the Holy Quran, and may Allah, the Compassionate, the Merciful bless us with power, riches, peace and feet planted firmly on the throats of our enemies."

The director made a slicing motion below his chin.

Yusuf's mouth fell open.

The director pointed at the television.

Moq'tar TV had cut away to its highest-rated talking heads. They would analyze the two unofficial speeches in depth—and hopefully hold the attention of one of the year's largest audiences for its advertisers—until coverage began inside the Assembly.

"Wonderful!" Zoraya exclaimed.

Yusuf turned to Bobby. "What do *you* think, Colonel?"

"Impressive, Sheikh!"

Yusuf smiled. "Short. Powerful. The ultimate sound bite." He fought the urge to sneeze and looked down towards the Great Hall. "It's still a toss-up, isn't it?"

"Maybe," Bobby answered. "Then again, maybe not."

Bobby stood three steps behind the roadblock as Yasaar's convoy approached along the Avenue of the Righteous. Behind him, a huge crowd had gathered in the plaza to witness the candidates' entries into the Great Hall and see their speeches on the now-familiar giant television screen.

A last radio check confirmed that all commanders and units were in place. None of the uniformed officers, Bobby figured, would know anything about bin Jabaar's demise that morning. On the other hand, bin Jabaar might well have brought a few senior and mid-level officers into the plot. Who they were, Bobby didn't know. At this point, he didn't care. Without their leader, they were likely to keep a low profile, let the election play itself out and float along with the tide. Officers in armies like Moq'tar's accumulated decorations like candy, but their medals tended to represent acts of discretion far more than those of valor.

Yasaar's limousine drew closer and halted in front of a line of security men Bobby had personally selected.

A slim Moq'tari captain in a fresh U.S. Army Combat Uniform stepped forward and positioned himself alongside Bobby near the right-rear passenger door. The captain saluted crisply, grasped the handle and pulled.

The door remained shut.

Three commandos carrying M4s each took one step forward.

The captain signaled to the passengers, driver and bodyguard in the front seat all to come out.

The limo's doors swung open in unison like the synchronized leg kicks of dancers in a Busby Berkeley musical.

Yasaar emerged.

Bobby stepped around him and leaned through the doorway. He glanced down along the plush bench seats and past the bar towards the driver's compartment. After holding his position for a moment, he withdrew to face Yasaar. "You haven't left anything in the vehicle, have you, Sheikh? No little surprises?"

Yasaar stared up at Bobby. His nostrils flared. He patted his chest as if checking for his wallet or cell phone in the presence of a pickpocket. He shifted his gaze down. "Accident, Colonel?"

Bobby glanced at the sling encasing his left arm. "It's nothing. Really. But you're very kind to ask, Sheikh."

Yasaar's eyes darted past Bobby to the Great Hall. "What can you possibly be thinking, Colonel? And where is General bin Jabaar?"

"General bin Jabaar seems to have gone missing," Bobby answered. "At Sheikh Yusuf's orders, I've assumed temporary command over the Ministry of Security."

A small bead of sweat slipped down the side of Yasaar's nose. Ignoring it, he displayed a renewed sense of calm as if he'd piloted a *dhow* through a difficult storm into the still waters of a welcoming harbor. "We are about to be chosen the next Sultan of Moq'tar, Colonel. Your assistance is unnecessary. Moreover, you have no authority over our vehicle or our people unless you are informing us that a coup is in progress."

"No coup, Sheikh. But Sheikh Yusuf's orders stand until the election."

Yasaar pressed his fingertips together. "Then be informed, Colonel, that following our election this afternoon, our first official act will be to terminate Crimmins-Idyll's contract. Not that we are unappreciative. The government of Moq'tar will pay for your first-class ticket on the earliest possible flight out of the country."

"That's kind of you, Sheikh."

"Then we understand each other, Colonel. Now, clear the way so that we may drive up to the Great Hall."

"Of course, Sheikh." Bobby motioned with his right hand. "We'll only need a moment."

Yasaar's eyebrows rocketed up like a field bird climbing steeply in a vain attempt to escape a pursuing falcon.

Half-a-dozen commandos moved Yasaar's bodyguards and advisors away from the limo. A heavyset master sergeant with a large mirror on a long pole stepped in front of the limo to examine its underside. Two commandos scrambled into the interior.

"Do you not understand us?" asked Yasaar.

"Just a precaution, Sheikh. If someone somehow planted an explosive your people didn't know about . . ."

"Something with which you are familiar, Colonel?"

A commando stepped out from the rear of the limo. "Sir!" he called to Bobby.

Bobby turned.

The commando pointed to the interior. "Under the rear seat, sir."

Bobby grasped Yasaar's right wrist and subtly guided him towards the open door from which he had exited. "I hope we haven't uncovered a terrorist plot, Sheikh."

Yasaar just as subtly pulled his wrist away. "What can you be talking about? In the name of Allah, do you think we would blow ourselves up?"

Bobby leaned into the limo, looked beneath the seat, pulled himself out and faced the Sheikh. "Might you have forgotten a personal item?"

Yasaar stood immobile.

"Sheikh, someone could punch a button on a cell phone right now, and investigators would be lucky to find a piece of any of us bigger than a thumb. Let me ask you one last time. Did you leave something in your limousine?"

Yasaar's clenching jaw made a grinding noise.

Bobby motioned.

The commando reached into the limo and retrieved a brick-size package wrapped in plain brown paper. He handed it to the captain, who handed it to Bobby.

Yasaar stepped back slowly as if he feared his foot might not come to rest on solid ground.

"Shall we clear the area, sir?" the captain asked.

Bobby held the package in his right hand then lifted it to his nose. Its distinguishing smell reassured him. "No need, Captain." He approached Yasaar and held the package out. "You're sure, Sheikh, that this isn't yours?"

"This is ridiculous, Colonel."

With a movement of his head, Bobby signaled the captain and the commandos to back away. His eyes fixed on Yasaar's, he again lifted the package to his nose and sniffed. "Sheikh," he said almost faintly as if they were sharing the deepest intimacy, "What we have here . . . and I've been around it in my various duties . . . is heroin." He hefted it in his palm. "Helps keep up with expenses, huh?"

Yasaar's eyes verged on crossing.

"This," Bobby continued, "places you in something of a compromised position. Worse, General bin Jabaar isn't here." He lowered his voice as if the two shared a conspiracy. "And frankly, I don't think you can count on him being with us again."

Yasaar's jaw dropped.

Bobby grinned. "Do bear in mind, Sheikh, that possession of heroin is a capital offense. On the books, at least. And the criminal code calls for beheading."

"You can not expect us to take your bluff, Colonel Gatling," Yasaar said in a hoarse whisper as if the bone of a small bird had stuck in his throat. "Do you think Moq'taris will believe anything so preposterous?"

"You've been burning a lot of cash, Sheikh. And a uniformed agent of the Ministry of Security just found a very incriminating package in your vehicle. Given your past . . ."

Yasaar's shoulders slumped like a fallen soufflé removed too soon from the oven. "This is not the reality, Colonel. Not the reality at all."

Bobby leaned closer. "Yet I suspect you'll be taking the next flight back to Geneva. Because you know as well as I do, Sheikh, that reality doesn't mean a damn thing. It's all about perception."

Allahu Akhbar! Allahu Akhbar! Allahu Akhbar!" roared the crowd in the plaza as they gazed up at the TV screen.

The newly elected Sultan of Moq'tar and his Vice Sultana stood at the podium in the Great Hall, their hands clasped over their heads in victorious celebration. The chanting from the crowd in the plaza pierced the walls and rang in their ears.

The Elders applauded. Many shot out triumphal screams, releasing the tensions and uncertainties of ten difficult weeks that had left the nation shepherdless and their own righteousness in doubt.

Yusuf and Zoraya lowered their hands to their shoulders.

The ovation continued. Men of all parties joined in traditional war songs. Many began dancing. Reenergized with new hope for the future, they snaked their way up and down the aisles.

Yusuf turned to Zoraya and whispered, "They love me."

Zoraya watched the Elders yield to ecstatic frenzy stirred by the wildly enthusiastic crowd outside. Perhaps the Elders and the people *did* love Yusuf. Perhaps he really *did* remind them of their beloved father in Paradise, a man so strong, so resolute—at least in the world he had once known and understood.

But she had her doubts. Both her heart and mind told her that another served as the object of their love and devotion. Their Vice Sultana. Their . . . she would never actually utter the heresy . . . goddess.

ʻAbriil

| April |

Twenty-five

Zoraya released a long, wistful sigh in spite of the lovely sunrise that promised an idyllic spring day. A mere heartbeat away from the throne, she had gone to her office at an unusually early hour ready to fulfill her responsibilities to the nation. Yet anyone who glanced at her calendar would bear witness to her exclusion from all serious matters of government.

She accepted that her election as Vice Sultana represented a political ploy. She applauded Yusuf for it. He might have won the election on his own had not Yasaar withdrawn at the last minute, but she wasn't convinced. Obviously, neither was Yusuf.

Now she felt as if the civic and charitable errands that had delighted her as a princess demeaned her in her new position. How could she be expected to tolerate such humiliation? She was a woman of the twenty-first century. Change would come to Moq'tar. This she knew. And it would come more quickly than Yusuf or the nation could imagine.

She swiveled in the ill-fitting chair behind her new desk and peered into a small, lighted mirror. The bronze metallic eye shadow recommended by Monsieur Pierre pleased her. She eagerly anticipated finding out if it would sustain her through the day ahead.

The buzzer on the gold intercom unit rang.

"It's him," proclaimed her executive assistant.

Zoraya closed her eyes to collect herself then picked up the telephone. The usual exchange of pleasantries required by Moq'taris and others in the region, often requiring several minutes of banal small talk, took only seconds after a simple acknowledgment of the lateness of the hour at the other end of the line. This kind of man, as the Americans said, cut to the chase.

She listened attentively. Her proposal had been well received.

"Very well then," Zoraya said, bringing the brief conversation to its inevitable close. "We have an agreement, Mr. Kantrowitz."

"You don't desire to make love one more time?" asked Ilana Svadbova, the bed virtually bereft of its blanket.

"Sounds great," Bobby answered. He finished tucking in his shirt and buckled his belt.

Ilana drew her thick pink lips together in an obviously feigned threat to sulk. "But you have a meeting."

"Actually, I do."

She raised her nightgown above her waist. She hadn't put on panties after they'd finally gone to sleep in her apartment following a chance meeting and a little too much to drink at the home of a mutual acquaintance.

"No, really. This is important, Ilana. I have to go back to my place and get ready."

"Last night was most enjoyable, Bobby. And this morning. You are very athletic for a man your size and age."

Bobby slipped on his shoes.

"I am thinking," said Ilana.

"Thinking what?"

"That I should divorce Jan so we can marry."

Bobby turned to face her.

"You don't love me?" she asked.

He froze.

She chortled. "April fool's! It *is* April first. Don't Americans play jokes on each other this day?"

"You're not American."

"Then you *don't* love me, thank God. Americans have this ridiculous belief that a man and a woman must be in love to have hot sex."

"I wouldn't know," Bobby responded. What he did know was that love had nothing to with the night they'd just spent. In spite of his initial misgivings, it worked for him.

"I am doubting, Bobby."

"Doubting what?"

"Whether we should do this again."

Bobby double-checked the pockets of his slacks for his wallet and truck keys. If he was confused before, he was more confused now. But feelings—if he had feelings—could wait. He had work to do.

"You don't think me cruel, do you?" she asked.

Bobby stepped over to the bed, kissed Ilana on the forehead and retreated to the door.

"*Ciao*," she called. "It really *was* lovely."

Bobby eased the bedroom door shut behind him and crossed the small living room. After letting himself out, he stopped in the hallway. Was this the way it was going to be for the rest of his life?

He shrugged and headed for the stairs. No sense in tormenting himself. Everything would work out fine. He felt it. He felt great, actually. Good sex made a man his age feel reborn. Sandi would have lectured him that he was supposed to feel empty and lonelier than ever after casual sex, but that's what wives—especially ex-wives—always said. Bobby wasn't all *that* big on guilt.

Screw the confusion, he thought. Damn, he felt good.

Bobby felt the urge to sing as he waited for the elevator to Sultan Yusuf's office for his weekly security briefing. He felt young and strong again. His knee was virtually free of pain thanks to Gulf temperatures approaching ninety.

Everything had come up roses. Following the election, any possible co-conspirators of Qasim bin Jabaar had buried themselves in the sand while the sultanate partied down. Assorted kings, emirs, princes and diplomats hosted feasts. The Chinese ambassador held an umpteen-course banquet at the Breath of the Dragon. Ambassador Kazanovitch presided over a dinner at the Club Metropol, complete with dancing Cossacks and vodka that flowed like the Don. Not to be outdone, every local tribal and clan chief threw a bash at his palace or home or favorite schwarma joint.

Only Moq'tar TV raised an alarm. An investigative report warned of the impending decimation of the sultanate's sheep and goats.

The roasting fires burned on.

As far as the USofA went, Ambassador Ellis laid on a Mexican buffet that elicited mostly positive reviews. Substituting pita for tortillas added a nice local touch, and the obvious lack of *carnitas* in deference to the State Department's no-pork, no-exceptions policy went overlooked thanks to the dwindling but still available plenitude of chicken, lamb and goat. More important, the margaritas would have passed muster on any beach from Puerto Vallarta to Santa Monica. And while the local mariachi band cobbled together by Dymme would have been booed in Topeka, a Beach Boys CD pulled America's reputation out of the fire.

Any way you looked at it, at least one small corner of the Persian Gulf had become a safer—and merrier—place.

After a week, sober reason exercised its prerogative. Sultan Yusuf pulled the plug on party season. Moq'tar had business to do. Ka-ching replaced ka-boom.

With Moq'taris standing firmly acquiescent behind their new Sultan, the pressure on Bobby and the Ministry of Security eased by an order of magnitude. Bobby resumed daily workouts at the Muscle Club. His sleep improved to semi-regular, which was now the new regular.

He also returned the package he'd borrowed from Makeen, who responded with a large envelope stuffed with ten thousand dollars worth of gratitude. Bobby declined it. True, the money would have brought him a little closer to the day he could devote all his energy to writing a book on counterinsurgency for which he'd developed a preliminary outline or doing doctoral work. But their relationship was personal not business. Pledges of brotherhood and allegiance would suffice.

Yet as Sultan Yusuf took firm control of Moq'tar, it was the Vice Sultana who reigned if not ruled. Zoraya's image graced supermarket tabloids and infotainment TV shows from Abu Dhabi to Australia to Alabama.

True to form, no political settlement could please all of the people all of the time. Riyadh responded to Zoraya's media exposure by ordering her face covered with a digital veil. Tehran vilified her as a prostitute and burned her effigy in Enghelab Square replete with the usual calls for death to America and Israel. Moreover, the ayatollahs claimed that the Jews controlled a blasphemous majority in the Assembly of Righteous Elders.

Al Qaeda, still seeking to be a force in the region, went apoplectic on the Internet. It claimed responsibility for a fire that damaged two of six chairs in a beauty shop in Newark, New Jersey while simultaneously calling for a worldwide boycott of all female hair products.

Everything was back to normal.

A security guard in a green blazer with a Moq'tari flag on the left pocket stood outside Sultan Yusuf's office suite. Bobby couldn't place him.

"Your identification, sir?" asked the guard.

Bobby's first response was to ream him out, but he felt too lighthearted and maybe just a touch light in the head. "Good one," he responded. He reached around the guard for the door handle.

The guard cut him off with a quick slide step and nudged his arm away. "Your identification, Colonel. You must wear it everywhere in this building. Regulations, sir."

Bobby's jaw muscles tightened as if he was biting down for an x-ray at the dentist knowing he had cavities to be filled. "I wrote those regulations."

The guard looked up into Bobby's eyes. He displayed neither fear nor hostility but resolution—just as he'd been taught. "Your identification, sir."

Bobby broke into a smile and searched inside his coat. He found the ID and presented it.

The guard opened the door.

Bobby approached Yusuf's executive assistant. The Sultan evidently had made another personnel change. A twenty-something man in a dark gray suit with black hair and a Bluetooth earpiece sat at the desk by the door to Yusuf's office. He looked like a fashion model or Hollywood's version of an up-and-coming, smarter-and-handsomer-than-everyone, always-lands-on-his-feet bureaucrat hiding a bad-boy past.

The executive assistant held up his right index finger like a school crossing guard hoisting a stop sign. He nodded. Then he flipped his wrist and pressed a button on his telephone console. "Colonel Gatling for the Sultan," he announced in English.

Bobby drummed his fingers on his laptop case.

The executive assistant stood, hesitated for a three-count and opened the door to the Sultan's office.

Bobby stepped back.

"Oh, hello there, Colonel," said Monsieur Pierre. He wore the kind of long-sleeve, jacket-like white shirt that catalogs sold to people who avoided the sun. His right hand held a white, wide-brimmed hat. His left grasped the handle of a large portfolio in a shade of brown that some copywriter had probably given a designer name like "marmoset" or "java jubilee."

Bobby stepped forward. The office was empty.

Monsieur Pierre nodded towards a door at the far side. "Just went to the loo."

"And everyone else?"

"I don't believe anyone else is expected, Colonel. I'm just leaving myself."

Bobby glanced down at the portfolio.

"We've been brainstorming," said Monsieur Pierre. "We're doing a complete makeover of this office. One of London's most fabulous decorators . . . I'm sworn to secrecy so I can't say a thing, but if you read *Interior Design,* you know who I mean . . . is flying in next week. As God or Allah or whoever is my witness, this office will make Meryl Streep's in *The Devil Wears Prada* look absolutely frumpy."

Bobby stepped aside.

Monsieur Pierre bounced through the doorway, whirled around and held out his right arm as if he was generously sharing the glory of his own perfect first-of-April morning with the entire Gulf.

"Colonel Gatling, I ask you. Would anyone have ever believed that Scott Sakowitz from Queens would be part of all this?"

Zoraya emerged from the Sultan's bathroom as if making a star entrance in the theater. She wore a thigh-revealing navy skirt and a white blouse that plunged only a little less dramatically than the cliffs below the Ram's Intestines. "Colonel Gatling," she chirped. "I am impressed by your punctuality."

"Thank you, ma'am. Just doing my job."

She strolled to the sofa at the left of the television and motioned Bobby to take a seat on the sofa opposite. "I am afraid Sultan Yusuf is not with us."

Bobby stood in place. "Yes, ma'am. I see that. I can wait outside."

Zoraya nodded towards the sofa.

Bobby sat and placed his laptop at his side. He rested his hands on his knees.

Zoraya went to the credenza below the television and collected a squarish bottle with a blue-and-gold top shaped like an onion dome. "Ambassador Kazanovitch was kind enough to present both my brother and me with a case of Jewel of Russia. Ultra. May I offer you a drink, Colonel?"

"It's a little early, ma'am. For me, that is. And I imagine that the Sultan will be here soon."

Zoraya affected a mild frown evoking the sham disappointment of a three-year-old who knows that ultimately she will get her way. She stepped towards the sofa and set the bottle on the coffee table between them, then sat and crossed her legs. The hem of her skirt rose well above her knees. "As it happens, the Sultan and his wife are in Moscow. I saw them off on a chartered flight just after midnight."

"Vice Sultana, why wasn't I told?"

Zoraya held a finger to her cherry-red lips then lowered it. She clasped her hands and settled them in her lap as if she was about to tell a story to a kindergarten class. "I am sorry to inform you that Sultan Yusuf suffered a sudden and very serious medical problem last evening." She raised her right hand and placed it over her left breast. "His heart."

As Vice Sultana, she had taken the responsibility of seeing Yusuf placed in the hands of the finest specialists. The Sultan's care in America would be first-rate without question, but Moscow was so much closer.

She lowered her hand. "I shall make an announcement on television this evening."

Bobby pressed his palms together. "I know the Sultan put on a few pounds over the last few years, and he's had an episode or two, but . . . What do his doctors say?"

Zoraya stood and circled behind the sofa. She closed her eyes and released a long, low sigh. "The Sultan has gone to his fathers."

Stunned, Bobby rose. "Please permit me to offer my condolences and those of my government."

Her eyes still closed, Zoraya motioned Bobby to sit.

Bobby lowered himself onto the sofa.

"I assure you, Colonel, you have no cause for alarm."

An amendment to the constitution approved by the Assembly of Righteous Elders the day following the election made Zoraya Sultana with all appropriate powers in the event of the Sultan's absence—whether temporary or, as was sadly the case, permanent. A new and lawful shepherdess would guide her people with a hand both gentle and firm.

"We'll have security issues, ma'am," said Bobby. "We should meet with the Ministry staff immediately."

Zoraya's eyelids rose to reveal the same cunning and determination Bobby had seen in portraits of Catherine the Great, Empress of Russia.

"I appreciate your concern, Colonel, but you may stand down. That is the phrase, is it not? General bin Rashid has preparations well in hand."

Bobby blinked to clear his head. "Fawaz bin Rashid? *Major* bin Rashid?"

The skin around Zoraya's mouth remained supple and alluring while her eyes projected a calculating distance. She might have been taking the measure of the courtiers and petitioners gathered in the Winter Palace at St. Petersburg. "I have elevated him over several more senior officers, but he has earned his promotion. You yourself wrote a very positive review of his performance."

Bobby nodded. He might have been short on the details, but putting the big picture together, in spite of Ambassador Ellis's opinion, was a piece of baklava.

Zoraya leaned forward. Her hands—the long, tapered nails matching her lipstick—grasped the back of the sofa like a hawk's talons securing a grip on its perch. "Colonel, may I confide in you?"

Bobby flashed on a nature show he'd once seen on TV. A snake swallowed a frog. At first, the frog struggled valiantly. But once firmly imprisoned in the snake's jaws, the frog surrendered any pretense of struggle and stoically accepted his fate. "Yes, ma'am."

The details painted anything but a pretty picture. Yusuf had compromised his viability as head of state. Zoraya possessed a multitude of files detailing business dealings not only shameful in themselves but of great embarrassment to the United States. Many involved the Chinese through a commingling of personal and family assets with those of the sultanate's sovereign funds. Accounts at the People's Wealth & Happiness Bank of Shanghai and several in Switzerland received regular payments from dummy corporations in Shanghai and Guangzhou. Those accounts also swelled with contributions from American and British oil companies, and an American construction firm with powerful connections in Washington. Additionally—and she found the disclosure almost too painful to relate—significant assets had been diverted from U.S. military and economic assistance packages.

There was also the basketball team. The Ambassador and Mr. Shen both held sub rosa positions in the franchise, which, unfortunately, the League no longer saw as viable. However, they would be handsomely if quietly rewarded when she sold the team for twenty-five million dollars more than the partners had paid for it. The League would relocate the franchise to Moscow.

If Moq'taris blamed their humiliation on the United States, she would understand. The situation might even arouse unsavory elements to act out. She had the greatest confidence, however, that General bin Rashid would keep any protests peaceful and orderly. Even as they chatted, he was detaining a modest number of potential anti-government plotters—no more than one hundred—for an indeterminate period. "A ruler's first duty is to establish order, don't you think, Colonel?"

"Slick!" Bobby said to himself.

"Colonel?"

Bobby shifted slightly in his seat. "May I ask when the Sultan's body will be returned?"

Zoraya swept a stray hair from her right cheek. "Quite soon."

"Unannounced."

"Security issues."

"A massive coronary."

"In spite of clear signs of deteriorating health, a shock to us all."

"No autopsy or toxicology report."

"Respect for our family's privacy."

Bobby studied the vodka bottle's blue and gold top. "Not that a report from Moscow would reveal anything of a suspicious nature."

Zoraya poured two drinks and held one out to Bobby.

Bobby hesitated. "Excellency, why have you told me all this?"

Zoraya put Bobby's glass down and stroked the bottle with a slender finger. "Given the way matters transpired on Election Day regarding my brother, Yasaar, I had a reasonable concern that you might cause me some difficulty."

"*Had* a concern?"

"Having shared a great confidence with you, I have concluded that you and I are quite capable of reaching an understanding."

The image of the frog again appeared before Bobby. Zoraya could have done the obvious and left him in the dark. Anyone else in her position probably would have gone that route. But she'd figured correctly that he'd start looking under rocks as soon as she made her announcement. So she threw him a curveball that achieved the intended result. He knew enough to understand what had happened to Yusuf—and why he couldn't do anything about it.

No question, Washington's suspicions would be aroused as soon as Zoraya went on TV. In due time, the grimy details would reach the White House. Whether testimony from Bobby might speed the process was arguable. More certain, whatever size file the CIA had on Yusuf—and it was probably thicker than the rejected Mickey Green's playbook—the President's advisors would never permit the release of information so embarrassing to the USofA.

Bobby could, of course, step up to the plate in defense of truth, justice and the American way. But the powers that be would view him as a threat. They'd cut off his income by making him impossible to hire. They'd probably find a way to block his pension. The IRS would attempt to bleed him dry. And if nerves in Washington still remained frayed after all that, they'd go for blood.

"An understanding," Bobby said. He didn't take his honor as a warrior and a patriot lightly, but all he could do now was evaluate his options.

"I shall be terminating Crimmins-Idyll, although I will praise your efforts on behalf of the late Sultan."

Bobby nodded in a meaningless attempt at gratitude.

"However, I should not wish you to think me unkind. As you face a substantial reduction in your anticipated income for this year, I wish to offer compensation."

The deal was straightforward. The Ministry of Security would place Bobby on retainer for the critical next two weeks before the Sultana's new security advisors arrived from Moscow. In payment for services rendered—or not—the Royal Bank of Moq'tar would transfer fifty thousand dollars to Bobby's bank or brokerage account.

"You seem hesitant, Colonel," said Zoraya. "I always think of you as a man who acts quickly and surely."

Bobby made no reply.

"One hundred thousand then," said Zoraya. "Nothing more than a simple business agreement."

"A simple business agreement," Bobby repeated. Wasn't that all his involvement with Crimmins-Idyll represented? Military service reflected duty to country and a willingness to sacrifice out of all proportion to monetary compensation. Military contracting concerned itself with love of profit rather than love of country.

Now, in spite of Bobby's best efforts, the company's bottom line was about to take an unanticipated hit. A letter of praise from the Sultana of Moq'tar might spur conversation at cocktail parties, but it wouldn't comfort the accounting staff in Alexandria. With luck, Bobby would be kept hanging with the promise of a new assignment at some time in the future.

With less luck, doubts and recriminations would be cast about from a few people at Crimmins-Idyll whom Bobby—for valid reasons—rubbed the wrong way. Someone with Allen Crimmins' ear might even suggest that Bobby fall on his sword in homage to Washington's addiction to pointing fingers. He'd have lots of company. Millions of other Americans were out of work.

Bobby glanced at Yusuf's empty recliner.

"*Two* hundred thousand," Zoraya said without a hint of anxiety as if she were negotiating the price of dates or pomegranates on a nostalgic outing at the Old Souk. "That, I am afraid, is the limit which must be placed upon my generosity."

Bobby stood.

Zoraya stepped out from behind the sofa. "I would not wish to rush your decision, Colonel. Take twenty-four hours."

"One thing," he said.

"Yes?"

"The Sultan's son."

"My darling Little Muhammad," Zoraya cooed.

"He succeeds to the throne on his eighteenth birthday."

Zoraya took Bobby's hand as if she were comforting the little boy who'd just lost his father. Her grip was delicate, seductive and unyielding all at the same time. "Colonel Gatling," she purred, "what kind of woman do you think I am?"

Twenty-six

$\mathcal{B}$ obby stretched his legs beneath the undersized table perched on the stone terrace of the beach bar across the Corniche from the Shepherd Palace. It seemed as good a place as any to say goodbye to Moq'tar.

He'd yielded to Dymme's insistence on treating him to a farewell dinner in spite of last-minute arrangements to be made for the film festival. With Makeen called to Damascus on business and Ilana off at a conference in Amman—assuming her willingness to bid him a fond and final farewell—Bobby had nothing better to do. He might even enjoy himself. In spite of their little dustup prior to the election, he and Dymme remained on the same team. And he had to give Dymme his due as a professional.

A breeze set the blue, white, red and green table umbrellas fluttering.

Dymme pulled at the collar of the white guayabera he'd picked up on an interesting jaunt to Havana. He'd considered wearing it at the opening of the festival in three nights but decided on his all-purpose blazer and a dress shirt without a tie. "Maybe you won't believe this, Colonel," he said, "but I'll miss you. I'll be glad to give you a ride to the airport tomorrow." He smiled sheepishly. "I've ditched the Jeep for the Escalade."

Bobby spun his glass of Pikesville Supreme between his thumb and index finger. "So much for saving the earth."

Dymme raised his glass—a full-bodied Syrah with a pleasing hint of chocolate.

"Anyway," said Bobby, "I've got a limo coming."

"Going out in style. I like that." Dymme gazed out at the blue waters of the Gulf. "I'm not a maudlin type, but too bad about the Sultan. He wasn't quite forty."

Bobby's father's funeral tumbled out of his memory. He saw himself standing at the grave haltingly reciting *Kaddish*—the Jewish prayer for the dead—reading a transliteration from the Aramaic on a small card and following the rabbi's pronunciation as best he could. He had no idea what the words meant or why they were so important to a man who had buried his past—and himself—for so many years. But his father had requested that he say *Kaddish* at his funeral—and at his mother's when the time came—and then each year on the anniversaries of their deaths. Bobby did the best he could. He understood duty. He understood as well that the dead were too easily forgotten.

"Colonel?" Dymme asked. "You okay?"

Bobby let a sip of rye ease itself down his throat. "Somehow I don't think you're shocked," he said as if his brief withdrawal form the conversation never happened.

Dymme smiled. "Not in my line of work. We've got it pretty much figured out though. There's quite a commotion in Washington, I can tell you that."

Waves tumbled relentlessly onto the beach as whitecaps dotted the Gulf. Behind them, traffic along the Corniche rumbled on in accustomed starts and stops.

"So where do you go from here?" Dymme asked.

"Back to Virginia Beach."

Dymme looked over his shoulder to the Shepherd of His People Mall. A huge Moq'tari flag hung at half-mast. Large signs advertised SULTANA BLOWOUT | HIGH FASHIONS, LOW PRICES. "You'll miss this."

Bobby fingered the lone cigar in his shirt pocket and decided to hold off until after dinner. "How's your boss taking the situation?"

"If you mean Ambassador Ellis, he's still shaken up. I think Washington's got him on a very short leash."

"Screw it," Bobby muttered under his breath. He removed the cigar from his pocket and lit up. Pleasure delayed was pleasure denied. Life, after all, kept everyone on a short leash. "I suppose Margaret's finally coming out now that things have settled down."

Dymme eased back in his chair and stared out over the Gulf as if he was calculating the split on a complex dinner tab. Satisfied, he looked into Bobby's eyes. "Margaret and I haven't lived together in years. Not a secret by any means, so don't think there's a security problem on my end. It's Marc who's coming out."

"Marc?"

"My partner. That doesn't screw up our dinner plans, does it?"

Bobby shook his head. He'd been wrong thinking that Dymme had no more surprises left. His personal philosophy, however, remained simple. To each his own.

"Listen, I'm not prying or anything," Dymme said, "but are you okay? Financially?"

"I've got my retirement," said Bobby.

"Sure, but that only goes so far."

Bobby closed his eyes and took in the scent of his lit cigar. It smelled like success—like the USofA on a good day. He'd enjoy every puff. Not that he'd be living like a monk after this, but he'd be cutting back on cigars. Expensive ones, at least. Honor came with a price.

Dymme stood and left cash on the table. "Shall we?"

Bobby pictured the New York steak he'd dig into at the Lone Star. He drew on the cigar, opened his eyes and eased himself onto his feet. Damn if his knee didn't feel nice and loose.

They strolled towards the Corniche not quite shoulder to shoulder. "Colonel," said Dymme, "this could have been the start of a beautiful friendship."

Bobby clapped Dymme on the back. "Only in the movies, Dymme. Only in the movies."